HOLLYWOOD
HEARTBREAK

HOLLYWOOD HEARTBREAK

A HEART OF THE CITY NOVEL

C.J. DUGGAN

hachette
AUSTRALIA

hachette
AUSTRALIA

Published in Australia and New Zealand in 2018
by Hachette Australia
(an imprint of Hachette Australia Pty Limited)
Level 17, 207 Kent Street, Sydney NSW 2000
www.hachette.com.au

10 9 8 7 6 5 4 3 2 1

A catalogue record for this
book is available from the
National Library of Australia

NATIONAL
LIBRARY
OF AUSTRALIA

ISBN: 978 0 7336 3956 2 (pbk)

Cover design by Keary Taylor
Cover photographs courtesy of Shutterstock
Author photograph courtesy of Craig Peihopa
Text design by Bookhouse, Sydney
Typeset in 11/16 pt Minion Pro by Bookhouse, Sydney
Printed and bound by Clays Ltd, Elcograf S.p.A

*For all those who live without filters on
their photos*

Chapter One

I lay motionless; the machine's long, pained beep sliced through the room. The infamous tone was drowned out only by a heart-wrenching scream as a body collapsed over mine, gripping and yanking at my limp corpse, causing my nasal cannula to be pulled out.

'No, dear God, no!'

'I am so sorry – we did everything we could.'

My hand was crushed by a vice-like grip as another voice entered the fray, a deep, sexy whisper.

'Goodbye, my sweet Cassie.' A kiss warmed the back of my hand. 'I will never forget you.' A hand cupped my cheek, as the very same lips pressed gently against my mouth. 'Always and forever.'

He spoke the promise upon my lips, lingering for a long moment before the darkened shadow lifted and his warmth was gone, leaving me with the over-perfumed woman sobbing at my shoulder – Stephanie Vanderbelt.

'Damon, wait – where are you going?' she cried.

'To find Kane,' he gritted.

'To tell him?'

'No . . . to kill him.'

I heard the hospital doors swing open so violently that a breeze brushed against my cheeks, leaving behind the long, haunting beep of the machine and the wailing sobs of Stephanie at my side.

'Oh no, Damon, nooooooo!' She screamed loudly again, her voice bouncing off the walls. Her tears dripped on my cheek while her arm draped dramatically across my chest.

One thing echoed through my mind: *Get. Off. Can't. Breathe.*

'Annnnd cut! Thanks, everyone, that's a wrap!'

I waited until the applause sounded, then I opened one eye, then the other, seeing the crying Stephanie continue to hold me as if I had indeed slipped from this life. I guess I kind of had. Slowly pulling myself to sit upright, I had little time to remove the oxygen cords when Damon – or, rather, Scott Johnson – burst back through the hospital doors so fast the fake wall frame shook.

'Great job, everybody. I really think we nailed that scene. Especially you, Abby; I mean, wow! Powerful stuff.'

A coldness swept over me as I plucked off the wires taped to my body, my brows pressing downwards.

'Trust you to compliment my acting when I play dead.'

'Yeah, well, I can appreciate it wasn't as easy as it looks,' he said, shoving his hands into his pockets. He was trying for sincerity, but it only made me want to glower some more.

What a total suck.

I peeled back the covers. I could appreciate how awkward I was making the situation, but whenever Scott was around I couldn't help exuding a certain amount of disdain. Whenever I looked into his big, stupid, sorrowful eyes, I felt the urge to imprint his cutesy, crooked grin on my knuckles.

Derek, the director, never missed a thing. He hovered between us, and asked perhaps the most overused question of the past few agonising weeks: 'Are you alright?'

There was no way to prepare for this. Right now it all seemed so surreal as I passed my chair with my name on the back. Well, the name I had come to think of as mine these past three years.

Cassie Carmichael, the youngest daughter and heir to the Carmichael shipping dynasty on Australia's number one drama, *Ship to Sea*. The cast jokingly referred to the show as *Shit to Sea* because, for a small coastal town, a whole lot of shit went down. Over the years I had survived a bushfire, a flood, a hostage situation, an explosion, three broken hearts, a pregnancy scare and a mystery illness. I had survived it all, until the tragic car accident that had spelled my end. But all of the above situations were a walk in the park compared to what I had to face on a daily basis.

Calling upon my professionalism, I smiled brightly – my finest acting performance of all time. 'Fine, absolutely fine.'

I pushed past Scott and the set crew, slamming my palms on the makeshift hospital doors and padding my way down the corridor, sporting a butt-crack gown and a thick bandage wrapped around my forehead. I was glad no cameras were allowed on set to capture my glamourous ensemble, set off by the novelty pink flamingo pyjama bottoms I sported beneath the gown and the lime-green Crocs I slipped onto my feet. I stole a biscuit from the refreshment table before continuing my storming, squeaky steps down the hall.

I was getting those looks again; sympathetic glances, this time accompanied by whispers of concern for the crazy lady. Usually I wouldn't be caught dead in my weekend slob attire but, let's face it, I didn't have anyone to impress. *Well, not anymore*, I thought bitterly, stepping up into my trailer and slamming the door behind me. I slumped against the rickety barrier, wishing it were made of something stronger, a sturdier defence against the realities of the outside world.

I felt strangely numb, but not due to shock that my character had been killed off. You see, the *Ship to Sea* executives had chosen something different with this season's cliffhanger. We had all been given three alternative endings to the season – three alternative deaths – so none of us knew who was really going to die – a ploy to keep the tension high. But I knew Naomi Kline's bee-sting death was the most likely ending; Naomi's contract was up and, rumour had it, she had her eye on a new pilot for an opposing network. It was the worst-kept secret ever and, safe in the knowledge that we'd be staying in the show, we'd embraced our death scenes. My car-crash-coma death seemed kind of mundane, though, considering Brian Formosa's character had been killed off by suffocating in a shipping container. How did they come up with this stuff?

I fell into my favourite chair in my trailer, the one that I spent hours in remembering my lines. I tried not to worry about the energy I wasted on my death scene that would go nowhere, which was a tragedy in itself. A smile crossed my lips as I recalled the looks on the faces of the crew and audience at the end of the scene; it felt bloody amazing to shove it in the faces of the naysayers. I didn't want to admit it, but a large part of me wanted to impress Scott, my on-screen – and, at one time, off-screen – love interest. We had kept it on the down-low, but we'd been pretty bad at it.

My smile slipped away, the way it always did whenever Scott entered my mind, which seemed to be every damn minute of my solitude. That's why I wanted to keep busy: to pause was to remember, and I really didn't want to remember. But as my eyes landed on the corner of a tabloid magazine sticking out from underneath my script, images flashed in my mind.

Scantily-clad lovers embracing on what I had thought was a private beach, but long lenses have a way of seeking you out. We were laughing, having a good time, and my arms were wrapped around Scott's shoulders as he grinned down at me like I was the only girl in the world. Unfortunately, as the magazine stated, I was not the only one he had eyes for. I know you are not meant to believe everything you read, but when 'Homewrecker' is the caption under your picture it makes you sit up and take notice.

I stared at the caption now, having slid the offending publication out from under the pile. The magazine was tattered and dog-eared, thanks to the fit of rage that had seen me throw it across my trailer, then attempt to rip it in half. As I looked over the pictures again, I saw nothing but ugliness. The dimples of cellulite on my thighs, the sandy wedgie of my bikini. The shot of Scott checking his phone while I sunbaked beside him held a whole new meaning. As I'd blissed out on our weekend getaway, little did I know that waiting at home was Scott's very pregnant girlfriend. Reading over the article for the hundredth time, it still didn't seem real.

Scott Johnson had been dating Sydney model and socialite Danielle Kendall for the past eleven months. I thought back to all the dinners, the late-night talks, the trips we'd taken over the past year – it just couldn't be possible, could it? I felt sick. I really needed to get rid of this magazine.

Instead, I slid it into the drawer, at the ready should I feel the need to torture myself again. I felt dead inside, a fitting emotion considering my last scene. I recalled the feeling of Scott's lips upon mine, the first real contact we had since I'd whacked the shit out of him with the rolled-up magazine.

He hadn't denied it.

Guess he didn't have much of a defence when her Instagram was loaded with photos of them together. Thanks to a fake alias, I'd managed to get myself befriended onto her private profile for a bit of detective work. I wasn't proud. It wasn't my finest moment, but neither had been discovering all of their happy snaps on their loved-up weekends away, and even mountain family get-togethers. It was like shoving a dagger into my heart and twisting it. We didn't remain Insta friends for long; I couldn't stomach it.

A part of me had wanted to be killed off from the show, so I wouldn't have to see Scott every day, and act in emotion-laden scenes with him that hurt like hell. Though it probably made me look like an amazing actress, my feelings were all too raw, too real. Had it not been for the support of my manager, Ziggy Forsyth, I might have given up long ago.

And just like that, as if I had summoned her from my very imagination, a knock sounded on my trailer door, and she whipped it open – as always – before I'd given permission to enter. But as she stood before me, still, silent, in a way I had rarely seen before, I knew something was wrong. 'Cyclone Ziggy' was always filling the space with movement and noise, but not today, and that could not mean anything good.

I straightened in my chair, still wearing the hospital nightgown and head bandage. I cared little for how I looked as I focused on Ziggy's solemn face, her wild, woolly hair and cherry-red glasses failing to soften her expression.

'What's wrong?'

'Crisis meeting.'

'How bad?'

'It's bad.'

'On a scale of one to ten?'

Her lips pressed together in a grim line. 'Put it this way, I think we might have broken the machine.'

Oh shit.

Chapter Two

I had only ever been in two crisis meetings in my time. The first was the intervention for legendary stage and voice actor Robert Stanton for his binge-drinking habits and his wandering hands in the make-up chair. He had called it a witch-hunt, but everyone else had simply called him out. He was killed off in a flash-flooding disaster. But when the front-cover spread hit, serious damage control was necessary, and I was called to my second crisis meeting.

Scott was a reigning Gold Logie winner, and Damon and Cassie's tumultuous relationship was a huge ratings driver; it was widely believed that if our characters ever got married, the event would break the Internet. The photographic proof of our real-life liaison had surely sent the Interweb into meltdown, not to mention the studio heads we were forced to meet with.

We had built a brand, a fantasy for young, daydreaming housewives and wide-eyed teenyboppers, and now one magazine article had smashed that dream. No one wanted to see Cassie as a homewrecker, and people certainly couldn't get their heads around Scott's secret, pregnant girlfriend. But as I sat in that room, it hadn't taken me long to realise that I was the only person unaware that Scott was in a relationship with someone other than me. It was almost incomprehensible how blind I had been to his many, many flaws.

I'd declined the stress leave that was offered. I wanted to stand my ground, to show that I wasn't the villain here, the cheater. He was the homewrecker; it just so happened that the title was under my picture. I'd been mad, madder than hell, and Ziggy had been equally outraged by the double standards. The men's club had sheltered their commodity. It had left a sour taste in my mouth, and the prospect of another stoush with those old dinosaurs caused my spine to tingle unpleasantly.

'What now?' I sighed, unravelling my bandage and moving past the divider to my little bedroom to ditch the flamingo PJs, probably not the best attire to front the big bosses in.

Ziggy took a seat and waited, which was unnerving, silence falling between us as I pulled on some jeans and a top. I sat opposite her at the small table, my stomach churning. 'Do we have to meet with Sal?'

'Yes, he wants to see us now.'

Okay, this was bad. Really, really bad.

'And you're here to give me the heads-up?'

Poor Ziggy – being the bearer of bad news seemed to be her job of late, tentatively sliding magazine covers in front of me before schooling me in damage control. But today, mercifully, there was no magazine to be seen, and I felt a bubble of relief inside of me. It didn't last very long.

'Danielle Kendall has given an exclusive interview to *The Desk*.'

My blood ran cold. *The Desk* was a primetime topical news program, with killer ratings and award-winning interviewers. I had appeared on the program myself – it was the go-to place for promotion.

I sat in silence, unable to press for more, but Ziggy continued regardless.

'Look, I am not going to sugar-coat it for you, Abby. I think you need to hear it – all of it – before you meet with the heads.'

I nodded. 'Hit me.'

'Based on the teary snapshots they have been promoting, it's going to be brutal. She's pregnant and popular, and you are the scarlet woman, the villain.'

I closed my eyes; it was everything I had predicted.

'I'm going to try to talk to her again. She needs to know that I had no idea they were together. If I had known, there would be no way I would even – '

'It's no use, Abby, she's going to stand by her man and play happy families. There's no amount of talking to her that will help, and I seriously advise against it.'

I could see it now, on the cover of a women's magazine. Danielle and Scott dressed in white, standing in their white kitchen, holding their little bundle of joy, under the title 'The gift that saved our relationship'. Tabloids were nothing if not predictable.

'What do I do?'

'Be calm, professional. We have your back, Abby. Sal is a reasonable man. He has known you a long time, and this is not their first rodeo.'

'Is Scott going to be there?'

'He's in a separate meeting right now.'

'Good,' I nodded. I just couldn't see him right now.

I hoped that they were telling him to mop up his mess, do an interview himself to confess his sins, take responsibility for being a two-timing rat, flirting and feeling me up in my trailer. Stolen kisses and promised futures. All a big fat lie. I knew I had to be professional, but if saving my reputation meant throwing Scott under the bus, then so be it. Despite the situation being far from ideal, I was filled with a new sense of calm and confidence. Or maybe that was the power of Ziggy, who was always preparing me for my most important roles.

I rubbed my clammy hands along my thighs. 'Okay, well, let's do this.'

Ziggy stood, moving to the trailer door and opening it for me.

'Remember, Abby: cool, calm and professional.'

~

'*You have to be fucking kidding me!*'

Ziggy's nails dug into my knee so hard that I felt their bite through the denim, but in that moment I welcomed the pain: maybe it would wake me up from this nightmare.

I stood abruptly, my chair flinging back and falling to the ground. 'You're killing *me* off?'

I thought Sal might have looked troubled. Lord knew Derek was squirming in his seat. Ziggy's hands were now on the table, clasped together so tightly that her fingers matched the red-coloured tips of her manicure.

'We think it would be for the best, in light of what is unfolding.'

'Unfolding? I'll tell you what's unfolding – Scott's over-sized tongue of lies.'

'Abby,' Ziggy warned, but I wasn't listening. Apparently being told that you were going to be killed off derailed any form of logical thinking.

'Scott's a separate issue,' said Derek, causing a stern look from Sal, who apparently thought he had said too much already.

'So is he going to get killed off too? A boating accident, maybe? A mudslide? Freak kite-flying accident causing decapitation? Seriously, you guys should be writing this stuff down.'

Derek's lips pressed together in a grim line; his expression told me everything I needed to know.

I scoffed. 'Of course, nobody drops the golden boy.'

'Believe me, Abby, we do not make these decisions lightly,' Sal countered.

'Sure, but hey, just think of my death ratings, right? I bet it made it a little less difficult.'

Sal's grey eyes sliced straight through me. I could tell he was trying his best to remain professional, when all he really wanted was to slam the door behind me. I was obviously not doing myself any favours, but I didn't care. My world as I knew it was falling apart and there was nothing that I could do about it.

Then, bless her, Cyclone Ziggy rose to her feet. 'Naturally Abby's financial contract will be honoured in light of the "situation". We wouldn't want there to be any further news stories about discrimination or workplace bullying.'

'Now listen here, Zig – ' Sal's words were cut off by Ziggy raising her hand.

'Save it, Sal; full entitlements will be paid, and a statement will be given by Abby, not you, about her decision to leave the show to pursue a career outside of Australia.'

My head snapped around. What was she doing? Had she lost her mind?

Sal grinned, and it was cold. 'Oh, pursuing other avenues already? Sounds like I'm doing you both a favour, then.'

Ziggy matched his smile. 'More than you realise.' It was a smile that said, 'Don't fuck with me.' As much as Sal could be frightening, Ziggy in business mode was down-right terrifying.

We walked out of the office together, me feeling nothing but hopelessness, while Ziggy seemed energised, a fiery spark in her eyes.

'What am I going to do, Zig?' I tried to keep tears from welling in my eyes.

'Oh, I wouldn't worry. By the time I'm through with him you'll have your entire trip funded.'

'Trip?'

Ziggy smiled, and she was terrifying again. 'Time for a change, Abby Taylor!'

Chapter Three

'We're going to die!'
    The man in front of me turned in his chair and gave me a filthy, twisted look.

Oh shit, did I say that out loud?

I smiled weakly; okay, so he wasn't overly worried about take-off. Turning in my own seat, I looked around, desperately seeking out another terrified soul, but there was no one. Everyone seemed unfazed, save for one young Korean couple who were trying to shove an oversized carry-on into the overhead compartment. *Yeah, that's not going to fit.*

'Excuse me, ma'am, can you please pull your blind up? We're preparing for take-off.'

I blinked, looking up at the Amazonian flight attendant with the high-wattage smile. Make no mistake, if I didn't comply she would not hesitate to have me tasered and escorted off the plane in a heartbeat – I read it in her eyes. My eyes shifted to the window, then I slowly slid the blind upwards to reveal my worst nightmare: the plane's wing.

Why was it that I always got sat on the wing, ensuring I would be the first to see it burst into flames and snap off? At least I wasn't in the emergency aisle – truth be known, in the event of an evacuation I would be throwing women and children over my shoulder and hurdling over seats like an Olympic champion.

How had I let Ziggy talk me into this?

I knew it was all too good to be true: escape the tabloids, the drama, start afresh, expand my career in a way I never could at home, especially since Danielle Kendall had become Australia's latest darling. And now I was going to die in a blaze of twisting metal and melted flesh. I didn't know which was worse: thinking about what I was leaving behind, or the very real terror I was suffering in the present moment.

I studied the emergency-landing guide intently, while simultaneously watching every single gesture and instruction from the flight attendants. My attention only wavered when I craned my neck to see if the people in the emergency aisles were paying attention.

A woman was switching off her phone, a man in his mid-twenties had his headphones on – *headphones!* – and a solid, bald man gave the hostess a glance or two; still, come crash-time I was sure he'd be able to pry open the door like the jaws of life. *Follow the lights on the floor, and follow the bald man – good plan.*

Now, don't get me wrong, this wasn't my first flight. I had been on planes lots of times, but it never got easier.

In fact, as Cassie, I had almost perished in a simulated plane crash on *Ship to Sea*, which, as you can imagine, only heightened my fear, though my acting was superb. The thought of being in the air for thirteen hours had me looking for the sick bag.

'It's going to be alright,' the lady next to me said comfortingly; apparently my nervous energy was rather obvious. I wondered if placing the sick bag in reach was the giveaway. 'There's nothing worse than a phobia of flying,' she said.

'Yeah, it's not fun,' I admitted, hoping that she might confess that she too suffered, that we could bond over it. But looking at her serene disposition, I realised this would not be the case, and I kind of hated her, as well as everyone else on this plane who wasn't paralysed by fear. Damn them all, lazily flipping through their inflight magazines, yawning, and adjusting their seat belts without a care in the world.

Oh. So. Smug.

'Look, this might help.' The lady next to me looked over her glasses and tapped on her screen. She looked just like my mum did when I was showing her how to log in to her Facebook account. Luckily there were no passwords this time. After a few mistakes and a lot of backtracking, the lady seemed rather pleased with herself. 'There, this will tell you exactly where the plane is, and how long until we reach our destination.'

My brows lowered at the flight path, a tiny little plane over a vast, expansive ocean to LAX.

'Oh, hell, no, I cannot look at that,' I said, recoiling in my seat and wishing to God I could erase the image from my brain.

The woman looked taken aback. 'Oh, my dear, is it really that bad?'

I simply nodded, not daring to look left to the wing, right to the flight path, or straight ahead to where the sick bag poked out of the pocket. There was no place to go and no way to fight this feeling. I could feel the tears well in my eyes, as my shaky hands tightened my seatbelt for the hundredth time.

The woman patted me on the shoulder; at first, I thought it was a means to comfort the basket case she had been lumped next to, but as she handed me a foil packet I realised she'd been trying to gain my attention. My brows lowered as she placed it in my hand.

Were we doing a drug deal?

'W-what's that?'

'Valium; the doctor prescribed them to me when my husband passed away at Christmas; they take the edge off your worries. I'm afraid there's only one foil sheet left, but that should help you get to where you're going.'

I read the back of the packet: Diazepam. I had seen it often enough in Caroline Quinn's dressing room to know that it would do the trick. I had a moment of hesitation: could this sweet old lady be planning to drug me and sell me as a sex-slave? But LAX had insane security and, even if the woman was successful in spiriting me away, I had no doubt that Ziggy would hunt me down and rescue me, singlehandedly. Besides, I didn't know how I'd survive the flight without medication. I pierced the foil packet and popped two tiny pills into my palm.

'Now you might only want to take one . . .'

Her words fell away as I flicked the tablets into my mouth and slammed them down with a gulp of water. *Oops*.

'Okay, well, they're only 5 mg, so they won't put you in a coma or anything.'

I almost spat my next mouthful of water into the back of the cranky man in front.

'I hope not; been there, done that,' I laughed.

The lady looked worried, possibly concerned that she had just aided a drug addict. I took in a deep breath and sat back in my chair, clasping my hands over my belly and closing my eyes as I willed the drugs to kick in.

Come on, you little white beasties swimming around in my belly, get to work.

And as the plane lifted off and no oxygen masks dropped from above, I smiled to myself, feeling quite at peace with the world. Long forgotten was the anxiety of leaving everything I had ever known. My family, my friends, my so-called dream job working with Scott-no-brains. I drifted off, my last murmured words slurred into my inflatable neck pillow.

'Hooray for Hollywood.'

Chapter Four

For a brief moment, as the laser scanned my drugged, bloodshot eyeball, I wondered if the steely-faced man at customs would have me escorted to a tiny room. At least I had two pills left, not that I planned to use them anytime soon. If all went well, my next flight would be on a private jet to a remote Siberian landscape to play the love interest in the next Bond movie; hey, you have to have a dream.

I hadn't even realised I was still wearing my neck pillow until I came to the counter to hand over my passport. I had simply followed the sea of people snaking its way through to the customs checkpoint, with, I can only assume, a serious case of bed hair and raccoon eyes; thank God nobody knew me here.

When arriving in Australian airports I made sure I looked fresh and sun-kissed, and wearing a light shift dress from a local designer, but there was no point here. Besides, if I had been at home the paparazzi would be dissecting me mercilessly, no matter how good I looked. Fortunately, customs let me through and I was once again swept up in the zig-zagging line of weary travellers on the way to claim their luggage; which, in my case, contained as much of my life as I could stuff into a suitcase.

I scanned the baggage carousel for my belongings, keeping an eye out for the red ribbon I had tied onto the handle. When I saw the same suitcase on its tenth rotation, the paranoia started to sink in.

They've lost my bag. They've lost my bloody bag.

Then, just to prove me wrong, my bag appeared, rolling around out of reach. I cursed under my breath, then ran after it, edging past bystanders, tripping, and dodging luggage until I lost sight of it completely. I stopped my scrambling and decided instead to move to a clear space right in front of the carousel, waiting for my bag to make its way around again.

Finally, it came into view; I was ready this time. Nothing was going to stop me from grabbing it, even if it meant I was dragged onto the belt and taken around for a joy ride. I yanked the fifty-kilo suitcase to the ground with a loud crack.

As I considered the potential damage, the support belt of my suitcase unclasped, snapping open like a broken rubber band. I clawed at it, desperately trying to edge myself away from the crowd. My suitcase felt like it was crumbling with each desperate drag. The zipper bulged and a corner piece of my case was left somewhere behind me. This was bad, really bad.

I finally made it to the ladies' toilets, breathless, then rummaged around in my carry-on for my mini make-up bag. I planned to emerge from arrivals fresh-faced and lovely-smelling, with the fine people of LA none the wiser.

But as I stared at my smudged mascara and shaggy, blonde mop I had never been so glad to be anonymous. Back home, public toilet situations were a nightmare. If I never heard 'Aren't you Cassie Carmichael?' again, I would be completely fine with that. It was why I had chosen LA as the city where I would further my career and escape the ghost of Cassie. The UK wasn't really an option, with *Ship to Sea* having a cult-like following there. If I was going to reinvent myself, what better place than the city of angels in the land of opportunity.

I couldn't wait to reunite with one of my dearest friends, Billie Martin. We had met on the set of *Ship to Sea* where she was the apprentice make-up artist. Now, after two years in Hollywood, she was living the dream, working for some big television network. She had made a good life for herself here, and now thought of LA as home – she'd even developed a slight American twang, which I relentlessly teased her about.

Now after a whirlwind two weeks of planning I was going to be able to tease her in person. I popped the top of my compact and checked my reflection, decidedly more at ease with my appearance now, and positively giddy knowing that my next destination was Billie's arms, a reunion I sorely needed. Billie had not only offered me a bed, but inauguration into LA life that would no doubt have me wondering why I hadn't taken the leap sooner.

The friends and acquaintances that had come and gone through the show seemed to take one of two main paths: LA or London. Thus, I had friends in both parts of the world, but more in the US, a group of people living the dream and hashtagging themselves as #LAfamily. I had watched on from the social media sidelines, envious of their sun-kissed skin, mirrored glasses and carefree lifestyles; an existence where the biggest concern seemed to be which club to hit next. Now I was here, and soon my two-hundred-thousand-odd Instagram followers would know it. I had already planned the first pic: it would involve a palm tree, it just had to. With a final after-travel facial spritz and one last hair scrunch I was on my way, rolling my beast of a suitcase to my new life.

Walking through international arrivals I knew I'd soon spot Billie's bright auburn hair shining through the crowd, better than any beacon. Friends, lovers and business associates greeted each other, lingering in awkward spaces and causing me no small amount of difficulty as I shifted around them with my faulty roller bag. Despite the noise and the threat of my arm getting dislodged from my socket, I smiled widely, so happy that I was here. I continued to search the sea of faces, wondering where she could be. Was she late? Finding a park? Was there more than one arrivals gate?

I was about to approach airport security for assistance when something caused me to pause, my smile falling slowly from my face. I blinked, sure that I was hallucinating. Was this some weird Valium side-effect? There before me was a sign scrawled in black sharpie:

Cassie Carmichael

Was this a joke? Attached to the makeshift sign was a very hot, tall, dark stranger. Most definitely not Billie. I had envisioned my welcome to be filled with squeals and tears – that I'd be jumping around with Billie like a loon. But, all things considered, this guy was quite the welcoming party.

I took a moment to stare at the unsuspecting hottie, taking in his well-cut denim, white tee and shades. He casually chewed gum, which somehow made him look even more gorgeous. I usually hated the act, after years of waiting for Scott to park his gum before every kissing scene we had. But he made it look cool; a suave effortlessness radiated from him, even as he checked his watch.

It was that small action that snapped me out of my trance, just in time to save me from tripping over a small child in front of me. With every step towards him, my nerves increased.

He can't be waiting for me.

Could he be a driver? Was this what taxi drivers looked like in LA? Christ. Oh God, what if he was actually waiting for a girl called Cassie Carmichael, and this was just some cruel joke that Fate was playing on me. The universe had pulled its fair share of pranks on me lately, and using a sex god to taunt me, bearing a sign with my character's name, no less, was certainly a clever way to do it.

I lingered awkwardly in front of him, smiling nervously.

'Hey, um, I'm Cassie Carmichael,' I said, waving like a total dork.

His attention shifted to me, his dark sunglasses masking his eyes; was he glaring, surprised, cross-eyed? It was impossible to tell, but the set of his mouth made him seem so serious. He looked at me for a long moment, giving me the strangest urge to apologise, though I wasn't sure what I should apologise for; I just felt so incredibly small under his inspection.

'I mean, I'm not really Cassie, like, in the literal sense, but she's kind of like a part of me in a way, like an alter ego, I guess, you know, having spent so long pretending to be someone, they're like kind of a part of you, especially after so many years, it just feels natural to say, yep, I'm Cassie.'

Oh God. Stop. Talking.

I cleared my throat. 'Hi, I'm Abby!' I said, thrusting my hand out to him so forcefully that he reeled back a little, his brows rising in surprise.

I had a moment of panic wondering if 'shaking hands' was not the go in America; had I been seriously uncool? Well, obviously, but was my attempt at a handshake making it worse?

Where was that sick bag? I suddenly felt very ill.

After another beat, the man lifted his shades, propping them on his shortly cropped hair to reveal intense, dark eyes, making me forget my name, real or fictional.

I would have stopped breathing in that moment, if an impossibly bright smile hadn't formed across his face.

'I'm Jay,' he said, and I could tell he was laughing at me, not with me, as he took my hand and shook it. If I had felt small before, I felt completely tiny now, his hand engulfing mine in a firm handshake that I could still feel long after he let go.

A silence fell between us, and he flipped his shades back into place; apparently he was a man of few words.

'Um, so Billie isn't here?' I asked, looking past him, half-expecting her to leap from behind a concrete pylon and yell, 'Surprise!' I wouldn't have put it past her. Examining the scrawled black handwriting on the sign 'Jay' held, I knew that it was Billie's handwriting; oh, she was sooooo funny.

Jay handed me the sign and reached for my bag. 'No,' he said, stating the obvious as he extended the handle of my suitcase, then paused to examine my baggage.

Oh fuck!

A giant pair of undies was spilling out of my busted suitcase – the bright yellow ones with 'Bootylicious' embossed on the back of them. This comfy weekend pair was not meant to be seen by anyone but me.

Oh, sweet Jesus, of all the pairs, why them?

I yanked, then yanked some more, literally tearing them free before dropping them at his feet, then stooping to pick them up. My cheeks burning, I shoved them into the deep, dark recess of my bag.

Yep, nothing to see here, folks.

'Lead the way,' I croaked, making an effort to not look up at the smirk I got a glance of before.

Without a word, he rolled on.

Staring at his broad shoulders as I walked behind him, trying to not die of mortification along the way, I had one very clear thought: *I'm going to kill you, Billie Martin!*

Chapter Five

My baptism into LA life having begun so disappointingly, I was glad to get out outside and shake off my embarrassment. The sun was barely up but the air was warm already, promising a fierce summer day. I couldn't wait to bake myself in it.

Tearing myself away from my plans, I noticed that my very attractive driver was lifting my suitcase into the back of a very attractive black Mustang.

Definitely not a taxi.

'Ah, so, how do you know Billie?'

Friend? Acquaintance? Lover?

'We're neighbours,' he said, slamming the trunk closed like a full stop.

Watching the cords of his biceps strain as he lifted my suitcase into the car like it weighed nothing, I had been momentarily distracted, but his two-worded response had my attention.

'Oh, right, cool,' I said, wondering what kind of neighbour picks up a friend of a friend on a 6 a.m. flight from Australia. Clearly a damn good one.

It wasn't until the Mustang's guttural engine revved to life that I moved into action; maybe it was the remnants of the Valium wearing off or jetlag, but I was slow on the uptake. I leapt to the passenger door, opening it and sliding into it. I felt the plush leather seats beneath my legs and noted the impeccable cleanliness of the interior; I knew jack about cars, but it was immediately obvious that this car was dearly loved.

'Nice car,' I said, struggling to think of anything else to say.

Jay didn't respond; instead, he watched and waited, ready to manoeuvre out of his space and into the stream of traffic exiting the airport parking lot. Naturally, he wanted to concentrate; in fact, he might not even have heard me, the radio was up so loud. Small talk was clearly futile – best to let him do his thing.

Damn if I wasn't excited speeding and darting in between lines of traffic, the likes of which I'd never experienced before. One of the things I'd heard about LA is that you either love or loathe it; despite the pollution clogging my pores and the dry smoggy heat of the morning causing a scratchiness in my throat, I knew I would love it. The concrete sprawling highways twisted and turned us as if we were on some grand amusement park speedway in a way that both horrified and thrilled me. There seemed to be two speed limits here, fast and faster, and we obeyed the latter. As far as grand entrances went, this was going to be hard to beat.

Maybe this was why Billie had organised for Jay to pick me up; as far as I knew, she didn't have a Mustang at her disposal, nor did she drive like she was being chased by the cops. I wondered if I could grab a pic of my ride; it would sure trump a palm tree.

'So, is Billie okay? Did she have to work or something?' I gripped the edge of my seat, thinking that if I concentrated on the road it would encourage Jay to do the same, but he seemed far more relaxed than I was, one hand resting on the gear stick, the other resting lightly on the wheel. His shades were still firmly in place so I could only hope that he was looking at where he was going.

Just when I was sure he wouldn't answer me, he gave a casual shrug. 'I have but two instructions: pick up Cassie Carmichael, then bring her back via the scenic route.' He said it so unenthusiastically that I realised he was doing Billie a huge favour; I'm sure he had a number of things he'd rather be doing on a Saturday morning than navigating LA traffic. I tried not to think about that; instead, I shifted in my seat, sitting up eagerly at the words 'scenic route'.

'Really?' I said, hopefully.

I was at the mercy of his mood, but despite his apparent reluctance to play tour guide, a little smirk tugged at the corner of his mouth as he glanced at me. 'Really.'

I fought an urge to clap my hands together like a child in a highchair being presented with her favourite food; instead, I played it cool, resting my elbow on the window ledge and nodding.

But like any tourist I couldn't help but press my face to the glass as we travelled along the Sunset Strip, past Chateau Marmont where John Belushi died and Greta Garbo lived, or the gritty darker corners of the Viper Room and Whisky a Go Go. There were palm trees, for sure, dotted along the concrete stretch of patchy roads and mismatched buildings, and nestled in the towering shadows of giant billboards, popping against the blue California sky. It was dirty and surreal, and as uninteresting as it must have been to Jay, I wanted to drive until the sun went down and neon lit the way to the soundtrack of the pounding live music that Billie had talked of.

I had definitely made the right decision leaving Australia. My fears and uncertainties were not going to keep me up at night – there was far too much living to do, too much adventure. I wanted to start building my career in this new and exciting world. I almost wanted to urge Jay to drive faster so I could start sooner, not wanting to wait one more minute to settle into my new life here. If ever I'd wished to be snapped by the paparazzi, it was now: cruising the Sunset Strip in a Mustang, next to a sexy, mysterious man. But maybe, for now, anonymous was good.

For now.

~

The scenic route could have been the normal route, I would never have known. Everything was so chaotic and ever moving, no rhyme or reason to the landscape. I wasn't sure what I expected to see: to drive past the Hollywood sign, get stuck at a traffic light next to Matthew McConaughey, or see Reece Witherspoon crossing the road? Yeah, it wasn't exactly like that. Still, the day was young and there was plenty of time for star-spotting, especially since my new home was in West Hollywood, a stone's throw from all the action.

Jay parked in front of a large, futuristic building that was reminiscent of a giant sugar cube, with black windows and high-tech security. My breath hitched at the sheer luxury, and that was just the outside.

'Wow, is this it?'

Jay laughed. 'Not exactly.' He pointed in the opposite direction. I followed his outstretched finger to an older, more modest, two-storey, Mediterranean-style building. It sat behind a black iron gate that matched the wrought-iron balconies, a narrow walkway leading through the arched entrance. It wasn't exactly lux but it definitely had charm, and a real sense of Old Hollywood.

'Disappointed?' Jay probed.

'Nah. Who wants to live in a giant sugar cube anyway?'

I knew he was looking at me – I could see it in my peripheral vision – but there was no use meeting his eyes; I already knew the look he was giving me. It read: *This*

Aussie girl is a bit of a weirdo. Luckily for him, his time with me was over. He had done his neighbourly good deed for the day – and he exceeded his quota when he grabbed my bag from the trunk and started across the road with it. I was about to insist that it wasn't necessary until I saw the long, steep tile staircase.

Yeah, nope, you're good!

Jay swiped his keys to activate the gate, then pulled it open. Standing aside, he nodded his head for me to go first. I darted in, then waited for him to lead the way through the giant stone arch that split the façade of the building. The cool, dark tunnel was a welcome reprieve from the hot morning sun. It led out into an open-air courtyard. Still much cooler than the stark concrete roadside, the courtyard was leafy and overgrown with clinging vines and potted palms – a veritable urban jungle. Or perhaps an urban oasis, for in the centre of the lush, green space was a large, tiled in-ground pool, the star attraction of the communal area.

I don't know why I was so surprised: Billie had spoken often enough about being poolside, and there had been plenty of Insta evidence. Gappy thigh shots of her lying on these very sunbeds, #LAdreaming #thegoodlife #californiagurl #sorrynotsorry.

As soon as I laid eyes on its emerald-green glory, I knew I too would be as obnoxious as her in no time – that all my old friends back home would hate me as much as I hated Billie. I couldn't wait.

Jay seemed to be humouring me, allowing me to move slowly about the space, openly gawking at my surrounds. The courtyard was empty, except for an older woman sitting at one of the wrought-iron tables, dressed in a kaftan and feeding her little white pooch a piece of toast.

'Morning, Mrs Simms,' Jay smiled, nodding his head. It was the most animated I had seen him in the entire time I had spent with him; he even patted the little dog.

'Oh, good morning, Mr Davis.' She beamed.

Davis. Jay Davis.

The lady looked expectantly at me, then back to Jay, waiting for an introduction, which, of course, was not forthcoming. He was clearly too busy patting the dog; he probably couldn't even remember my name.

'Hi, I'm Abby,' I said, stepping forward and shaking her hand.

'Nice to meet you, Abby; Veronica Simms, medium and clairvoyant to the stars.'

'Wow, really? Anyone I know?'

'Oh, my dear, confidentiality is the cornerstone of my business practice. I simply mustn't divulge any information about my celebrity clients.' She placed her hand on her heart; her hot-pink nails matched her kaftan and lipstick. Even little Rover had a pink diamanté collar.

'Well, as an actress, I can completely respect that.' I laughed.

Veronica sat up straight. 'An actress? How exciting!'

Jay scoffed. 'Yeah, just what this town needs, another actress.'

My smile fell; slowly I turned to look at Jay. He had removed his shades, so I was able to look into his eyes and see that he wasn't joking. It was the most he had said since we had left LAX, making his choice of words even more offensive; maybe it was just as well he rarely spoke.

'Excuse me?' Maybe it was my tone, or the incredulous look that spread across my face, but Veronica's dog started to growl, no doubt picking up on the sudden tension.

Just as Jay was about to speak, his words were interrupted by a high-pitched scream that brought our attention to the second-storey balcony behind us.

'Abby!' Billie squealed, jumping up and down and clapping. 'Oh my God, you're here! Stay, right there, I'm coming down!' she yelled, before disappearing back through the doors to her condo.

My eyes shifted back to Jay, who still had the same steely gaze, and the tension was back again. I wanted to give him a piece of my mind, or let Veronica's poodle do it for me, but the animated squeals and fast-approaching footsteps saved him. Besides, it would be a shame to ruin the courtyard with a chalk outline of a body, no matter how tempted I was.

Jay Davis had gone from knight in shining armour to grade-A jerk within two point five seconds. As soon as he had dragged my heavy suitcase to the second level, I would be more than happy to see the back of him.

Chapter Six

There was no chance of Sorscha the toy poodle attacking Jay. Her barking, snarling attack seemed to be directed solely towards me and Billie, as we finally had our laughing and jumping scene. Veronica seemed overjoyed for us; Sorscha and Jay, however, were not amused.

'Oh my God, I can't believe you are here,' Billie said, cupping my face, checking that she wasn't imagining things.

'Me either – it's insane!'

Our laughter was interrupted by the scraping sound of my suitcase handle being repeatedly extended and retracted, as Jay gave a less-than-subtle hint.

'Jay, you are a legend! I owe you one.'

Jay extended the handle again, clicking it into place and grabbing it. 'You owe me four.' He looked at Billie rather pointedly.

Billie chose to ignore his tone. 'You're hilarious.'

It then occurred to me that I hadn't yet thanked him for picking me up; could this be the reason for his lack of personality thus far? Before I had a chance to remedy the situation he began to move towards the stairs.

'Where do you want it?' he asked Billie, as if I wasn't there. He had been so nice to Veronica and her dog but couldn't seem to bring himself to make eye contact with me.

'It's okay, I've got it,' I said, stepping forward and reaching for my suitcase, which he tipped back out of my reach.

'Do you?' he asked, his brow curving, as if the very notion of me rolling a bag was ridiculous.

'I think I can manage,' I said, reaching again, only to grab at fresh air.

'Listen, I don't know what you have in here, but dragging it up those steps ain't going to be easy.'

'Well, I guess I shouldn't have packed all my acting props, you know, my wigs and feather boas.'

'Is that what was spilling out of your suitcase . . . a prop?' Jay smirked, watching as I flushed at the memory of my canary-yellow undies.

'Shut up!' I said, marching on towards the stairs and leaving him with the stupidly heavy bag; it wasn't until I got to the foot of the stairs that I realised I had no idea where I was going.

'Ah, this way?' I pointed to the stairs.

Billie's eyes flicked from Jay to me with a sparkle of

interest. 'Yes, that's the way,' she said, whacking Jay in the side. 'Come on, muscles, let's get the girl settled in.'

An image of Jay tucking me into bed while Billie read me a bedtime story flashed in my mind. I quickly turned and started for the very long, very narrow, stairs. I was suddenly ever so grateful that I had not won that argument; it was hard enough to get myself upstairs, let alone my excess baggage. If anything, I took great pleasure in hearing the clunk, clunk, clunk of suitcase wheels being dragged up each step by the begrudging Jay.

'Turn left up here,' said Billie. '2C.'

A small hall led into a little alcove that had a gold, slightly crooked 2C on the left, and 2D on the right. I guessed that was Jay's door, and tried not to notice its close proximity as I heard the rolling of wheels approach.

He was trying to keep his breath even but, as Billie worked on unlocking her door, I could tell he was a little worn out.

'Thanks, I think I can take it from here,' I said, reaching out for the handle; this time he didn't fight me, and my hand brushed over his as he slowly let go. It was the strangest sensation, almost as if an electric shock had passed between us, and I could still feel the warmth of his skin against mine. Our eyes met for a brief moment then we quickly looked away as Billie pushed the door to her condo open.

'Home sweet home!' she sing-songed. 'Hey, thanks again for helping out, Jay.'

I pulled my bag inside the doorway. 'Yeah, thanks,' I said, probably sounding a little ungrateful. The truth was if I never saw Jay Davis again, it would probably be too soon. The sight of his cocky, lopsided smile as he unlocked his own door only strengthened my resolve.

Rather than say 'anytime' like a normal, polite person would, he looked at my broken suitcase and shook his head, then stepped inside his door.

'See you around, ladies.'

~

Billie's West Hollywood condo was beautiful: the charming, bright space matched the perfection of the vintage building and its idyllic location, being just steps away from the fabulous dining and entertainment that the Sunset Strip had to offer. A cosy kitchen opened into the formal dining room, light hardwood floors flowing through out the space. Natural light flooded in through the windows that looked onto the terrace, and the coved ceilings and arched doorways had the charm and character of Old Hollywood. Billie had added her own distinctive touches to the place: a large framed picture of Frank Sinatra sat above the fire-place, and the room was furnished with her attractively worn leather couches, eclectic rugs and boho cushions.

'Um, I think I need to get a gig as a make-up artist,' I said, running my hand along the marble countertop of the kitchen.

Billie laughed. 'You mean, what's a girl like me doing in a place like this?'

'Oh, no, sorry, I didn't mean it like that.' I winced.

'How can I possibly afford it?'

It was the very question burning a hole in my brain, but I wouldn't come out and say it.

Billie plonked herself on the couch, tucking a cushion in her arms. 'That's okay – I totally can't afford it.'

I stilled, turning to her. 'Jesus, Billie, you're not a squatter, are you?' I seriously wouldn't have put it past her.

She burst out laughing, turfing a cushion at me. I caught it, much to my own amazement.

'No, I am not a squatter, I am simply a very charming individual.'

I threw the cushion back and collapsed on the couch next to her. 'Well, I know that.'

Billie tucked one leg underneath the other. 'One of the best jobs I've ever had here was a short-lived production for a Hallmark Western with Nancy Satora and Jack Seddan.'

I blinked, rolling the names around in my head.

'Who?'

'Trust me, they're big in the midday movie world.'

'Okay, right.'

'Anyway, there was this really amazing character played by the legendary stage actor Molly White, and because I was the new kid on the block, I was assigned to do the make-up of anyone over seventy on the shoot.'

I laughed, shaking my head at the vision.

'Not that I minded. Nancy was so up herself, and Jack Seddan had wandering hands, if you know what I mean. Plus Molly was a hoot – I used to love going to work just to listen to her repeat the same stories about her young Hollywood days. I honestly think I was the only one that ever had the time or the patience to listen to her.'

'That's kind of sad.'

'Yeah, yeah, it was. Especially as she could out-act anyone.' Billie spoke with a faraway look in her eyes, reliving a fond memory, before blinking back to the here and now. 'So, anyway, production wrapped, we caught up for a top-shelf lunch afterwards and she was horrified to learn that I was couch-surfing in some dark, downtrodden corner. She lives in Florida but has had a condo here for years and said that I'd be doing her a favour to keep it dust-free for her.'

'Wait, this is Molly White's place?'

'Yeah. I'm her favourite tenant – have been near-on two years now.'

'Wow, that's awesome.'

'She's awesome! I pay her every week – much to her disgruntlement – and water the pot plants. Before Molly, I was *this* close to packing it all in and moving home, so I intend on taking full advantage of the card I've been dealt for however long it lasts.'

I looked at Billie, slightly taken aback at her confession. I'd had no idea she had struggled here; she had never given that impression. But then again, everything in the online world had a giant filter – I could attest to that.

'So, does Molly know I'm staying here?'

'Oh, yeah, of course – she was actually thrilled. She constantly worries about me being on my own.'

I slapped my hands on my knees. 'Well, Miss Martin, be careful what you wish for because you are definitely not alone anymore.'

'Yaaaaay!' Billie clapped her hands together in delight. 'Come on, I'll give the grand tour: first stop, your new room.'

My room was sparse compared to the living areas, but it mattered little as I stepped towards the sliding door to the small patio that overlooked the pool.

'Ah, yeah, thought you might like this room.'

I tore my eyes away from where Veronica and Sorscha still sat in the shady part of the courtyard. 'It's bloody awesome,' I said, moving over to her and wrapping my arms around her. 'I can't thank you enough.'

'Don't mention it. No friend of mine is going to stay on some flea-ridden couch.'

I took in the space again. With white walls, plenty of light and a double bed, it was a blank canvas. Just what I needed for my new start in a new town – a new adventure.

'Oh, and before I forget.' Billie grabbed my hand and dragged me out of my room, through the living area and into the kitchen. 'Look.' Billie pointed to perhaps the most beautiful thing I had ever seen: an industrial coffee maker. 'Please tell me you are still addicted?'

'Worse than ever,' I said, stepping closer and admiring its beauty. I had died and gone to heaven.

'You can have coffee on your balcony and learn your lines,' Billie smiled. It was as if she was trying to convince me to stay, but she seriously needn't have bothered – I was already well and truly sold!

Chapter Seven

Oh, jetlag, you filthy mistress, you.

What goes up, must come down, and no coffee, no matter how impressive the froth on top was, could save me from hitting a wall, yawning with each fold of my clothes I retrieved from my suitcase. I showered, pressing my forehead against the Mediterranean tiles in the impressive shower cubicle that was bigger than my bedroom back home. I washed away the grime from being trapped in an enclosed space for thirteen hours, not that I had remembered a lot of it.

As I walked through the living room, towel-drying my hair, the delicious aroma of onions and spices filled my dulled senses. Billie was stove-side, working on a feast for lunch; fresh lettuce, tomatoes and avocados were strewn over the kitchen countertop. She was making my favourite: Mexican. I shook my head; how would any other day live up to the epicness that was my first day in LA? A relatively painless flight, a Mustang escort – well, that wasn't exactly painless; maybe I should have knocked back my final sedative to make the silence a whole lot more bearable. Since the moment I had closed the door on Jay, I couldn't help but wonder what his deal was.

Wrapping my hair in a turbanesque twist and firming the tuck of the towel wrapped under my arms, I padded towards the fridge, which I guessed was my fridge now too.

'So, what's the go with Jay?' I had to raise my voice over the sizzling of the frying pan and the exhaust fan over the stove.

Billie turned. 'What?' she said, frowning and reaching for some seasoning. 'You might want to put some clothes on.'

I was a little taken aback. Billie wasn't a prude; surely I could walk around in a towel?

'I said, what's the deal with the hottie next door?'

Billie turned from the stove; her eyes popping.

Oh God, she had turned into a prude.

'I mean, don't get me wrong, he sure is nice to look at, but he needs a personality transplant.'

'Abby!' Billie seemed really distressed; if she'd been wearing a pearl necklace she would have been clutching it. Who was this woman before me? She had the perviest mind of anyone I had ever known; her observations usually made me squirm. Had America tamed her wicked ways? Surely not. And as unsettling as it was to think that my friend was uncomfortable with what I was saying, I kind of enjoyed pushing her buttons and watching her mouth gape.

I shrugged. 'What? I'd fuck him!' I said, grinning from ear to ear until I saw her horrified eyes flick over my shoulder.

A chill swept over me, and it wasn't due to the fact I was merely wrapped in a towel; there was something in Billie's face, the sheer look of utter shock that made my insides twist.

Oh God, he's right behind me, isn't he?

I slowly turned to see the very image of my nightmares standing in the alcove of the dining room, seemingly entranced by the placemat on the table. But there was no mistaking the twist to his mouth.

He had heard every single word.

I wanted to die.

I could throw myself over the balcony. Or get the next drug-induced flight home. It wasn't enough that I had to completely humiliate myself with my gutter mouth and insults, I had to be standing there, wrapped in a tiny pink towel, with no make-up and no dignity.

'Um, Jay said you left your bag in the car,' Billie stammered, gripping the wooden spoon intensely, looking like she wished the ground would swallow her up too.

My widened eyes dipped to the bag he was holding. My bag.

'Oh,' I said. 'Thanks.'

Jay cleared his throat, not really knowing quite where to look as he placed my bag on the table. 'I'll just leave it here.'

'Yeah, um, great, well, I'm just going to, ya know . . .'

I side-stepped out of the kitchen, not daring to lift my gaze to the dining area, then raced to my room, tightly gripping my towel. The very last thing I needed was to do a nudie run.

I shut my door and resisted the urge to slide the chest of drawers across it to barricade myself in. My Hollywood dream had turned into a Hollywood nightmare. I mean, Christ, I was joking! Surely they knew that? I was totally taking the piss, deliberately trying to shock Billie.

I covered my face with my hands. 'Oh my God.'

Why hadn't she tried harder? Flung herself across the kitchen and slapped me with a wooden spoon? My hands fell to my side; I bit my lip, whimpering in despair.

Okay, maybe it wasn't that bad. I could just head back out there, tell them I was kidding and have a good ol' laugh about it. A memory flashed vivid in my mind.

He needs a personality transplant.

I cupped my burning cheeks, shaking my head. What must he think of me? First, I had flashed him a rather shady-looking pair of undies at the airport, and now I had insulted him while talking like a horny construction worker.

A half-naked one.

I felt the bile rising at the back of my throat.

In order to put on my big-girl pants, I would first have to put on some pants . . . and a top. But where to from here? Putting on a full face of make-up seemed over the top, and blow-drying my hair wasn't something I did for

an afternoon at home. Still, we had company; that's if he
hadn't already headed for the Hollywood Hills. Opting for
the fresh-faced, casual-California-girl look, I found myself
sitting on the edge of my bed, thinking and overthinking
what I might say. Maybe I could pretend that I knew he
was there the whole time. Yeah, I could get away with
that – use the old 'You should have seen your face!' line.

But before I could work up the courage to show my
beetroot-red face again, I heard the condo's front door open
and close. I placed my ear to my bedroom door, listening
intently for the sound of voices.

There were none, only the distant clattering of kitchen
utensils and running water.

Had he gone? He was obviously too mortified to stay.

I didn't know how I felt about that; I certainly didn't
feel any less nauseated. I heard Billie's voice call from the
kitchen. 'Abby, the coast is clear!'

I whipped the door open so fast that the kickback of
air pushed my half-wet hair back across my shoulders as
I padded out into the lounge.

'Seriously, could you not have told me he was behind
me?'

'I tried to stop you.'

I sat on the stool near the kitchen bench, burying my
head in my hands. 'Next time just yell at me to shut up.'

Billie laughed. 'Next time?'

My head snapped up. 'Please tell me he's not coming
back.'

Billie salted the pan in front of her before stirring some more. 'Nope.'

I sighed. 'Good.'

'I am guessing this is more to do with your humiliation than not liking him, because you have only known each other, what, seven hours?'

Yeah, seven hours too long.

Billie watched the contemplative musings in my expression with great interest. 'He's a good guy, Abby.'

I shrugged, tucking a wet strand of hair behind my ear. 'Clearly not a fan of actors, though.'

'Oh, I think he's just a little jaded, that's all.'

My ears pricked up; was Jay a washed-up actor? Well, where he had failed I was sure to succeed.

'He's kind of surrounded by all that, all the time at work. Lots of part-time actors and actresses waiting to hit the big time.'

'Uh, he does know he is living in Hollywood? If he has such an attitude about it maybe he should move elsewhere. What does he do, anyway?'

'He's the owner-manager of the Saloon Bar.'

I did a double-take. 'Owner?'

Billie smiled. 'Yes.' She always loved to shock me.

I knew of the Saloon Bar – hell, everyone did. Its VIP corners and wild, high-class parties made it synonymous with the Hollywood Strip. No wonder Jay was driving a Mustang.

'You seem surprised – you didn't think he was living next door due to the kindness of another ageing actress, did you?'

Whatever I had thought, this was definitely not it. Now I really had lost my appetite.

How could someone, seven hours in, have got so under my skin? And, more importantly, how had I managed to show him so much of mine?

'Well, if I don't see him in a really, really long time, that would be quite alright with me.'

Billie rolled her eyes. 'Uh-huh. Lunch is ready.'

Chapter Eight

Angling my phone in the most ridiculous and unnatural angle, I snapped a picture of my torso and legs, slightly bent, the glistening pool beyond my feet, my stomach held in until I desperately needed air. On the fourth take I was satisfied enough to flick through the selections of filters, choosing the one that made my legs look tanned and the pool extra emerald. I smiled to myself, hitting next and captioning 'This is what I call Monday' #californiadreaming #Hollywood #sorrynotsorry.

'Post.' I smiled, smug as I placed my phone to the side and reclined on my sun bed, the view of blue sky and palm trees muted through my sunglasses. The first week I had been plagued with emotional doubt, jetlag and the unwavering anxiety that I had made the worst mistake of my life. I almost became nostalgic for front-cover exposés and cellulite snaps of me at the beach. There was comfort in the known, and getting used to my new situation was, well, a little uncomfortable.

Making plans with Billie was not the easiest thing to do. Her work was often either long days or short, broken-up hours, depending on what she had booked. I was often alone, and that was strange. I spent my days by the pool and my nights surfing Netflix. I couldn't wait for Ziggy to get to LA next week and not only wine and dine me but fill me with hope about my promising future. My ego was in desperate need of a stroke. I picked up my phone to check if anyone had liked my photo and got the feels I needed from the comments.

'Damn gurl!'

'I kind of hate you right now.'

'You are so beautiful. Cassie and Damon 4EVA.'

'Sooooo jelly!!'

'Come back Cassie, Damon needs you!'

And then there were the trolls, and a part of me delighted in their attention, too.

'You're so up yourself!'

'You need to eat a burger.'

'HOMEWRECKER!!'

I flinched at the last word. It gutted me every time I saw it. I skimmed over it and moved on down the list, liking the comments that didn't tell me I needed lipo. Then I paused at one comment.

'Abby in the hood! Can't wait to catch up, babes – we'll paint the town red. Xo.' OfficialSiennaBailey.

Ugh, Sienna Bailey.

Sienna was the golden girl of *Ship to Sea*, and a season favourite until she got killed off in a scuba-diving accident eighteen months ago. She was pretty and popular and vivacious, and it seemed that everything she touched turned to gold.

I couldn't stand her.

She had been in LA for less than a month when she landed herself a prime role on an original Netflix series that had been an incredible hit. Now there were rumours about who she was dating every five minutes, and heavenly food snaps from exclusive restaurants. The shots of her hiking in the Hollywood Hills in activewear, without so much as a drop of sweat, made me sneer, as did the pics of her linking arms and toasting cocktails with her #LAfamily. Meanwhile, my LA family consisted of Eduardo the groundskeeper, who was scooping up what looked like a dead bird from the pool. Not the greatest start to my day.

Just when I thought my mood couldn't get any blacker, the screech of the gate sounded and a figure appeared in the corner of my eye.

Oh shit.

I quickly put my phone down and lay still. Eyes closed, I wished him away. I hadn't seen Jay since utterly humiliating myself last week, for which I was incredibly thankful, but now his footsteps neared. I suddenly felt very exposed in my barely-there bikini. If I pretended to be asleep maybe he would walk on. He didn't. Instead, a shadow came over me.

I lifted up my glasses, and there he was, arms crossed and looking down at me with a sceptical curve to his brow that said 'nice life for some'.

And indeed it was, until he came along.

'You're blocking my sun,' I said.

'Shouldn't an actress be worried about tan lines?'

'What?' I said, looking at the spaghetti strap at my shoulder, calculating how many hours I had been out here. 'Well, thanks for your concern, but I think I'll be fine. Besides, I happen to know a brilliant make-up artist.'

'It would be good for her to get some practice in,' he said.

'I hardly think she needs me for practice – she's doing it every day.'

Jay said nothing, and I lifted my glasses again. Silence wasn't a foreign concept for him but this time it didn't sit right, and neither did the way he was looking at me.

'She hasn't told you?' he asked.

'Told me what?'

Jay shifted. For the first time he didn't look so confident; in fact, he looked decidedly unsure. 'Listen, it's not for me to say,' he said, and with that he started to walk away.

'Hey, wait a minute,' I said, sitting up. 'You can't just leave it at that.'

I scooped up my towel and phone and padded after him, trying to keep up. 'Jay, stop!' But he was intent on escaping to his condo. Breathless by the time I reached the top floor, I pushed on and threw myself in his path, blocking him along the breezeway.

'You cannot leave me hanging like that. Why would she need practice?' I stepped from side to side, mirroring his moves, blocking his path.

'Abby,' he warned. Hearing him say my name for the first time kind of threw me. He took advantage of my momentary lapse of concentration and dived past me, moving the final distance to his door.

'Why would she need practice, Jay?'

He opened his door with expert ease, not allowing me enough time to ask the question. Had I been wearing shoes I might have stuck my foot in the door; my dramatics knew no end.

'I'm keeping out of it,' he said. Surprisingly, he didn't slam the door in my face; instead, he stood there looking down at me as if he wanted to say more. Just as I thought he was going to reveal all, his eyes glanced down, and up again quickly. 'Ah, you, ah, might want to, ah . . .'

I frowned, looking down.

Oh my God!

Worse than any red-carpet nightmare, there it was, loud and proud, coming out to say 'HELLO, BOYS!' My left breast. Of course, of all the times to have a nip slip, it had to be while I was arguing with an incredibly hot man.

I. Wanted. To. Die.

As I cupped my boob, mortified, Jay stared up at the ceiling, his face twisted like he too wanted to just disappear.

I tucked myself into place and crossed my arms; if he found the ceiling fascinating, I found the floor intriguing. How do you exit such a situation? Why hadn't he just slammed the bloody door in my face? I could scurry back to my condo and wait for Billie to come home to see if she was willing to relocate to save me from ever running into Jay again, or I could be totally mature about it. I mean, what was there to be ashamed about? I had nice boobs, an ample B, and they were real, which was not something that everyone could claim in this town.

Jay, having moved on from his ceiling investigation, scratched the back of his neck and offered me a small, awkward smile.

'Well, considering you've seen my boob, the least you can do is tell me about Billie.'

Jay smiled more broadly. 'Do you always extract information this way?'

I rolled my eyes. 'Oh, sure. It's a really useful interrogation method.'

'It's certainly a distraction. I don't know how to end this now . . . it feels kind of wrong to shut the door on a girl who I've practically been to second base with.'

'Pfft, second base, you should be so lucky.'

'Hey, listen, it's not my place to say, but maybe just talk to Billie. She could probably do with a sympathetic ear.'

Jay seemed genuinely sincere. I hated to admit it but I kind of respected the fact he wasn't going to divulge anything about Billie. I mean, who was I? He didn't know me; sure, I was Billie's roomie and friend from Oz, but I was just a stranger to him – albeit one who had just flashed him her assets. Still, I wasn't going to give him credit for being a good guy.

'Fine,' I said. 'Clearly I am not going to get any information out of you so I'll just ask her myself.'

Jay nodded. 'Maybe just go in with the questions a little bit more gently than you did with me.'

'Gently?'

'You did chase me up two flights of stairs and block my path.'

Oh, yeah, *that*. 'I guess I can be a little . . . over-the-top,' I conceded.

Jay scrunched up his face, struggling to keep it together.

'Yeah, just a little,' he said, closing the door.

Chapter Nine

I had planned to sit in a chair, in the dark, waiting for Billie to arrive home. I didn't have a cat to stroke like your typical Bond villain, but I could click the lamp on next to me for added dramatic effect. The thing was, I never knew when Billie was coming home, and I'd definitely get bored waiting for hours in the dark. Instead, in an effort to distract myself from memories of my embarrassing afternoon, I opted for Skyping Ziggy; her effervescent, unwavering belief in me was always my go-to. However, her vibrant, manic hello soon turned to business.

'Now, honey, I've booked you in for an acting class on the fifteenth – write that down.'

Acting class?

'Oh, I kind of thought I would just hit the ground running.'

Ziggy cut me a look up through her funky red-framed glasses. 'Have you met with your dialect coach yet?'

Oh shit.

I would have to act the shit out of this corner I was being backed into; truth be known, I had been too scared to navigate Hollywood without Billie showing me around.

'The fifteenth should be okay. I'll pencil it in,' I said, looking intently at my diary.

'Abby.' Ziggy's tone commanded attention. She never freaked out, and was the first person to tell me everything was fine and I was doing great, so when her voice took on that tone I got worried. 'Abby, sweetie, your cute little Aussie accent may get you a free drink from a hot American in a bar, but it's not going to land you a coveted role anytime soon.'

'Yeah, I'm sorry. I completely forgot about calling Faye. I've just been so flat out.'

Sunbaking by the pool.

Ziggy stared at me for so long that I thought the screen had frozen. 'Ray – his name is Ray.'

Double-shit.

I coughed. 'Ray, yes, of course. I'll call him first thing.' I wrote down a note.

'Well, make sure you do. I'm not going to organise any meetings until I get there next week. I expect some serious groundwork done by then; I know you've been settling in but it's time we got to work.'

I nodded. 'Absolutely. I am dying to get into it.'

I would do whatever Ziggy wanted: acting, elocution lessons, work on my posture, diet, Kabbalah, anything. I was kicking myself about how distracted I had allowed myself to become. This wasn't a holiday, this was my career, and now was the time to start taking it all a bit more seriously.

'I'll do anything, Zig, you name it!'

'Excellent, because I have organised a lunch date with Sienna Bailey. She'll be an invaluable connection while you're there.'

Anything but that.

Sienna fucking Bailey, my nemesis. Having lunch with Sienna at some avant-garde restaurant while she told me all about her success and her social life was cruel and unusual punishment. I thought maybe Ziggy was trying to end the conversation on a bit of a zinger, but she was deadly serious.

I wanted to protest. I wanted to scream that a huge part of Sienna's success was due to luck, because it surely wasn't based on her talent. I bit the inside of my cheek. Sienna had never had a single acting class, and had learned her American accent from watching hours of *90210* reruns. She was an utter fluke, and it killed me!

I forced a smile, knowing that Ziggy could see right through it. 'Sure, I'd love to catch up with Sienna. It's been ages.'

'Great, I'll send you the details. I think you can learn a lot from her.'

Her words were like a dagger to the heart: not only did I need acting lessons, but now Sienna fucking Bailey was going to be my mentor. This conversation was meant to make me feel better, not worse. While she'd stuck to our agreement – that is, not mentioning the aftermath of the complete shitstorm that brought me here – by the time we signed off I was eating ice-cream straight out of the tub.

So, Billie was keeping something from me, I'd flashed the neighbour, been told I needed acting lessons, and now I had a lunch date with my nemesis. What would tomorrow bring?

The sound of the front door and the jingling of keys halted my pity party.

'Honey, I'm home! I also hunted and gathered for us.' Billie appeared, dumping her make-up travel kit that she took everywhere with her – which I now eyed suspiciously – before dumping some takeaway bags on the counter.

'In-N-Out burgers!' she announced.

How could I stay mad at her? I quickly placed the lid back on my ice-cream, thinking it probably wouldn't be long before Ziggy suggested I join a gym. No one wanted a gal with a gut; I would have to watch my 'holiday' mode. Tomorrow it was back to business.

'How was work?' I asked, with genuine interest. It was hard to gauge Billie's reaction when I was staring at her back, but her voice seemed even enough.

'Crazy, but good crazy,' she said, unloading the chips from the bag. I snared one, munching on it thoughtfully as I rounded the counter.

'Well, I had an interesting day. You won't believe what happened.'

'You got an audition?' Her eyes lifted with hope.

'Ah, no, nothing like that; I ran into our favourite neighbour, Jay.'

Billie's demeanour changed instantly and she sighed. 'You weren't weird, were you?'

My memory flashed to chasing him up the stairs, blocking his way, harassing him at his front door and inadvertently flashing him.

'Define "weird".'

Billie scrunched up the empty takeout bag. 'Goddammit, Abby, what is your problem with Jay?' she snapped.

I was taken aback; her defence of him was rather over the top. I paused.

'Wait, do you like him?'

Billie did a double-take. 'What? No, of course not,' she croaked.

'You clearly do – you're always defending him.'

'I am not. I just think you have been a little judgemental about somebody you don't even know.'

'Ha! Judgemental? He judged me from day one!'

'And you haven't done anything to be judged on?'

I couldn't believe this; Billie was supposed to be on my side. We were meant to roll our eyes and bitch about boys, sisters before misters and all that. I felt kind of betrayed.

'I know you probably think he's just some cocky guy, but he's not. He's really helped me out.'

My interest piqued, while something strange twisted in my gut; why should I care if Billie and Jay had a thing? I completely didn't care. Really, truly.

'Have you been listening?'

My mind snapped back to the present.

'Sorry, what?'

'What did you do today? What was so weird?'

I cleared my throat, reaching for my chips, avoiding her questioning eyes at all costs. The whole spectacle wasn't even about me, so I wasn't going to start making it that way.

'Nothing, really; Jay just alluded to something, and when I pushed for more information, he shut down.'

Billie shifted uneasily. 'What did he allude to?'

Here was the moment to confront her. But now, seeing something in her eyes, I didn't feel so confident about it. I knew what it was like to be questioned. But if Billie was keeping something from me, how long would it be before it built up into something else?

'Is there something you're not telling me, Billie?'

Her face told me everything I needed to know. She was definitely keeping something from me, and it was something big.

All of a sudden, I felt nervous. What could cause such a look? Were she and Jay lovers? Ex-lovers? Was this condo really a gift from a sweet old actress or had Billie murdered her and hidden her body in a laundry chute? What was it?

Billie's chin began to tremble, and I instantly felt like shit.

'Damn Jay, why couldn't he just keep his mouth shut?' she said, moving to the lounge and flopping onto it like a moody teenager.

'Well, h-he didn't actually say anything,' I said, following her out and panicking at her tears. Now I was the one defending Jay. I sat next to her, touching her shoulder as she buried her head in her hands. 'So I guess he really is a good guy because, believe me, I tried to get more out of him.'

'And what did he say?' Billie sniffed.

'He said to ask you.' I winced.

Billie shook her head. 'I didn't want to say anything. I wanted you to want to come here, to think that I had my shit together.'

I didn't press – I felt bad enough as it was. I grabbed an In-N-Out Burger serviette from the counter so she could blow her nose, and then sat quietly, waiting for her to go on, if she wanted.

'I don't have a job . . . well, not the job you think. I came here thinking that I would be this big-time make-up artist to the stars, that I would be riding golf carts around the back lots of studios and be lining up for buffet lunches with crew members, but it's not like that – it's never been like that. I've applied for everything from make-up artist in a dodgy-ass "glamour" photo place to theatre restaurant work, and I've got squat. My biggest gig was the one with Molly White. If it weren't for her and Jay, I would have come back home with my tail between my legs long ago.'

My brow creased in confusion. 'But I don't get it – your Instagram . . .'

Billie laughed, so maniacally I thought she had truly lost it. 'Oh, Abby, please. Haven't you heard of fake it till you make it? Crop a pic, chuck on a filter and sell the lie. Everyone back home thinks I'm this big success, living the dream, but I'm a big fat failure.'

I could hardly believe what Billie was telling me; for the past week she had left with her make-up bag, talking about clients and her long days; the effortlessness of her lies was disturbing. I looked at her broken demeanour and wondered how long she had been living this way.

'Jay is the only person who knows the truth, and he has never judged me for it.'

'And that's why you defend him, because he's been a really good neighbour, a friend to you,' I said. It all made total sense now.

Billie shook her head. 'He's so much more than that,' she said, and my chest clenched like a vice. Billie and Jay were a thing; despite all her woes, she had actually bagged herself a sexy-as-hell man, who was successful to boot. Something primal surfaced in me. I really didn't want her to tell me, to confide all the sordid details, and yet, despite the voice screaming inside me, I pressed her for more.

'Oh?' I said, cocking my brow.

Billie's mouth curved as she looked at me with blood-shot eyes.

'He's my neighbour, my friend . . . and my boss.'

Chapter Ten

'Your what?'

'I work for Jay . . . at the Saloon.'

I stared at her, waiting for her to tell me she was joking.

'Yep, the big-shot make-up artist waits tables on the Strip – and that is the look I've been wanting to avoid.'

I blinked, trying to gather my thoughts. 'Sorry . . . It's not a bad thing, I am just – why didn't you tell me? I don't care, Jesus, it's not like you're topless table dancing or anything . . . you're not, are you?'

'Abby!'

'I'm sorry, of course you're not.'

'I *work* on the Strip, I don't *do* it.' She half-laughed.

'Okay,' I said, kind of embarrassed. I'd heard enough about the Saloon Bar to know it wasn't that sort of club.

'It's actually a really cool place; I mean, if I'm going to be a failure and have a plan B, it's a pretty funky plan B.'

My shoulders slumped. 'Billie, you are not a failure, you're just taking a detour until you get to where you're going, that's all. I mean, you're still here, surviving; that's a success story.'

'I'm just lucky in a lot of ways.'

'That's what everything is based on in this business – pure luck.'

'You being here isn't about luck – you worked for it. You are driven and talented, and I just know that you're going to get what you want.'

Ziggy's voice echoed in my head. *I expect some serious groundwork done.*

'Maybe. Ziggy thinks I need acting lessons.'

Billie frowned. 'I'm sure she meant that as a positive – you know, to hone your craft.'

Maybe that was what she meant, but there is always a part of you that believes you're a natural, a regular Marlon Brando. I bet that Sienna hadn't spent time clucking like a chicken or doing mime work to develop her acting diversity.

'Yeah, well, whatever it takes, right?' I sighed.

Billie nodded. 'Whatever it takes.'

'So now that we have all that sorted, can we make some house rules?'

'Sure,' said Billie, hesitantly.

'No more secrets, okay? After all that I have left behind, the one thing I can't stomach is people keeping secrets from me.'

Billie knew what I was referring to. I had told her about how things had gone down back home, knowing I wouldn't be able to move forward unless I was open with her.

'Oh, Abby, I'm sorry – of course, no more secrets.' She nodded adamantly.

'So if you are secretly waitressing topless in your spare time, speak now or forever hold your peace.'

Billie laughed, almost shoving me off the couch. 'Shut up.'

We laughed, feeling the tension lift from us; there was a lot to be said for keeping it real between friends. I kind of wanted to ask her about Jay, if there was ever anything more between them than just neighbours and colleagues, but I figured we'd had enough drama for today.

'So what about you – anything you want to tell me while we're clearing the air?'

I bit my lip. I wanted to recoil from the vision that haunted me but, seeing as we were being honest, I thought it was better to come from me than Jay.

'Well, speaking of being topless . . .'

~

I had thought Billie might offer me some comfort, some friendly reassurance to make me feel better, but instead she fell to the floor, flailing around in complete, hyperventilating hysterics.

'Oh my God, I wish I could have seen his face,' she breathed, wiping a tear from her eye.

'Oh, shut up – I hope you get carpet burn,' I said, making for the kitchen, hoping to soothe my sorrows with a microwaved burger, but Billie rolled over and grabbed at my ankles.

'Wait, wait, tell me more,' she giggled.

'What's there to say? I never want to speak of it again; in fact, is there any chance we can relocate to the Hills where we will never, ever run into Jay?' I pulled my legs from her grasp.

Billie rolled over and rested her head on her hand. 'Nope, no chance, sorry.'

'Well, can you give me his work hours or something, so I can avoid him?'

'Sorry, doesn't work like that, especially for Jay; his hours are all over the place.'

'So, he's the manager?' I asked, placing my plate of burger into the microwave and grimacing at how disgusting and soggy it was going to be.

'Ah, owner-manager; he's the "big" boss, remember?'

I was curious; Jay couldn't have been any more than, what, thirty? How had he landed on his feet? What was his story? The microwave beeping pulled me out of my reverie.

'He's really great to work for, firm but fair. I can't believe you two don't get along.'

'I wouldn't say we don't get along.'

Billie snorted. 'Are you kidding me?'

I thought about our track record in the short time we had known one another; the foundation of our acquaintance was built on shoddy ground at best.

'Well, the man has seen my nipple, which is the basis for all good friendships. I'm sure we'll get along just fine.'

Chapter Eleven

Most aspiring actresses would have given their right arm to receive a phone call for a lunch date from Sienna Bailey. I, on the other hand, wanted to fake my own death and enter a witness protection program.

The call came far sooner than I anticipated; luckily, Billie and I had discussed tactics prior.

'Meet her on your turf! Don't let her whisk you to one of her fancy locals – bring her to you,' Billie had said.

It sounded like we were gearing up to stake a vampire through the heart, which, all things considered, wasn't too far from the truth.

Billie's eyes were alight. 'Get her to meet you at the Saloon.'

'I don't know.' I wasn't sure that was even neutral ground for me.

'Come on, I'll be working and I will totally serve you; it might just stop you from committing self-harm.'

I was about to ask if we could make it a day Jay wasn't around but thought better of it. Apparently, he could do no wrong, and I had made a conscious decision to be mature about all things Jay. Meanwhile, I secretly hoped I could avoid him for the rest of my life, so going to the place he owned was not the brightest move. I had stayed non-committal, until Sienna rang.

Despite my scheming with Billie, Sienna caught me off guard and I panicked. I found myself not only agreeing to meet her but also uttering, in an animated, high-pitched voice, ridiculous phrases like, 'Can't wait!' and 'It's going to be epic!' Billie simply shook her head, looking at me like I was a stranger. I rolled my eyes, cupping the receiver.

'When's your next lunch shift?'

Billie grinned from ear to ear. 'Tomorrow.'

I sighed deeply, unblocking the phone and returning to our conversation with the confidence of a woman who had lived in LA all her life.

'How's tomorrow at the Saloon Bar? Great, meet you there at 12 p.m. Awesome!'

I ended the conversation feeling utterly sick.

'Awesome,' Billie mimicked.

'Oh, shut up! How am I going to get out of it?'

'You can't – you just have to grin and bear it.'

'I don't know if I am that good an actress.'

'What did I tell you?'

'Never leave home without eyeliner and a nice bra?'

'Fake it till you make it.'

'I thought we'd decided that tends to backfire.'

Billie shrugged. 'Sienna isn't the sharpest tool in the shed.'

'Perhaps, but, at the end of the day, she's employed, I'm not.'

'You will be.'

I wondered if this was what I sounded like when I reassured Billie; it was really annoying.

'Do you think she knows about . . .' I really didn't want to say Scott's name, but I didn't need to; apparently the look on my face spoke for me.

Billie shook her head. 'Seriously, you've got a blank slate here. All of the LA Family are so self-absorbed they can barely see past the end of their nose jobs.'

'You really think so?'

'Trust me, in this town you are a complete nobody.'

I laughed. 'I don't know exactly how I should feel about that.'

Billie smiled. 'You should feel awesome.'

'Oh yeah, why?'

'Because here, you can be whoever you want to be.'

The title 'homewrecker' flashed in my mind, and I felt a shiver run down my spine.

'Fake it till you make it, huh?'

'Yep. Welcome to Hollywood!'

Chapter Twelve

The Saloon Bar was reminiscent of a giant Aspen ski lodge: wood, stone, sweeping balconies and an expansive courtyard garden. The beers were big; the steaks were plump. Why had I let Billie talk me into bringing Sienna here? She was probably expecting an Ivy-esque atmosphere; shellfish canapés, white linen tablecloths and fresh floral arrangements, and I had brought her to a bar and grill. Sure, it wasn't just any bar and grill, but somehow I just couldn't see her sitting on a stool, chowing down on some southern biscuits.

I hadn't thought this through at all; here I was, looking like Elly May Clampett in shorts and singlet, while she was a vision in crisp white, floating towards me in designer sunglasses, Yves Saint Laurent handbag on her arm. I could smell her perfume from a mile away, probably French and expensive. She was my age but she was dressed like Grace Kelly – like she had just stepped out of a salon, not into a saloon. If she felt out of place she never showed it. Instead, spotting me from a distance, she lifted her sunglasses, a huge, bright, white smile spreading across her radiant face.

'Abby!' she called out, waving as she made her way over to me. I slid off my stool knowing she would be a good foot taller than me; now I'd literally be in her shadow.

'Oh my gosh, look at you.' She embraced me with her long, bony arms; I only hoped I didn't get make-up on her shoulder. She pulled away, looking me over from head to toe.

Sienna actually looked thinner than I remembered her on set, maybe it was all that trekking in the Hollywood Hills. Her hair was shiny, her skin was aglow, her teeth were extra white: she represented everything that Hollywood success was about. If she thought we had anything in common and could hang, I was really at a loss as to why; maybe seeing me would make her feel better? Seeing her only made me feel worse. Maybe I should have left *Ship to Sea* two years earlier, and hit LA when Aussie actors were a hot commodity. Was it too late? Had I missed my time?

'I can't believe you're here,' she said, sliding onto the seat opposite mine. She placed her bag on the tabletop, label facing my direction. 'Isn't it insane?' she said, shaking her head, staring at me as if my presence was just too much to wrap her head around.

'Well, we are in La-La Land,' I said, sipping on my Coke.

'Right?' She laughed way too much for my terrible joke.

'Did you want a drink?' I asked, looking around for Billie, who, I hoped, was lurking in the shadows, ready to come and save me.

'I would kill for a sangria, but I have to go to this god-awful red-carpet event with Leon tonight.' She rolled her eyes.

She didn't need to name-drop Leon's surname: every gossip rag had shown snaps of her, on several occasions, locking lips with Hollywood action star Leon Denero.

'Well, best walk a straight line,' I said, fixing my eyes on Billie, who was weaving her way to the bar to grab a jug of water; oh, she was loving this.

My attention was snapped away from the bar when I felt Sienna's hand clasp mine.

'Babe, tell me the truth,' she said earnestly. 'How are you going after that horrifically embarrassing break-up with Scott?'

I felt myself physically recoil from the mere mention of his name – and, worse still, the fact that Sienna Bailey was mentioning the core focus of my humiliation, the very thing I had been running from. Now it had caught up to me here, from the pouted lips of my nemesis. I blinked, pulling my hand away, desperately trying to think of the words, words that failed to come.

Mercifully, a voice sliced through our growing silence.

'Water, ladies?' Billie announced, placing the jug and two glasses down.

Sienna placed her sunglasses back on to shield her eyes from the sun, her attention instantly diverted by a notification on her phone. 'Do you have sparkling?'

'Why, Sienna, I recall you being partial to plain old tap water back home.' Billie placed her hand on her hip and looked at her expectantly. Sienna's attention snapped up from her phone. She slowly lifted her sunglasses, revealing a confused stare.

'B-Billie?'

'Hello, Sienna,' she said brightly.

'W-what are you doing here?' Once again came the head-to-toe look.

'I work here.'

'Really?' Sienna said, as if she expected her to say it was a joke, but when the punch line never came, Sienna's expression morphed from horror to happiness. 'Oh, awesome, it's a really cool place. Leon actually dropped me off – he said this was one of his night spots back in the day.'

There was the name drop again, and the little dig – 'back in the day' – didn't go unnoticed by Billie and me. *The Saloon Bar? Oh, that's, like, so yesterday.*

'Well, he knows what a cool place it is, then,' said Billie, pouring a glass of water for me.

If Sienna was finding it hard to believe I was here in LA, then Billie's presence was really leaving her lost for words. 'Wow, it's like a *Ship to Sea* reunion,' she breathed out.

'It sure is.' I saluted with my drink.

'Okay, I'll give you a minute to look over the menus, and I'll be back to take your orders; remember, tip big.' Billie winked.

I laughed, shaking my head and studying the selection, thinking maybe Sienna had found Billie's quip funny; after all, Billie was always the funny, entertaining one at work. But by the looks of Sienna, shaking her head and watching on as Billie disappeared, she didn't find anything the least bit funny.

'What?' I asked, looking up. I thought maybe she'd been shocked by the lack of vegan options on the menu, but she hadn't even opened hers up.

'My God, Billie Martin. Can you believe it?'

'Believe what?'

Sienna leant forward, lowering her voice. 'She's waiting tables at the Saloon Bar, like, totally tragic.'

It took every ounce of my control not to pick up my drink and throw it in her face. 'What's so tragic about that?'

'I just always thought she was doing well for herself, that she was this make-up artist killing it. I never thought she was . . . here.'

'Well, most artists have a second gig.'

Sienna laughed. 'She's a make-up artist, Abby, not some tortured painter or struggling actor; it's not the same.'

I remembered why I had detested Sienna so: it wasn't just because she was a completely talentless fluke, but because beneath the perfect veneer was a bully, a mean girl, and I couldn't stomach her.

'Excuse me, I have to go to the bathroom,' I said. If I didn't get away I was likely to stab her with my butter knife, I was so utterly furious.

I had to calm down. If I leapt over the table and attacked her, chances were there was a pap waiting in the bushes, and I really didn't need a mugshot to be my introduction to Tinseltown; I mean, that sort of thing usually came much later on. Lost in my furious thoughts and wondering how I would possibly survive the remainder of lunch, I stormed down a corridor and up a small flight of stairs, following the signs to the ladies' toilets.

Breathe, Abby, just breathe . . . 'Fuck!'

I slammed into someone so hard that the involuntary expletive shot out of me as I grabbed at my shoulder, feeling a sharp slice of pain as if I had run straight into a brick wall. And in a way I had, except the brick wall had a face and a name, and its name was Jay.

'Abby?'

'Hey, hi.'

'What are you doing here?'

It was the same question I had asked myself every second I'd been here.

'Oh, I, um, I'm meeting a friend, and Billie said the cookie-dough sundae was something to write home about, so I thought I'd pop down and have a crack.'

Stop. Talking.

I was blabbering like an idiot, trying to come up with an excuse as if I'd been sprung rifling through his filing cabinet. I had no way of dealing with running into Jay, especially when he was looking at me the way he was now, as if he found my ridiculousness so completely and utterly amusing.

'Cookie dough?' he mused.

'Yeah, love me some cookie dough.'

Honestly, how had I made it to adulthood? I had walked red carpet events in Oz, attended awards ceremonies, interviews and photo shoots with grace and dignity, and yet being near this man turned me into a complete basketcase.

Just when, for the second time that week, I was ready to seek out a second-storey balcony to throw myself off, I was saved by the intervention of Billie, who was bouncing up the stairs behind me.

'Oh, wow, she has changed soooo much.'

'Aesthetically, but she's still a mega bitch.'

'Her hair is ridiculously shiny. Do you think she's had work done? Her nose looks more like a ski jump than I remember.'

'Who are you talking about?' Jay interjected.

'Sienna Bailey,' Billie said pointedly, like he should know who that was, but his eyes were blank.

'You know, from that crime/mystery show made for Netflix, something "FX" – I can't remember the full title. She plays one of the main characters.'

'Oh, yeah, that's a really great show.'

I rolled my eyes. Was everyone mad?

'Yeah, I remember, she plays the main girl, has a really bad accent in it,' he said.

My head snapped around so quickly I almost got whip-lash. 'What did you say?'

Jay looked at me, probably taken aback by the manic look in my eyes. 'Ah, her accent is bad?'

'Really, how?'

Jay shrugged. 'Have you seen it? I think she's trying too hard. Her American accent is way over the top.'

I stared at Jay, overcome by the desire to kiss him square on the lips; with four small words, Jay had made my day, my month, and he didn't even know it.

'I think you might be my favourite person in the world right now.'

Jay smirked, a little intrigued and whole lot confused as he looked between me and Billie, not quite sure what to make of my weirdness.

Billie sighed. 'Sienna Bailey is Abby's arch enemy.'

'Oh, right,' he said.

'She has this way of sounding like she's being sweet while being a total bitch,' Billie said.

'And she's a terrible name-dropper,' I added.

'And just generally makes you feel beneath her, right?' Billie said.

Billie was on the money, and I couldn't even begin to imagine what she would think if I ever relayed what Sienna had said about her. The last thing she needed was a judge-mental idiot making her feel worse than she already did.

'And this is the friend you're meeting with?' Jay asked, perplexed.

Oh great, now he would think I was this giant two-faced bitch; maybe I was a hypocrite. Lunch wasn't my idea, exactly, but he wasn't to know that.

'Yeah, well, more of foe, really,' I said.

'Do you want me to make up an excuse for you to cut lunch short? An emergency phone call or something?' Billie asked.

'No, thanks, I'll be right. I'll use it as an acting lesson, an Academy Award–winning one at that.'

Jay folded his arms. 'Why don't you just leave? Why waste your time hanging out with someone you don't like?'

His completely logical advice annoyed me. 'Well, it's complicated.'

'Only if you make it complicated.'

'Abby's manager set it up for her,' Billie added in my defence.

Jay scoffed. 'Managers.' He said the word as if it had a bitter aftertaste; it was the same disdain he'd shown when he learnt I was an actress.

'Don't sweat it, Jay. I don't expect you to understand,' I said coolly, swapping one place I didn't want to be for another. Back at my table, Sienna was idly swiping through her smartphone, bored.

'Sorry, I was just asking Billie what the specials were,' I lied.

Sienna laughed. 'Well, she'd know,' she said with a little wink, like we were a part of some inner joke.

'Actually, I'm thinking of getting a gig here.' Another lie.

Sienna's eyes flashed up from her drink. 'What?'

'Yeah – I mean, I think I would just go mad if I spent my days jogging up to the Hollywood sign and sipping on vegan juices all day. I need to be in the thick of it, chatting to VIPs and rock stars. Come sundown this place is something else.'

Though I had little proof that the Saloon's reputation was, in fact, true, the kink in Sienna's perfectly manicured brow was enough to tell me she was intrigued.

'Here you go. On the house, the tastiest buttermilk biscuits you'll ever have.' Billie broke the silence, placing down the basket. 'Ready to order?'

'Ah, yeah, I'll have the kale and quinoa without the honey mustard vinaigrette, please.'

Billie smiled so brightly she almost blinded us. 'Of course you will,' she said sweetly; then she turned to me expectantly.

'And I'll have the chicken tacos, with extra sour cream and guacamole,' I said without apology. If my memory served me rightly, Sienna loved her food, and the thinly-veiled disappointment in her voice when she had ordered told me as much. I would have great pleasure watching her face fall when our plates arrived.

'Abby was just telling me what a hoot this place is,' Sienna said.

Oh God, I wished I could telepathically communicate with Billie right now; please don't undo my lies.

'Yeah, haven't you been here on a Thursday night? The place is insane! You really aren't a local until you've experienced happy hour here.'

I had no way of knowing if anything Billie was saying was true, but it aligned with my glowing testimony, and I was relieved. Until I saw Jay making a beeline for our table. Mr Honesty-is-the-best-policy was on his way, and we were so screwed.

Chapter Thirteen

Abort! Abort! I really didn't want Jay to witness my ability to bullshit so thoroughly, but the larger part of me really didn't want him to meet the perfect Sienna Bailey, who was already straightening in her seat and brushing her long, blonde hair over her shoulder.

'Ladies, how are we finding everything today?' Jay flashed the most gorgeous grin, completely disarming any hot-blooded woman within a five-table radius. He had certainly never used it on me before, which was lucky as I already seemed to become a bumbling idiot around him at the best of times.

'Amazing,' Sienna almost purred; I glanced at her half-drunk water and the untouched biscuit and wondered what she had found so amazing. The LA air? That would be a first.

'Excellent. Hey, listen, I'm going to send over some champagne. I'm sorry I can't join, but hey, Abby' – he turned to me, pointing – 'we'll catch up later, okay? And a huge congrats on closing the deal. My lips are sealed, but, man, party at your place,' he said, with a parting wink.

It was official, Jay had lost his mind, and all I could do was blink, utterly confused, until Billie intervened.

'Oh my God, you landed a deal? Abby, that is *so* amazing, congratulations!'

My eyes shifted to hers; had I missed something? Had everybody gone completely bonkers? The moment I turned to Sienna, who was sitting on the edge of her seat, her eyes wild, I realised what was going on.

'What deal?' she asked.

An air of satisfaction rolled over me, seeing her so utterly desperate to learn more. But she knew just as much as I did.

'Look, I'm sworn to secrecy, and at this stage I have literally only just signed on the dotted line, so I'm keeping it on the down-low.' Lies, lies, lies.

So much for me being all about the truth.

Sienna laughed, almost nervously. 'Oh, come on, Abby, you can tell me. I am as silent as the grave.'

Suuuure you are.

'Sienna, I would tell you in a heartbeat, but I'm bound by confidentiality.'

The hole Jay had dug was getting deeper and deeper and, had I not been loving every single minute of watching the secretive deal drive Sienna slowly insane, I would have had some reservations. I could see the cogs turning in her head.

Movie deal, TV deal, book deal? Wouldn't she like to know.

'So, who is the gorgeous man?'

'Oh, that's Jay, Abby's special friend,' Billie added.

My head spun around so fast.

Whoa, whoa, whoa. It was one thing to get carried away with a little white lie, but let's not get fucking crazy.

'Don't you have work to do?' I muttered under my breath.

Billie giggled. 'Yeah, gotta keep the boss happy, hey?' she grinned. 'I'll be back with your meals soon.'

I drew in a huge sigh of relief watching her walk away, but it was short-lived. I turned back to catch Sienna's manic blue eyes. In four quick shunts, she moved her seat closer to me, leaning in as if to tell me a secret.

'Oh my God, Abby, you're doing alright for yourself,' she said, her eyes shifting to where Jay stood at the cash register, engaged in conversation with the bar manager.

'A secret deal and a hot man – looks like you're living the dream.' She said it in a way that tried to make out that she was happy, but there was a dead look in her eyes. 'You're such a surprise package.' She sat back in her chair, assessing me with amused interest.

'What's that supposed to mean?'

'Well, unlike Billie, you're kind of a closed book; you're not online very much, you have, what, eighty-one Instagram posts? Your profile page on Facey hardly gets any traction, and have you ever tweeted in your life?'

I felt my spine involuntarily straighten. 'Well, maybe I'm just a private person.'

Sienna scoffed. 'Oh, please, Abby, you know that privacy is just for people with low self-esteem – what you're doing is social suicide.'

I felt my insides twist at her words. What she was saying was every actor's worst nightmare, the thought of fading into oblivion, of not being relevant anymore. Back home, I was relevant. I was on the cover of magazines, in the gossip columns. In many ways it was a curse, but the one thing it did do, the one thing I really hadn't appreciated or felt until now, was that it put my name out there. But in LA, I was just one very small fish in a big ocean. Looking at Sienna's ice-blue eyes, I could see she was the shark.

'Listen, I'm just giving you some advice,' she said, as if I should be grateful. 'I just think if you have something, show, or tell.' Her eyes once again strayed towards Jay. 'If I had *that* I'd be screaming it from the rafters.'

I knew Sienna well enough to know what she was alluding to. All those pap snaps with her and Leon out and about were no accident. And he sure did feature on a few of her three thousand-odd 'candid' Insta pics, but that just wasn't me. Not after what happened. Sure, I could lift my profile if I were to post a few happy snaps with a sexy mystery man abroad, but that wasn't my style. Even if my eyes were lingering on Jay for a tad longer than I wanted.

Don't even think about it, Abby – you're already the scarlet woman.

'Well, whatever your grand reveal is, make sure the hottie is in on it. He is going to look mighty fine on a red carpet.'

I tried to control the snort that wanted to escape. Jay on a red carpet? He would sooner die, of that I was sure.

Sienna had her head tilted slightly, her eyes still towards the bar. 'It's so strange . . . it's almost like I know his face.'

I wanted to roll my eyes so bad; of course she would try that. Nothing was sacred. 'Well, you're a socialite, you probably crossed paths at some stage.' Although I seriously doubted it; Jay didn't exactly mingle with actors.

Sienna seemed troubled, struggling to place him.

'Maybe he just has one of those faces,' I said, trying to move the conversation along, wishing that we could just stop talking about him altogether.

'I don't think I would forget running into a man like that. It is annoying, he seems familiar but I just can't put my finger on it.'

Mercifully her trance was broken the minute Billie appeared. 'Grub's up! One kale, and one chicken taco,' she announced, plonking them in front of us. Billie took in our little huddle, Sienna now sitting so close that our elbows were almost touching.

'Listen, um, Jay says he doesn't mean to cut your lunch date short, but he has to leave by one,' Billie said to me. 'So if you want to get a ride to that thing of yours you'll have to hurry . . .'

Billie looked at me intently, trying to communicate with her eyes.

'That thing?' I repeated.

She nodded her head slowly and I mirrored the movement, until finally the penny dropped.

'Oh, right, that thing! Yes, of course, sure,' I said, wincing and turning my attention to Sienna. 'Sorry, I really have to eat and run.'

'Oh, no worries, secret deals and things have to be seen to.' Her words were laced with sarcasm; my rather intriguing life was simply eating at her insides, and I loved it. Billie was so right bringing me here; instead of going home depressed, I was going to leave so completely smug I could barely stand myself. I glanced at my watch and pretended to be disappointed that one o'clock would allow barely enough time to scoff down my lunch and hear Sienna's enthralling story about her summer on a yacht off the coast of Croatia.

When Jay appeared at our side, jingling his keys, the relief that washed over me almost numbed the intense case of indigestion that I was battling. 'You ready to go?'

Hell, yes, I was ready. So ready I was prepared to do a deal with the devil, and be whisked away in the devil's black Mustang.

Chapter Fourteen

The thing with lies is that you can never quite tell where they will take you. But to wind up this little tête-à-tête with Sienna, I was willing to go to hell and back.

'Ah, yeah, sure, we don't want to be late,' I replied to Jay, praying that Billie had given him the heads-up on the role he was playing in my elaborate exit.

'Sienna, I am sorry to have to end our catch-up,' I said, just as Jay coughed into his fist, no doubt trying to hide his smile. I wanted to kick him, hard, but I ignored him and stood, accepting Sienna's weirdly long hug.

'We should make a regular thing of this,' Sienna said, her eyes sparkling with excitement.

'Sure, sounds like a plan.'

Jay had now turned to the side, averting his face from us; he was clearly finding it difficult to maintain his composure with so much bullshit flying around his courtyard.

'Well, we have each other's numbers, so . . .' I stepped nearer to Jay.

Rather than waving goodbye, Sienna followed me and walked up to Jay, her eyes shifting between the two of us. 'I was just saying to Abby that I feel like I know you from somewhere – have we met before?'

Jay's eyes flicked momentarily across Sienna's face, then glazed over. 'I don't think so,' he said, shutting her down quickly, before grabbing my hand. It was such a shock I almost flinched. 'It was nice to meet you, though. We better run.'

Sienna laughed, a little embarrassed she had mentioned it, then brushed her hair aside. 'That's okay, thanks for lunch. It's a really cool place you have here. I might swing by with Leon one night and we can hang out.'

Jay's hand squeezed mine so hard I was tempted to dig my nails into his skin. 'Sure, any time,' he said in that charming way of his. Now who was full of it?

After a final, awkward goodbye with Sienna, Jay mercifully pulled me away, weaving through the tables and heading for the exit. I smiled to myself, enjoying the fact that Sienna was watching me leave hand-in-hand with hot Jay. I had no doubt that she had met me for lunch to gloat over her success and revel in my misery, assuming that I'd be down on my luck, friendless and unemployed. While much of that was true, Sienna didn't have to know it; 'fake it till you make it', right?

The moment Jay and I veered out the exit and into the alley that led to the parking lot, Jay let go of my hand; the ruse was over, one I'd had no idea he was a part of.

'Thanks, special friend,' I said, looking for a crack in his demeanour, which had returned to its usual stern state. And then I saw it; a dimple softened his cheek as he smiled. He took off his sunglasses and looked my way.

'Hey, blame Billie,' I went on. 'I think she enjoyed all that far too much.'

'I hope you tipped her big?' Jay laughed, and it was the first time I had heard it. So genuine, and undeniably lovely, was the sound that I couldn't help but look back at him as he went round to his car door, looking at me expectantly.

'Oh, you're really giving me a ride?' I was beginning to find it hard to decipher what was real and what was not. As far as I knew, the only 'thing' I had to attend to was defrosting chicken for tonight's dinner, a stark contrast to the mysterious plans I had alluded to earlier. I had gone from feeling quite smug to feeling like a bit of an impostor.

Jay's elbows rested on the roof of his Mustang. 'I said I would.'

'Oh, okay, well, thanks,' I said, shifting to the passenger door. 'But just so you know, I'm not tipping you.'

Jay's smile broadened as we opened the doors in unison and slid into the car.

~

Jay steered down the narrow lane of the alley over potholes and around graffiti-coloured skip bins, passing a couple of kitchen hands lingering near the back door, smoking. Jay lifted his finger from the steering wheel in acknowledgement, and rather than scurrying out of the path of the Big Boss like you might expect, they replied with jovial salutes and head nods. I took a moment to glance at Jay, wondering exactly what kind of boss he was. Billie liked him enough to defend, even praise, him, so he must be alright. The Saloon seemed to run smoothly and efficiently. The atmosphere was nice, the surfaces were clean, the staff were happy and friendly – all proof of a well-oiled machine. Maybe I had been too quick to judge. Maybe he really was a good guy; after all, he had conspired with Billie to help me with my nightmarish lunch with Sienna. I guess I owed him one. Just as I was about to say as much, even thank him, his words cut me short.

'You know, I think I've underestimated you,' he said.

Wait, what?

My mouth gaped a little, stunned by the unexpected words. 'Oh?' I pressed, the suspense killing me.

'You are a far better actress than I thought you'd be.'

My brows knitted together as I stared at his profile.

'Really?'

'Really; I mean, the way you delivered your lines to Sienna was particularly impressive: "thank you so much, let's catch up again". I mean, that shit was Academy Award–worthy.'

He mimicked me – fucking mimicked me! I could feel my blood boiling.

'Yeah, well, your performance was rather impressive, too. Tell me, do you often interfere with people's affairs on the job? Is that how your business has become such a success? Maybe I should try it sometime,' I spat, turning my attention out the window.

I didn't know if Jay was smirking or glaring my way, but I didn't really care; accusing me of being fake really hit a nerve, mainly because I knew it was true.

'If Billie asked me to walk over fire, I would,' he said solemnly. My attention snapped from the blur that was the Strip at high speed to Jay, wondering what on earth made them so fiercely loyal to each other. I just didn't get it.

'Yeah, well, you don't have to have any false sense of duty to me,' I said.

'I don't.'

'Good.'

'Fine.'

We drove on in silence; the tension between us was painful but neither of us was willing to give in. Luckily the condo wasn't far from the Saloon; in fact, I could easily have walked home, or maybe hung around with Billie and walked back with her. Somehow suffering through lunch with Sienna now seemed far more appealing than being in the presence of this man.

Had he not been driving so fast I would have taken my chances and leapt from his Mustang, army-rolling onto the pavement and flipping him the bird, before limping the rest of the way home.

Instead, I chose to be the bigger person. I could pretend to be nice; I'd just spent the last hour doing so with Sienna.

And if I managed to break through Jay's stone wall and build some kind of rapport, Billie would be really proud of me.

Where to start? His ego. I had tried complimenting his car last time and got nowhere, and the only other thing I knew about Jay was his business.

'I love the Saloon Bar,' I said, and it wasn't a lie. The vibe was great, the food delicious. It had been a pleasant surprise.

We were stilled at a set of traffic lights, and I could sense something in Jay shift. Could it be possible that his icy façade was thawing? It seemed like he didn't know how to respond to me; I guess saying 'thank you' would be kind of weird.

'Look, we're not exactly hiring at the moment, but if you have a résumé I can let you know when something comes up.'

Wait, what?

I laughed, astounded by his arrogance.

'I don't want a job, I was just saying . . .'

'Really?' he said incredulously.

'I don't need a job.' And if I did, working for him would be the last thing on earth I'd consider.

'You say that now, while you're living off your little nest egg, but believe me, if you want to be an actor in this town, you're going to need a day job.'

I crossed my arms; seriously, who did he think he was? He didn't know me or my situation. 'You seem to know an awful lot about actors.'

Jay smiled. 'Nikki, the floor manager, was a child star in the eighties; I think she's waiting on a call-back for a reality TV gig. Jimmy, my busboy, is currently reciting lines for a Levi's advertisement; my head chef is a classically-trained stage actor who works the matinee shift at a local theatre-restaurant on a weekend, which is a real pain in the ass to schedule around, but he cooks a mean chilli so I can forgive him. Charlotte, Marissa and Toni are casuals and models in the latest Walmart catalogue, and one of the bartenders, Josie, plays Super Girl on Hollywood Boulevard. And that's just to name a few. So, yeah, I know about actors.'

I snapped my mouth shut, hoping he hadn't noticed it drop.

'There's something you need to know in this town,' he continued. 'Everything you think you know about this place is wrong. Everyone is blonder, skinnier and richer than you, and at some stage in your "journey" you will be sitting in your car crying in a parking lot after yet another soul-destroying audition for a beer commercial where you won't even have any lines to remember because a panel of soulless men will just want you to turn in a bikini for them, with the promise of putting you on a Super Bowl billboard.'

'Wow. Someone is incredibly jaded.'

'I'm a realist.'

It all made sense now; Jay hated everything about my profession – that was clear. No doubt it would make rostering tough with staff cancelling or swapping shifts for yet another dead-end audition. He'd seen the ups and downs of promise and rejection, mopped up tears and suffered burst eardrums after an employee screamed with the joy of a call-back. Yeah, no wonder he had taken an instant dislike to yet another actress with stars in her eyes coming to town.

'Tell me, then, why do you live in Hollywood? Because it pretty much sounds like the very last place on earth you should be.'

Jay laughed, the irony not lost on him. 'You mean, a realist living in the land of dreams?'

'Exactly.'

As we paused at yet another red light, he rubbed at his jaw, pondering the absurdity of it before shrugging and looking at me with a smile. His eyes were dark but I saw a boyish sparkle there, and though I fought it, it made me smile. I cocked a brow, still waiting for his answer.

'Someone has to pick up the pieces.'

And in that moment, for just a second, I caught a glimpse of the real Jay Davis.

Chapter Fifteen

Jay dropped me off at the condo, having 'errands to run', and we parted on a relatively civil note. I couldn't help but think about all the motley crew that were on his payroll. It had planted a seed in my mind, one that I really didn't want to water and blossom.

Nope; with each determined step I took up to the condo a new resilience built within me. I would take acting lessons, I would work on my accent, I would go on a health kick and run up all the hills and drink all the water. I would start my integration into the #LAfamily scene and I would completely fake it till I made it, showing them all back home what I was made of. And if that meant taking snapshots, chucking on a heavy filter and making out I was living the dream until I really was, then so be it.

My dreams weren't going to end up on the scrapheap for the likes of Jay Davis to sweep up. If anything, his tales had only made me more determined to prove him wrong, to be different, to make it. I wasn't just some naive wannabe – I came from good Aussie stock and I knew a thing or two. And I knew exactly what I needed to do now.

First things first; I got out my cell and, fighting against every fibre in my body, I texted.

Hey Sienna, so great catching up today, sorry I had to go. Wanna catch up for a happy hour sometime? We can paint the town red, or whatever colour you want xoxo

Ugh, hitting send felt like selling my soul, but I also knew Ziggy was right. Making connections was vital in LA. I'd known that before I'd even stepped off the plane. I barely had enough time to unlock the door when my phone beeped in reply.

Hey Gurl, it was SO amazing seeing you today too, could have hung all day. We totally have to do happy hour together! What are you doing this Thursday night???

Nooooo, my brain screamed in protest, but I had to follow through. I had to get out of my comfort zone – that was all there was to it. I put my bag down on the kitchen counter, then collapsed onto the leather lounge. I waited a few minutes, wanting to appear casually cool, not desperate, then, with a nod of encouragement and a deep breath, I eventually replied:

Thursday – can do! Send me the deets . . . can't wait xx

Send and grimace.

Sienna responded straightaway; no waiting for her. Her enthusiasm was off the charts.

Yay! I'll text you the deets for your official #LAfamily outing. Woohoo!

This was it – this was the beginning of my life here, the path I was destined to tread, and there was no going back.

Just as I was about to text back another series of woohoos and kisses, my phone beeped again.

P.S. Bring that gorgeous man of yours! No excuses!! Xx

Oh God.

I chucked my phone to the ground, recoiling at the words I read on the screen.

'My man' – hah! Jay wasn't 'my' anything. As soon as Billie came home I was going to kill her. I was all about acting, make-believe was kind of my jam, but as far as Jay being my 'special friend'? Well, that was a bridge too far.

I thought back to his smile in the car, the boyish grin that lined his lush mouth. I found myself smiling again, and quickly shook the image from my mind.

'Okay, time to shut that shit down,' I said adamantly, slapping my hands on my knees and moving to stand. No more midday lounging, no more Netflix binges – and risking seeing another Sienna Bailey banner – no more dirty takeaways or pool lounging. Initialisation phase for *Abby Taylor: Version 2.0* was about to commence, and I was pretty bloody excited about it.

~

The look on Billie's face said it all. The moment she walked through the condo, placing her bag next to mine on the counter, she looked at me with a mix of trepidation and wonderment, like a tourist spotting a lion on safari. 'W-what are you doing?'

I knew very little about yoga, but I believe I was attempting the awkward, and utterly unattractive, 'down-ward dog' pose. Had the blood not been rushing to my head I would have told Billie exactly that; instead, I snapped.

'What does it look like I'm doing?'

Billie edged her way closer, leaning against the open door to the balcony, where I had my yoga mat rolled out; well, if you could call the boho floor rug I dragged out from the lounge a yoga mat.

'Wow, one lunch date with Sienna and you're donning activewear and putting a twist of lemon in your drink bottle.'

'Oh, shut up,' I said, collapsing to the mat and reeling at how unfit I truly was. 'I'm having happy hour with her on Thursday.'

'What? Are you serious?'

'Yep!' I pulled myself to sit cross-legged and reached for my water, popping the bottle with my teeth. I sipped and looked at Billie's horrified expression. 'Some place called the Skybar?'

'Wow, fancy.'

'Really?' I tried not to sound too excited.

Billie didn't elaborate, she simply straightened from the doorway. 'Well, I have to work that night, so you'll have to come up with your own escape plan this time.'

'Ah, yes, about that – Sienna also wants me to bring my gorgeous man with me.'

Billie grinned. 'Oh my God, that's hilarious.'

'No, it's not,' I said indignantly.

Billie's eyes brightened in that wild way they did whenever she had a great idea. 'You should totally ask Jay to go with you.'

'I don't think so.'

'Oh, come on, it would be hilarious. Sienna will rock up with Leon and God knows who else; believe me, you do not want to go into the LA Family snake pit alone, and Jay would be the perfect plus one.'

'And how did you possibly come to that conclusion?'

'Because Jay doesn't buy into the Hollywood bullshit, and there is no chance of him ever being starstruck.'

'I am perfectly capable of navigating these waters on my own, thanks.'

Billie turned, making her way back into the condo. 'Okay, but remember those waters are shark-infested.'

I rolled back onto my elbows, shakily posing in some form of made-up, butt-in-the-air, semi-planking position, mumbling, 'Tell me something I don't know.'

Chapter Sixteen

I swear, the moment my mind was made up, the universe provided; no sooner had I washed away the yoga sweat and towel-dried my hair than I received a message from Ziggy.

You're going to want to check your email! Z x

My heart raced, because I knew what that meant: she had something exciting to report. Sure, a call would be great, but Ziggy was a busy woman, often locked down in conference calls and lunch meetings, and I had learned not to be oversensitive to the lack of one-on-one time early on. An email was grand.

Especially when the title of the email read: 'You're going to want to jump on this.'

I clicked so quickly I missed the email window altogether, then I quickly realigned the mouse and drilled into the email.

'Oh my God!' My eyes ticked over the screen.

Casting call.

Sci-fi pilot

Jerry Fucking Bassman

It only took those first three lines to know that I was sold, that I wanted whatever part of it there was, even if it meant fetching lattes for the staff on set. But, reading through Ziggy's email, it was so much more than that. They were searching for a female actor for a strong supporting role in an intense end-of-days drama, exploring the battle of good versus evil and the fight for survival, skim, skim, skim . . . I had all I needed. I was perfect for the role, this was mine, and Ziggy had obviously thought so too.

Start prepping, MS attached, you go up Monday! Z

My mouth went dry. This was it. My first real, honest-to-God, serious audition for something truly amazing. I thought back to Jay's scepticism, of the picture he painted of lining up for non-speaking beer commercials, and I was even more determined to prep for this role of . . .

'Annika.' Description: *small but fierce.*

'I'm small but fierce.'

Can cut down full-grown men with a simple look.

'I can do that.'

Athletic.

I tried not to think about how red my face was – even now – after puffing my way through yoga. I mean, I did dance and gymnastics in my teens; I could get by.

Attached was a full backstory and the scene for the character, which was to be prepared for the audition.

'Way to go, Ziggy!'

I would hug the life out of her when she got here; this was what I was talking about, the very thing I had hoped for. If this came to fruition, who knew? Maybe I would have a real secret deal to allude to after all.

I printed off the manuscript, using the eco-friendly, recycled yellowish paper that Billie stocked the office with. It seemed like a bit of a crime to have such great writing displayed in such a way.

I found Billie painting her toenails in the lounge room. I helped her dry them by fanning them with my script, smiling from ear to ear.

Billie looked up at me, instantly recognising my giddiness. 'What is that?'

'A pilot of dreams.'

'That's not the name of it, is it?' Her face twisted.

'No, silly.' I bopped her on the head with it before sitting down and handing it to her.

'It's a pilot episode of a new sci-fi series produced by – '

'Jerry Bassman?' Billie blurted out. Her eyes widened as she flipped over the pages. 'Holy shit, Abby!'

'I knooow, right?'

'Christ, they don't need a make-up artist, do they? Someone to attach elf ears or something?'

I laughed, taking the manuscript from her. 'I don't think there are elf ears involved, it's more of a dystopian, sand-dune, end-of-the-world kind of thing. But for that the actors would need to look weathered and dirty – I'm sure you could manage that.'

'Hey, weathered and dirty is my middle name.' The minute the words left Billie's mouth, we looked at each other, frowning before bursting into hysterics.

'Okay, maybe not,' she said, grabbing the papers back from me and looking over them in awe. 'So, what now?'

'I have a meeting on Monday, so I'll be prepping for then. Get into the headspace, do some research – oh God, meet with my voice coach. Jesus, I have to call Faye!' I said, clutching my head.

'Isn't it "Ray"?' Billie corrected.

'Shit, yes, Ray! RAY! Christ, Ziggy is going to kill me.'

'Okay, just calm down, you've got this, and Ziggy wouldn't have put you up for it unless she knew it was a perfect fit for you, and it so is.'

'Could you imagine, name-dropping Jerry Bassman to the LA Family over happy hour?' I laughed, but Billie didn't find it funny. Her face pinched a little, as if slightly annoyed.

'Don't worry about them, or what they think – just worry about you and this,' she said, lifting up the script.

'Yeah, I know,' I said, feeling a bubble of defensiveness float to the surface. 'Well, I better get cracking with this.'

Lockdown began now.

'Hey, I'm making some carbonara, but don't worry, I have some cheap wine that will cut through the cream.'

My heart soared at the thought, but my mind quickly shut it down. 'I'm kind of on a health kick right now.'

Billie's brow curved. 'Oh . . . well, I'm fresh out of kale.'

I winced. 'I know, worst housemate ever. Don't worry about me, I'll grab something later. Just try not to fill the place with too many delicious aromas,' I said with a wink, before heading to my room and shutting the door, gripping the script tightly in my hands.

'You got this, Abby. You. Got. This.'

Chapter Seventeen

'Oh honey, no, honey, stop.'

These were the words I had become accustomed to the moment I sat down with the flamboyantly effervescent Ray Minogue, chief stage presence and part-time elocutionist to the clueless. He had a smart side part and a preference for stripes. He also had a real gift for telling you that you were awful and making it sound kind.

His gold pinkie ring glimmered under the stage lighting as he tapped his pen on his notebook for me to start again, only to stop me immediately. It certainly wasn't doing wonders for my confidence.

Ray sighed, throwing down the notepad and moving from his chair to circle me. He walked with his hands clasped behind his back, head held high, as if in deep, contemplative thought.

'For today's actor, the ability to speak in a flawless standard American accent is essential. After all, it is becoming commonplace for film and television production companies to cast American roles using non-American actors.' He stopped, turning to look at me pointedly. 'But make no mistake: in order to land the role, your standard American accent must sound *truly authentic.*'

'And I'm guessing mine needs work.'

'You guess correct; now, from the top!'

After an hour of going over vocal focus and sound placement, general American cadence, emphasis and stresses, the dominant American 'R' sound, vowel sounds and consonants, nuances and observations, I was spent. I had truly underestimated the complexities of faking an American accent, so I booked a session with Ray every day until Monday to help me nail it. He told me several times that he was 'squeezing me in' because he was terribly busy; if it weren't for my connection with Ziggy, he wouldn't have given me the time of day.

Again that word: 'connection'. If you didn't have connections in this town you were in serious trouble. It made my decision to ask Sienna to happy hour drinks feel like a smart move. I needed to infiltrate the #LAfamily, which kind of sounded like I wanted to join the mafia, which wasn't too far from the truth. The circles Sienna ran in were well documented on social media; the who's who of the Aussie acting scene who had set off to forge their careers were indeed a tightknit bunch. They were beautiful, buff and tanned, with artistic, exotic Instagram accounts that were extremely staged in order to appear effortless. A bit like the pic I just snapped of the beautiful exterior of the old picture theatre where I met with Ray. I put a moody filter on the slightly angled photo. It made it look rich and mysterious, especially with the cryptic caption, 'And so it begins.' Was I on set? Filming, a fashion shoot? Nope, just sitting in a dusty old theatre being rapped over the knuckles for how terrible my accent was. Yeah, I thought it better to leave that part out.

As per usual, I gained enough likes and comments to make me feel validated, after I blocked the trolling comments of course.

And why shouldn't I feel validated? I was on my way to improving my craft. I was eating a low-fat, no-sugar yogurt as a snack. I had drunk nearly three bottles of water; I was going to be fabulous! So why did I feel like utter death? It was probably due to this being my second sugarless day – *way to pick a time to quit sugar, Abby. Yeah, let's detox when you're trying to remember lines in an accent that isn't your own. Brilliant.*

It was a deadly combination: hungry and angry – 'hangry' – and now, rather than soothing my soul by eating a donut, I had to wash it down with vitamin water.

'Mmm, delish.'

Hopefully by Monday I would be past the darkest days of the detox. I wanted to fill the void in my life with something other than sugar, and instead glow with radiant, shiny hair that would make Sienna Bailey's look dull in comparison. I walked aimlessly with my thoughts until one urgent thought broke through.

Where the hell was I?

I had arrived here without incident, thanks to an Uber, but how would I get out of here? Where *was* here? The sooner Billie's car got out of the shop the better. I could have a go at driving and exploring LA myself; I just had to make sure I piled on the extra insurance cover, the kind that would probably be equivalent to a mortgage repayment. An extortionate yet necessary cost when dealing with LA traffic chaos.

One thing I had learned in my short time in LA was that it was unlike most world metropolises, where you could step off a plane and onto a train that would whisk you into the heart of the city. LA was far too spread out, its treasures strewn across the whole town and there wasn't one bus or walking trail that could take you to each and every one. Right now I was somewhere in Downtown LA, a once dead zone that was now a walkable hub of restaurants, bars, performance theatres and museums. These eclectic, if slightly smelly streets were a far cry from the hilly hikes through Griffith Park, the orgasm-worthy Dim Sum in Gabriel Valley and the Westside's glorious beaches. I had so much to discover, so many opportunities to get lost, as I was right now, knowing I could get myself back on the right track. After all, if I was going to become a local (accent and all), I was going to have to be self-sufficient. I couldn't always be chauffeured around in a black Mustang, even though I probably wouldn't have said no to a lift right now.

Standing in the middle of a busy street, I figured it was probably time to search for a bus stop, because the sooner I got out of here the less likely I would be to give in to the siren call of Subway and smash a twelve-inch sandwich, its sign a neon arrow of temptation.

I had to be strong, I had to remain focused; *oh God, they had cookies, too.* No! I really had to get out of here and, as if the universe was interjecting again, I saw the sign, quite literally.

Bus stop, dead ahead!

~

I was panicking; two days in and I still couldn't remember my lines. I was in the blackest mood, no thanks to the pending catch-up with the LA Family tomorrow night and Ziggy's imminent arrival, upon which she'd no doubt be expecting to hear my fluent American accent. What was I thinking? I had to focus – I had to clear my foggy mind. Despite the weakness of my poor sugar-starved body, I had to snap out of this rut and learn these lines!

Even if it killed me.

Now, in the late hours of the night, with Billie at work, I actually stood a chance. The condo was in complete silence. I sat on my bed with a cool breeze filtering through my opened balcony door, with only the sound of a distant chopper overhead and the usual street traffic that I had become accustomed to. What I had not become accustomed to was the yapping of a little dog in the courtyard below. No doubt the culprit was Veronica's precious little Sorscha, and she didn't sound happy. In fact, she sounded like she was alerting the neighbourhood to trouble. I had visions of a masked man climbing up to my second-storey window, the very window that, right now, was wide open and welcoming. He probably had a gun – because everyone had guns here, right?

I slowly leant across to my side lamp and turned it off, now in complete darkness. In the safety of the shadows I edged off the bed and crept to the balcony, squatting down to peer through the wrought-iron railings to see what all the fuss was below. There was Sorscha, giving someone exactly what for and shaking with the effort. Someone had clearly disturbed her late-night toilet run. Good little guard dog.

Veronica suddenly appeared, her long white night-gown flowing behind her; it was only then that I saw who Sorscha was accosting.

'Oh, I'm sorry, Jay. I hope she didn't startle you.'

There, standing by the end of the pool in nothing more than shorts, abs lit by the soft pool light, stood Jay. A towel was draped over his shoulder and his bright white smile shone at Veronica as he unfastened his watch.

'I think I startled her,' he said, his voice carrying up and hitting me in the chest. How had I not seen him earlier?

Veronica scooped her up. 'Say sorry to Jay, Sorscha. You can be very rude sometimes.'

Jay let Sorscha smell his hand before patting her on the head. 'Oh, it's alright, she's just telling me who's boss.'

'You and the entire neighbourhood,' Veronica laughed.

Jay smiled. 'Well, better get to it,' he said, turning away from her.

'Yes, of course, your nightly laps. I'm sorry to interrupt you. But before I let you go, can I ask if you've given my proposition another thought? About doing a reading for you sometime?'

Jay might have had his back turned to Veronica but, even from two storeys above, I saw him wince, before plastering on a false smile and turning back towards her.

'Sorry, Veronica, I've just been so busy at the Saloon I don't know when I could commit to anything.'

'Well, I'm not going anywhere – just let me know when you're free. I'm available nights as well,' she said, clutching her nightgown to herself and giving him a rather alluring look from beneath her blue eyeshadow. I had to clasp my hand over my mouth to keep from bursting into laughter. This was a classic Mrs Robinson moment, and I had the best seat in the house to watch Jay squirm.

'Ah, yes, well, nights are for laps, and I'm pretty beat, so . . .'

'Oh, of course, just putting it out there,' she said, smiling and stepping away, not breaking eye contact until she bumped into one of the garden tables. 'Oops! Better watch where I'm going. Night, Jay.'

'Night, Veronica.'

He watched her go, unmoving until he heard her flip flops make their way down the path and her door thud closed; only then did I see Jay's shoulders sag, like he was relieved to be alone. But he wasn't alone, not exactly. No, he had a voyeuristic neighbour sitting cross-legged on the balcony, head tilted, admiring the view. The unguarded, half-naked Jay. He placed his watch on top of his towel and moved to the pool's edge. The faint glow of garden lights lit the courtyard well enough, but it was the lights within the pool that really lit the space, giving his beautiful dark skin an emerald glow. He looked like a god, chiselled from stone, and someone had taken extra care carving out his sixpack. Jay was ripped, and though I couldn't guess what was responsible for his physique, it had to be more than cutting some laps in a pool.

I held my breath until he dove in, slicing through the rippling water. When he eventually surfaced, it was with the perfectly formed freestyle stroke of an Olympic champion, and he even did the flip and push at the end of the lap. Okay, it probably wasn't actually called the 'flip and push' but, hey, what did I know about sports or physical activity? I was hard pressed to do yoga without cramping. Jay's rhythmic laps were almost hypnotic, aided by the slosh of the water from his powerful kicks.

I leant my temple on the iron bars, transfixed, trying to remember what it was that I was meant to be doing. My eyelids became heavy and I stifled a yawn, not because the show was boring – anything but – but I sure was getting tired.

I was jolted out of my reverie when Jay stopped ten laps later – or perhaps it was a hundred; I hadn't been counting. Though, as Jay pushed himself out of the pool, I couldn't help but study his taut abs, which were now glistening in the courtyard lights, droplets of water running over his shoulders, down his strong back and over his drool-worthy chest.

I swear I didn't blink; instead, I felt my hand tighten on the iron railing as I bit my lip and whispered under my breath, 'Hello, Hollywood!'

Chapter Eighteen

What do you wear when you're meeting your nemesis and her posse? I opted for black, like my mood. I really didn't want to meet up with the #LAfamily tonight. I knew it was about making connections and forging a path through the Hollywood scene, but I really wasn't feeling it. I wasn't confident in my life choices – or, more precisely, in my ability to convincingly read lines in my fake American accent. I felt lost and underprepared.

Did I really want to surround myself with overachievers?

Among twisted blankets, propped up against my pillows, I did some research on the LA Family. Who made up the clique and what had made them so damn unapproachable? I skimmed over their highly filtered, seemingly perfect lifestyles. A tan, for one thing: time spent in the Californian sun (or, more likely, paid for at an exclusive salon) was definitely a part of their appeal. I glimpsed my pasty shoulder, then wrote in the margin of the notepad resting on my lap.

*Little black dress
*Spray tan

Unnaturally white teeth were obviously a thing too, but that would take time, and I kind of liked my teeth. I ran my tongue over the straight ridges, which were thanks to my parents' empty pockets and three years of braces in high school. What else? Luxe lunches and expensive outings, coastal drives in jeeps – and was that a human pyramid on the beach? I rolled my eyes. Of course it was, and who should be on top but Sienna Bailey. Surprise, surprise.

I looked at some of the familiar faces and tagged their Instagram accounts.

Dion Preston had been on a similar drama on a rival network, where he played the sexy doctor who ended up losing his memory in an explosion or flash flood episode – I couldn't recall, as I made an effort not to worry about the competition. He had been in LA the longest and had done pretty well for himself by all accounts, landing a supporting role on a pretty big movie franchise based on a bestselling series of books. As far as I had heard, Dion was going places; and if his gym pics were anything to go by, he thought he was going somewhere too. Confidence had never been his issue.

Jake Savage was a child star turned heartthrob who'd been a favourite detective on an Aussie crime show until his character got killed off in an underworld slaying. I had been addicted to his show until I had met him, drunk and slurring, at an awards ceremony. He had ended the night by vomiting into a pot plant and was whisked away by his team to avoid scandal. When I had seen him the next day he pretended not to know who I was, which I wasn't too precious about, though I vividly recall his one-eyed assessment of my 'cans', so maybe that was why he couldn't remember my face.

Nicole Towney was, from memory and reputation, a nice enough girl with a sweet, heart-shaped face. I had thought that she'd head for the London scene – she had played a leading role in a top-rated Aussie television drama to critical acclaim – but here she was, chilling with the LA crowd. It had kind of made me sad to see her posing with fish-pout lips.

I scrolled through the pics.

'Don't know you, don't know you – oh, yes, who are you again?'

Jessica Stine? *Okay, yeah, you were on that show that was cancelled, a New Zealander from memory.*

There were a few folks that I couldn't quite put my finger on, but I had the gist of the main crew. I threw my phone to the side, snuggling back into my bed, dreading the day that would soon slip into night. But what was that saying? The things you dread the most usually always turn out the best? God, I hoped so.

Rolling onto my side and hearing Billie's frenzied stirrings in the kitchen, I wondered why she'd never chosen to align herself with the LA Family. Had she not wanted them to know the reality of her career, or was she just an excellent judge of character?

'Hey, Billie,' I called out, 'we should start our own hashtag.' I picked up my phone and scrolled through yet more beautiful photos. My door creaked fully open, drawing my attention to Billie, who held a mixing bowl, flour colouring her cheek. She was wearing an oversized baseball top and jean shorts; she was adorable and uber cool, but she didn't think she was, which was part of what I liked about her.

'Yeah, hashtag desperate and dateless,' she said.

My brows lowered. 'Speak for yourself.'

'Well, it's a beautiful mid-morning and I'm baking cupcakes and you're still in bed, so . . .'

'I had a late night going over my lines.'

And Jay's lines, all the dips and curves and . . .

'Did you hear me?'

'What?' I asked, snapping back into the moment.

'Have you even managed to venture out and be a proper tourist yet?'

I sunk deeper into my cocoon. 'I've been too busy,' I lied. I may not have been a proper tourist, but I had read up enough about LA to be a bona fide expert on the place.

Billie rolled her eyes. 'Busy lying on your back.'

'Now, that's how nasty rumours start,' I said.

'So, what have you got planned today? I know you have hot plans for tonight.' Billie's words dripped with sarcasm, the way they always did whenever she made reference to the LA Family.

'Are you sure you don't want to come? I could really use a wing woman tonight.'

'Yeah, well, you get yourself into these situations. Besides, I am certainly not skipping work to listen to Sienna and her cronies dribble on about how awesome they are,' she said, saying 'awesome' in an American accent that was infuriatingly better than mine.

I rubbed my eyes; listening to Billie had me wanting to never leave bed again. Giving myself a quick mental shake, I reminded myself that I did, in fact, have a plan, and I had best stick to it. I peeled the blankets aside and dragged myself to the edge of the bed, yawning.

'Well, I had better meet the day. I have to find myself a tanning salon. Which one do you recommend?'

Billie stopped mid-stir. 'You're getting a spray tan?'

The hairs on the back of my neck stood up at her tone. 'Yeah, so?'

Billie shook her head. 'Wow, you'll be part of the Family in no time: some fillers and teeth whitening and you'll be all set,' she said, peeling herself from my door frame and heading back to the kitchen.

I really didn't appreciate the sarcasm, and I sure as hell wasn't going to admit I had contemplated teeth whitening as I moved to stand and follow her out.

'Shut up, I'm only having a few drinks with them.'

'That's how it all starts.'

I slid onto the stool on the opposite side of the breakfast bar, watching as Billie spooned some batter into paper cups.

'What starts?'

'Drinks, dinner, brunch: soon you'll be trekking up those hills in activewear.'

I know Billie was only repeating the same things we had both rolled our eyes over, but I couldn't help feeling that her words were coming from a darker place, as if she was jealous or something.

'Well, firstly, there will be no hill trekking, because my weak calves can barely handle "upward angry dragon", or whatever that bloody yoga pose is called, and secondly, since you don't want to come, I will have to relay all the cringe-worthy details later tonight.'

A small smile tugged in the corner of Billie's mouth. 'Look, I know you'll be fine.'

'Don't worry, I will not succumb to the wilder herd. It's simply about networking – a necessary evil.'

'Sometimes I am glad to be a lowly waitress.'

'Don't be like that.'

'But it's true. Don't think I didn't see the way Sienna looked at me, that look of horror and pity. What did she say to you?'

Oh God, our motto was to not keep secrets, to be open and honest, but I couldn't bear the thought of recounting how Sienna had referred to her as 'so tragic'. I really didn't want to pour salt in Billie's open wound right now.

'No, nothing,' I lied.

~

Karma was going to get me. It was only fair, seeing as I had lied right to my best friend's face. It would appear that I wouldn't have to wait too long for it to strike.

'I'm ORANGE!' I yelled.

'You wanted the Californian glow,' said the peroxided beauty technician, who also happened to be the receptionist, make-up artist, hair stylist and nail bar operator at this dingy shopfront in a back alley in Hollywood. I'd had reservations about going into the empty shop but a ticking clock does strange things to your mindset, so I'd walked in. I knew I should have taken the lack of clientele as a bad sign.

'I wanted a sunset glow, not neon-fucking-streetlight.'

'It makes you look thinner,' she said, tilting her head to the side, admiring her work as if she had no idea what my problem was.

'I look like an Oompa Loompa.'

'Is that some kind of Australianism or something?'

I gaped; she was probably barely legal, let alone qualified, but the fact that she wasn't versed in the genius of Roald Dahl made me even more furious.

'I'm not paying for this,' I said, picking up my bag and storming to the door. I'm not sure what she called after me – 'something-something bitch' – but I didn't care, I was too busy crying, which I continued to do for the whole walk back to the condo. I pulled my hair free from its messy bun, shaking my head and feeling ultimate humiliation. I had to cancel tonight; I couldn't go out looking like a giant orange! As it was, I would have to face the wrath of Ziggy when I met her tomorrow –

I stopped dead in my tracks.

Oh God.

My audition. Monday. Three days away.

I felt my stomach drop to my feet.

What have I done?

Maybe if I soaked in a lava-hot bath and loofah-ed off the top layer of my skin I stood a chance. I quickened my steps, a new hope bubbling inside me. I almost felt manic, and excited at the possibility of tackling this disaster before the colour soaked into every pore of my body.

But hope is a funny thing: it can die as easily as it comes. And die it did when, a moment later, I spied the condo, and saw Jay exiting his Mustang.

Oh God, please, don't let him see me, please, please, keep walking, just keep walking . . .

He looked back, stopping as he spotted me.

Fuck!

What had I done to deserve this? Was all this because of my little white lie to Billie? Or was this some kind of challenge – survive this week and score the role of a life-time – was that how it worked? Was this to be my sacrifice? After seeing the look on Jay's face as I neared, I didn't know if it was worth it.

'What happened to you?' he said, mystified as he looked me over from top to streaky toe; I felt about two feet tall.

'Not now, Jay!' I said, holding my hand up as I passed him, averting my eyes from his amused stare.

'Were you caught in a sandstorm?' He laughed.

I flipped him the bird over my shoulder, knowing he was following in my footsteps.

'Come on, Abby, don't be like that; seriously, what's wrong?'

Tears burned in my eyes once more. I didn't dare answer because I didn't want my voice to betray how furious I was, didn't want him to see the true depths of my despair. I forged a path through the courtyard to the back staircase, glaring at Sorscha, who broke into a series of barks and growls as she watched me approach; the apricot tinge to her coat looked far better on her than me.

'Shut up, you little furball,' I muttered, stomping my way up the first set of stairs, my jaw clenching as I heard Jay's voice behind me.

'Aww, it's okay, Sorschy, she doesn't like me either.'

I reached the top step, turning to glare down at him, my sudden halt bringing him up short to look at me with raised brows. Either I had surprised him by turning to confront him or he was really taken aback by how hideous I looked. But something dimmed in his eyes, and his smile fell away as he started up the steps once more, coming to stand next to me, my vantage point changing as he towered over me.

He looked serious, contemplative even, as his dark eyes ticked over my face. I really didn't need his judgement as well.

I thought he might say something smart, or make me feel worse, but instead he did something completely unexpected: he reached out and wiped away a tear, so gently.

'There are white lines down your cheeks,' he said. 'I think it will wash off.'

'Great, all I need is to soak in my tears.'

Jay smirked. 'Or . . . in a saltwater pool,' he said, kinking his head over his shoulder.

'Somehow I don't think the tenants will appreciate an orange slick on the top of their pool.'

Jay laughed, deep in his throat; the sound almost had me forgetting my woes.

'I look like a freakin' clown,' I said, examining my arms. I cringed at the thought of the little black dress I had laid out on my bed, chosen in order to show as much skin as I could.

'It's . . . not that bad.' Jay said it so unconvincingly that I knew he was trying to be nice, which was such a foreign concept I didn't really know how to react.

'I look like a terracotta nightmare.'

'You are kind of blending in with the steps.'

'I bet you've never managed to do something so bloody stupid,' I said, glancing down at my striped legs; not only had she done the wrong colour but she had also done a shitty job. I glanced up at Jay, who was biting his lip in an attempt not to laugh.

'No, I can't say I have ever had the need for a tan,' he said, lifting up his arm and examining his naturally dark complexion. I instantly felt like an idiot.

'Oh no, I didn't mean, it's just . . .'

'It's okay.' He laughed. 'But I did have a girl ruin my sheets with that stuff once, so I know how potent it can be.'

I felt something stir inside me; the thought of a girl in Jay's bed made me feel funny, and I really didn't like the feeling on so many levels.

'So, I guess the only kind of advice I can give is don't panic-scrub – you'll make yourself blotchy, and that's not a great look either. Maybe just bunker down for a few days.' He shrugged.

It was actually really sound advice, but my shoulders still slumped. 'I'm going out tonight.'

'Oh.' Jay winced, as if feeling my pain. Which only made me feel even more hopeless. 'Can you cancel?'

'Not exactly, and even if I did I still have to front up to my manager tomorrow, who is going to totally kill me as I have a really massive audition on Monday.'

'Oh yeah?'

Jay leant against the railing, his attention fully on me.

'It's okay, you don't have to pretend to care.'

Something flashed in Jay's eyes, like he was surprised at my words. 'I don't hate you, Abby.'

My eyes snapped up; his expression was earnest, his words a complete shock in their admission. I found myself standing in stunned silence, until I finally realised something: 'You just hate what I do.'

'Let's just say I am not a fan of the entertainment industry.'

Jay was such a mystery to me; sure, he had been burned multiple times by his flaky, shift-swapping employees, but was there more to it? Had the girl who'd oranged his sheets been an actress too? A model, a stripper? Another poor wannabe in search of the California glow?

'Why do you hate actors so much?'

'I told you,' he said, shifting uncomfortably.

'Tell me again.'

'No,' he said, moving past me on the stairs; now it was me who was following him, and he was the one no doubt wishing I would disappear.

'Come on, Jay. You choose to work in a town crawling with people chasing their dreams. You can't be so jaded by them.'

'I'm not jaded.'

I laughed, reaching our little alcove, both in search of our keys. 'Oh, I think you are.'

Jay turned, looking me over again in a long, drawn-out assessment.

'What about you? You still have that twinkle in your eye, living the dream?'

It was a low blow, and I would have taken exception to it if he hadn't made an attempt to lift my spirits in the last five minutes.

I lifted my tank top to reveal my stomach, showing just how bad my spray tan was. A large dark orange circle the size of a dinner plate was smack-bang in the centre of my abdomen. 'Does it look like I'm living the dream?'

Jay broke into a broad, brilliant grin, the kind that was contagious, as he worked on opening his door. 'You just can't seem to keep your clothes on around me, can you?' he said, pushing his door open.

'I'm just showing you my tan!'

Jay laughed, shaking his head as he stepped inside his condo. 'A likely story.'

Chapter Nineteen

felt like I had gone through some kind of decontamination procedure, and my skin was raw and tender. I'd removed as much of the terrible tan as I could, short of a full-body chemical peel. As long as I avoided fluorescent lighting, particularly on the stubborn streaks on my legs leading down to my muddy-looking ankles, I should be fine, right? Or had I just stared at myself for so long I couldn't remember the real colour of my skin?

Where was Billie when I needed her brutal honesty? I had to run the standard pre-outing questions by her: 'Does my bum look big in this?' and 'Do I look like a faded peach?'

I opted for a dress that covered a bit more skin, with my hair down, covering my shoulders. I shifted from side to side in front of the mirror, pangs of anxiety clawing at me. God, I really needed a second opinion.

Someone who would give me the most honest opinion, who wouldn't pull any punches, who had seen me at my most orangey worst.

I stilled.

Surely I couldn't.

What? Ask Jay if I looked alright, actually invite his criticism? How ridiculous. Weren't men programmed to lie when responding to such trick questions anyway? I sighed, looking over my reflection once more.

'Only one way to find out, I guess.'

I made a determined line down the hall, opening the front door and stepping into the small alcove, stopping to take a deep, steadying breath.

Desperate times called for desperate measures.

I squared my shoulders, stepped forward and rapped on Jay's door. I made sure my knocks sounded strong, confident. After all, this was no big deal.

After waiting a long minute I was ready to duck back into my door and pretend I was never here. Seriously, what the hell was I thinking? Jay and I weren't friends. Just because he'd admitted that he didn't hate me didn't mean he was my confidant. But it was too late; the moment I turned Jay's door swung open, whipping an aroma of delicious spices from his place into my nostrils, causing my stomach to rumble involuntarily. Jay stood there, drying his hands on a tea towel. If he was surprised to see me he didn't let on; he simply leant against his doorway, waiting for me to stop staring.

I was frozen in the breezeway, caught between my door and his, confused about what to do now. Jay kinked a brow at me, waiting for me to say something, but my mind went blank. How could I possibly stand here and ask how I looked? While I was at it, perhaps I could do a twirl and lift out my legs for him to examine – which, by the way, he already was, giving them a long, lingering assessment in my heels and knee-length black number, this one with sleeves and covering a little bit more of my orange-tinged skin. This had been such a dumb idea; I would simply ask for some sugar or something.

Just when I was about to stammer my way through some lame excuse, Jay saved me from myself. 'You look beautiful.'

My jaw went slack – I was now frozen for a completely different reason, no less awkward but far more surprised. I double-blinked.

'R-really?' I asked, disbelieving that those words had come out of Jay's mouth.

'Really,' he said, finding my shock extremely amusing. 'Hey, listen, can you give me ten? I've just got to take this off the simmer and then I'm pretty much ready to go,' he said, pushing off the door jamb and heading back into his apartment.

I stood there, confused, edging forward and slowly peering through his open doorway. 'Ah, go? Go where?' I called out, seeing nothing but a narrow hall curving off into the unknown, the mirror image of Billie's entryway.

I stepped inside tentatively, listening in case he replied. But all I could hear was clattering and movement in the kitchen, running water and the tapping of utensils. Before

I thought through what I was doing, I stepped down the hall, following the sounds and being lured by the mouth-watering aromas.

I moved into the opening near the kitchen, expecting to find Jay standing in a space identical to our own next door. But apart from the layout, Jay's place had nothing in common with ours and it really took me aback. It was a whole other world away from Billie's boho, eclectic faux furs and fabrics, potted greenery and eccentric clutter. This was sleek and minimalistic, but uber-stylish.

I took in the glass tabletops, glossy hardwood flooring and high-tech surround sound system; everything was modern with sharp edges, decorated sparingly with carefully planned placement of items that obviously had meaning. Unlike Billie's dated kitchen, Jay's was stainless-steel perfection that any chef would be happy to have. There was a serious amount of money outlaid in his condo, though it wasn't showy and denoted a great sense of style – undeniably Jay. It was strange to watch him in his natural habitat, moving around and working on seasoning a pot, stirring and then sliding to the sink to run water over his spoon.

'Do you like chilli?'

I flinched, coming back to my senses. I was surprised he knew I was here; I had kind of been lurking in the shadows, watching him, which really needed to stop. I cleared my throat and stepped fully into the light.

'Is that a trick question?' I asked, my heels clicking on the hardwood floor into the kitchen as I came to stand beside Jay. I looked into the pot he was stirring, surprised by the simplicity of the dish.

'What? You expected duck cassoulet?' He laughed, clearly reading my surprise.

'Isn't chilli something you cook when you're on a budget?' I mused, looking curiously around his plush apartment. Perhaps Jay had spent all his money on his flash car and décor and now had to eat like a pauper.

Jay tapped the side of the pot. 'Chilli is a classic.'

'If you say so. All I know is that John Wayne ate it in a Western I watched once.' I shrugged.

Jay laughed. 'Is everything you know from a movie?'

I thought about it for a moment. 'Yeah, pretty much.'

Jay skimmed a sample of chilli onto his spoon, bringing it up to his mouth and blowing on it, cupping his hand underneath to prevent possible drippage onto his immaculate kitchen tops. I watched on in casual amusement, my hip cocked, leaning near the stove. Only when Jay held the spoon out to me did I straighten.

'Have a taste.'

I scoffed. 'Ah, no, thanks; I don't like spicy food.'

Jay smiled, broad and wicked. 'It's not that spicy.'

'Well, forgive me if I don't believe you.'

'Whoa, what does a guy have to do to earn your trust?' he said, relenting and taking the spoonful for himself, his

eyes rolling as if he was a culinary genius. 'Man, that is
so good.'

So modest.

'Okay, that's done – give me a sec to change and then
we can go,' Jay said, running his hands under the water
at the sink, speaking those same confusing words again.

'Go? Where?'

Jay looked at me, drying his hands. 'Billie said you
needed a lift to Skybar.'

I was going to kill her!

'Oh God, you don't have to take me. I have it all worked
out – it's pretty direct,' I lied. I actually only had a vague
idea of where I was going and how I was going to get there,
which had given me an immense amount of anxiety and
caused me to practically beg Billie to go with me (which she
had strenuously declined – again). I'm sure Billie's request
for a night off would have thrilled Jay no end: 'Oh, hey,
Jay, can I take the night off to accompany my best friend
to drinks with a bunch of fellow actors that neither of us
like?' Yeah, I could understand why she turned me down.

'It's not direct without a car.'

I had wondered if that was why Sienna had chosen the
location, guessing that I mightn't have a car yet. I wouldn't
have put it past her.

'Still, you must have plans – better things to do than
drive me around.'

Jay sighed, looking at me like he wished I would just
stop talking. 'Abby.'

'Yes?'

'Take the damn ride.'

I smiled, but only a little because I didn't want the full extent of my relief to be so apparent. 'Well, if you insist.'

Sitting on Jay's black leather couch, waiting for him to appear, I started to doubt everything. Maybe I could call off the drinks; I mean, look at my legs! Had she finger-painted me? What time did the sun go down in LA? Did the bar have mood lighting or harsh lighting?

'I think I'm going to go and put pants on,' I called out, moving to stand only to be stopped by Jay appearing from out of his bedroom, shrugging on his jacket and fixing the collar of his stark white shirt. He looked gorgeous: cool, casual but oh so smart. He knew the scene, knew this town like the back of his hand and should he choose to drive me around the entire city, who was I to argue?

'What did you say?'

I blinked. 'Oh, nothing. Let's go.'

Chapter Twenty

West Hollywood was a grid of wide boulevards and narrow residential streets. The neighbourhood also had a concentration of the most avant-garde restaurants in Los Angeles (rivalled only by the burgeoning restaurant scene Downtown). So it was little wonder this was the neighbourhood of choice for the entertainment industry's up-and-comers. Producers, directors, writers and aspiring actors called this area home, or so Jay informed me.

Taming the wisps of hair that whipped around my face in the cool evening air, I managed a side glance at Jay, wondering again what he was doing here, in this town, in this scene. He looked every bit the part of a Hollywood star. Jay conversed effortlessly, pointing out landmarks and telling stories, a stark contrast to our first car ride together, in which he'd seemed barely able to construct a sentence. Tonight, he seemed relaxed.

'So what's this place like? Will the lighting be harsh on my skin?' I said, studying my arm, paranoia at an all-time high.

'Relax, I've called ahead and organised for you to be slipped in through the back entrance, through the kitchen under a blanket.'

'Oh, ha-ha,' I said.

'You look fine,' he said, but I really wanted him to tell me I looked beautiful like the first time; geez, when had I become so needy?

'Why do you care so much anyway?' Jay asked. 'Your manager, the audition, sure, but why is drinks with your friends worth stressing over?'

I scoffed. He really had no idea.

'They're not my friends.'

Jay flicked me a glance. 'What?' he smirked.

'I don't even think I like any of these people and, truth be known, I actually feel physically ill at the thought of catching up with them tonight.'

Jay stared at me, confusion evident on his face. He studied me until the car behind us honked to let us know the lights had changed. Jay quickly moved into gear.

'Okay, so let me get this straight: not only do you have lunch dates with people you don't like, you have drinks with them too?'

'Well, yeah, same girl you met at lunch, Sienna Bailey and the "LA Family".'

'The LA Family?'

Oh, I really should stop talking. As the words tumbled out of my mouth, they sounded juvenile and ridiculous. But how would someone outside of this world understand the need to network, which, more often than not, meant socialising with people you didn't even like.

'I know it sounds crazy,' I said, looking down and smoothing my dress across my lap. I really didn't want to get into the dynamics of the LA Family, especially to Jay. At this point I really just wanted him to drop me off so I could get this night over with, and be left to stress about my meeting with Ziggy tomorrow. Best to just focus on one thing at a time.

I didn't know exactly what to expect. I know we had a private booking – Sienna had ensured me as much. But what did that mean? Would I wink at the doorman as he unlinked a velvet rope for me? I had no idea how it worked.

Luckily, Jay seemed to pick up on my terrified energy and took the lead. He parked the car across the street and, without a word, slid out from the driver's side and made his way around to my door. If he hadn't opened it up for me I probably wouldn't have moved from my seat. There was a long queue outside and a couple of men with cameras lingering nearby, waiting for a newsworthy shot. I was very much a nobody, able to skim through the crowds in obscurity, although I was sure that certain members of the LA Family wouldn't be as lucky. Knowing them, they wouldn't care. Whether it was a protective measure or Jay thought I was actually more of a big deal than I was, he led me away from the paps loitering down the street, and I laughed.

'Good idea – imagine how the tan would look under flashlight.'

But Jay didn't laugh, instead marching me across the street until we were safely curb-side. Looking down the street and over his shoulder, he was one earpiece away from being a bodyguard; were we in a dodgy part of town? My smile dimmed, seeing the trademark serious façade slam down over Jay's previously relaxed demeanour.

'What's wrong?'

Jay's focus shifted back to me and he tried to force a smile. 'No, nothing. So you think you'll be right from here?'

'Sure, I'll just join the queue and name-drop at the door.'

He nodded in hesitant approval, but he didn't seem happy about it. Glancing down the street once more, he seemed eager to leave.

'Thanks for the ride. I'll find my own way back,' I said, but it fell on deaf ears.

'Okay,' he said, stepping away without so much as a 'see ya'. I would have been a bit offended had a deafening squeal from behind us not completely destabilised me.

'There you are!' Sienna Bailey's heels clicked to a run – well, the closest thing to a run as she could manage in her skin-tight skirt – wrapping her arms around me. 'I am so happy to see you,' she said, pulling back and cupping my face as if she was committing it to memory, before her eyes lifted and her face brightened. 'And you brought Jay, awesome!' She beamed, stepping forward and wrapping her arms around him, closer and longer than she did me.

Jay's eyes shifted to mine, his horror evident, as if he were a fly caught in a spider web, which was not so far from the reality of the situation. Before he could protest, Sienna slipped her hand into his and grabbed mine, dragging us into motion.

'You're going to love this place – it has some of the finest views of LA,' she said, hauling us past the long line of patiently waiting customers and straight up to the doorman.

'Leon Denero party.'

And as if she had summoned him by magic, Leon appeared from behind us, on his phone, nodding at the doorman in a 'what's up' gesture as his bodyguard barked at the crowd to keep their distance. I felt Jay's hand at my back, guiding me inside as the doorman stepped aside, allowing us in just as the paps starting yelling for Leon's attention.

'Leon, man, right here, brother! Come on, give us a wave, yeah?'

'Leon, Leon, are you excited for the next *Hero Squad* movie?'

'Leon, are the rumours true? Did Mexico happen?'

It was fast and confusing, much like the plotless movies Leon was linked to, but he didn't flinch at the attention; he simply smiled wolfishly. 'What happens in Mexico stays in Mexico.' He winked, leading his entourage, which somehow included Jay and me, into the bar.

'You can go if you want,' I said in a low voice, feeling terrible for subjecting him to a world he was clearly repelled by.

'Ah, yeah, about that,' he said, glancing down at Sienna's arm, firmly linked through his, pulling him into the restaurant.

'Fashionably late,' called out Dion Preston, moving from his position at the bar and heading towards Leon.

'You know it, brother.' He laughed as they slapped hands and bumped fists in the most elaborately choreographed handshake I had ever seen. Disappointingly, it didn't end with a synchronised chest bump. I wished I could telepathically communicate with Jay to gauge what he was thinking about all this, yet his sneaky little brow rise clearly said, 'What fresh hell is this?' And I kind of adored him for it.

Billie assured me that there was no chance that Jay was going to get starstruck anytime soon, which made him the perfect, if reluctant, wingman. Much to his surprise, I linked my arm through his, the other side still occupied by Sienna, who appeared to have permanently fused herself to him. Meanwhile, Leon worked the waiting group inside with more secret handshakes and back slaps.

'Leon, these are the two I was telling you about,' Sienna called out over the noise, but Leon didn't seem to hear her, or didn't want to.

'Oh, man, it's so loud in here.' She laughed, waving at her face as if the temperature was also a factor. 'Be back in a sec,' she said, squeezing Jay's arm and weaving away from us. We simply stood at the bar, watching on as the clique chatted around us. I felt hugely deflated, and very insignificant.

I now knew better than to make a judgement in the first few minutes of meeting someone; I mean, I had judged Jay and had since learned he wasn't quite so bad after all. But I couldn't help it; Leon Denero seemed like a complete douche.

'Why is he wearing sunglasses? It's night-time.'

A huge grin spread across my face as I peered up at Jay. 'Must be all those paparazzi lightbulbs out front,' I said.

'What's the bet he tipped them off that he was going to be here?'

'Surely not.'

Jay shook his head as he looked at me. 'So naive, so innocent,' he teased.

'Yeah, well, some things I don't want to know,' I said, looking on as Sienna lingered next to Leon. She was yet to gain his attention as he spoke to his 'boys', who were all laughing and lapping up his conversation.

Jay grabbed my arm and guided me towards the bar. 'There's only one way to get through a night like this.'

'But you're driving.'

'Not me, you.' He laughed, slapping his palms on the marble bar before drawing the attention of the barman, who slid us over some drink menus.

'Hey, look, this one's for you,' Jay said, a line drawing between his brows in concentration. 'Mediterranean sunset, to match your tan,' he joked.

I tilted my head, squinting at his utter hilarity, before studying the menu myself. 'Wow, this place is made for us; look, you can get an ale called "Arrogant Bastard". You sure you don't want a drink?'

Jay's mouth lifted a little in the corner, as he pretended to ignore me.

'Hey, can I have a bottle of Rosé Perrier for the woman?' Leon's voice rang out over all others as he slid in next to Jay and ordered the thirteen-hundred-dollar bottle for his 'woman' whom he suddenly realised existed. It appeared he now registered our existence, too, looking our way and dipping his shades. 'Hey, you're that chick.'

'And you're that guy,' I said, wondering where exactly this stimulating conversation was leading.

'You're Sienna's bestie from Oz,' he said, but he was directing his conversation to Jay while he sized him up.

'We used to work togeth—'

'Hey, man, I'm Leon.' He cut off my words, holding out his hand to Jay, who took it and shook it slowly, old school-style. 'Sorry, I didn't catch yours.'

Jay smirked. 'I didn't throw it.'

Something flashed in Leon's eyes before he burst out laughing, shaking his finger. 'Heeey, I like you.'

Before Jay could respond, Sienna moved between them. 'Here you all are, my favourite people.'

'Yeah, just speaking with the mystery man here,' Leon sneered, hooking his arm over Sienna, who could only laugh.

'This is Abby's boyfriend, Jay, he's the owner of the Saloon on Sunset – you know, the place I was telling you about?' Sienna looked at him, imploring him to remember, no doubt like so many things she had told him.

'Oh yeah, right, I love that place. Haven't been there in a while, but hey, we might have to change that. Do you think you can hook us up with some VIP treatment?' Leon winked, grabbing the bottle and glasses.

Jay didn't say a word, watching as Leon moved away.

Then Leon stopped and turned, clearly perplexed. 'Have we met before?'

Jay shrugged. 'I don't think so.'

'Maybe you guys met at the Saloon?' Sienna added helpfully.

Leon's stare was unmoving. 'No, that's not it.'

'Guess I just have one of those faces.' Jay smiled.

'Yeah, you really do,' Sienna nodded.

'Hey, grab your drinks and head upstairs – we'll teach you what VIP is all about. You might even pick up some tips for the Saloon, J-Man.' Leon laughed, signalling to his posse to make a move. I could feel Jay's body tighten next to me as he turned to the waiting barman.

'One arrogant bastard.'

'A beer?' The barman questioned.

Jay breathed out a laugh. 'No, just an observation.'

Chapter Twenty-One

How did the night pan out like this?

There was no networking or bonding with potential new friends to be had. Apart from Dion Preston and Sienna, I didn't know any of these people, and no one went out of their way to introduce themselves. There was nothing sunshiny, friendly or welcoming about the clique, no matter what kind of filter you put over this. I felt so bad for subjecting Jay to this; if I didn't want to be here, I could only imagine how he was feeling. And instead of working the room with the flair and confidence that I might have done back home, I selfishly used Jay as my anchor in the storm. Would he ever know how grateful I was that he had stayed?

At least the view was spectacular, even if the company wasn't.

Jay led me away from the hollers and high fives of the group to the outer edge of the impressive rooftop pool of the Skybar, an open-air, ivy-covered pavilion. It was the hottest new LA lounge and, come daylight, would make you feel like you were floating in the clouds, if not for the custom-made furniture: luxurious lounge seating accented with yellow-and-gold reflective glass surfaces evoking the twinkling city views. We stood for a long moment, almost enjoying ourselves, until we heard a loud cackle and jostle break out between two of the group, drunkenly play-fighting and threatening to drag one another into the pool.

'You know what? A bowl of chilli looks really appealing right now.' I laughed.

I turned to Jay, lifting my glass to my lips, only to pause at the way he was looking at me.

'What?' I asked.

'Abby Taylor, are you trying to be fresh with me?'

I rolled my eyes. 'All I'm saying is, I'd rather be anywhere but here.'

'Well, it's not like you're making an effort.'

My eyes snapped up. 'What?'

'You have to work at it, introduce yourself, make new friends; isn't that why you're here? Go get a sip of that expensive wine.'

I didn't know what to say. I guess I just kind of expected Jay to be on my side, to validate my feelings by saying what a nightmare this was, maybe even throw in a cutesy offer to reheat some chilli for me. I really didn't expect this.

'I don't know what I'm meant to do,' I admitted. It was the first time I didn't feel like I could face something. I was usually the life of the party, and now I just felt completely insignificant.

'Yes, you do,' he said, almost annoyed.

'I really don't; if anything, I should be at home in sweat-pants rehearsing my lines and – '

'Feeling sorry for yourself.'

I glared up at him; now he was starting to ruin the first not completely awful part of the night. Our twosome was now suffused with tension; if he turned on me, I would have no place to go.

Jay sighed. 'Okay, you see that girl over there? The brunette in white, burgundy lips.'

I followed Jay's eyes, unnerved by how my chest tightened at how he noticed the colour of her lips. She was an absolute stunner, sitting casually on the edge of one of the daybeds and talking to some of the others.

'What about her?'

Jay stepped closer to me. 'That's Alexis McKellen – she's a really big deal in daytime TV.'

I looked more closely at her. She did seem familiar, but apparently so did Jay so I didn't think too much about it.

'She's sitting with some big-time producers. And here's the clincher: she's not an asshole.'

I smiled, turning back to Jay. 'Really?'

'Really.'

'How do you know so much?'

'I may not have a rooftop pool at the Saloon, but I get people through the doors, more than once.'

'So, what do I . . .'

'Just play along; you can act, but can you improvise?' Jay said, taking my drink and tipping it out, much to my horror.

'Of course I can.'

'Okay, then, follow me.' Jay carried both of our empty drinks past the pool, right near where Alexis was sitting; he didn't have to say a word before a bright, happy voice sliced through the air.

'Jay?' Alexis clocked him the moment we passed, bringing us to an abrupt halt.

'Hey,' he said, like he was surprised to see her; it was kind of unnerving how effortless he was in playing the role.

'What are you doing here?' She stood, embracing and kissing him on the cheek, which registered with a violent jolt inside my stomach. I had expected to stand to the side like I had done all night, play the subservient role as Sienna did with Leon, but I needn't have worried. Alexis's shining eyes moved straight to me and she held out her hand.

'Hi, I'm Alexis,' she said.

'Abby,' I said, instantly warming to her. 'Lovely to meet you.'

'You're Australian?'

'Guilty.'

'Oh, I just adore your accent! Do you guys want to come join us? Come, sit, speak Australian to me.' She laughed, sitting down and tapping the spare space next to her. I turned to Jay, who looked triumphant.

'We were just headed home, but I could grab us a couple of refills,' he said, lifting up the empty glasses.

I smiled broadly. 'Absolutely.' I liked how he implied we were leaving together; the openness of it gave me a kind of thrill.

'Oh yeah, stay! We have been so bored – come wake us up.'

Alexis's friends were already making space for us.

'Well, let's get the party started, then. What are you ladies drinking?'

A stocky blonde girl dressed more for business than pleasure lifted her glass enthusiastically to Jay.

'Mediterranean sunsets,' she said.

I closed my eyes briefly, willing myself not to turn and see Jay's broad smile.

'Sounds delicious,' he said, and I didn't have to look at him to know just how smug he felt.

~

Abby Taylor was back! Proving there was life outside of the Family, I had successfully ventured out to chat to Alexis, bonding over terrifying auditions, LA cliques (not mentioning any names) and the sheer vastness of the city. It was refreshing to know that Alexis also had to work really hard at her accent, shrugging her natural southern drawl to work on her show.

'Now I just speak like this all the time; once I start saying "y'all", I'll be done for. Although, a few more of these and I will be saying it, guaranteed.'

'Yeah, it really comes out when she's drunk,' said Brenda, the thin, dark-haired girl who blushed anytime she looked Jay's way. I couldn't exactly blame her. After a few sunset cocktails, I, too, felt my skin flush anytime he smiled, or when I felt his jean-clad leg pressed against mine as we sat side-by-side on the day bed. I could feel the heat of his body, the vibration of his laughter, his casual, relaxed warmth as he engaged our group. Maybe it was the alcohol or maybe I could put it down to improvising, but I let my wrist casually lie on Jay's knee as I leant forward, gripped by Alexis's story of when she nearly choked on a buffet meatball at work.

Our group expanded when a few of Alexis's friends rocked up and joined in. The night was filled with laughter, genuine laughter, aided by a few drinks. A long, interesting conversation led to an exchange of business cards with Jonathan, who worked in Star Network's wardrobe department. His boyfriend worked in make-up and was really keen to recruit some new blood for the team. I tried not to snatch the card out of his hand, giddy at hearing 'we are desperate to find someone with actual experience'. Thinking of Billie, I wanted to scream from the rooftop, and wished more than anything she was here with me.

I had gone from coy wallflower to actually wanting to get up and dance; gone were all my reservations. I accepted Jay's dare and dragged Leon onto the dance floor, which surprised him, but it didn't take him long to start busting some old-style dance moves that the nineties wanted back.

I had even been in high-enough spirits to hug Sienna, telling her how much I loved her and how we had to catch up more. It was at this point that I knew I'd partaken of one (or two) too many cocktails.

By the time Jay steered me by the shoulders towards the ladies' bathroom, I really knew I had.

'I can walk,' I insisted, banging into the side of the hall.

'Sure you can,' he laughed.

'I can't believe no girl wanted to go to the bathroom with me, it's like our rite of passage to go in a group; I feel so betrayed.'

'They probably didn't want to be legally responsible for you if anything went badly.'

'Oooh, that's right, people love suing people in America, don't they?'

'I think you've watched way too much TV.'

I hiccupped. '*Judge Judy* is awesome.'

'Okay, here we are.' Jay grabbed my shoulders, pointing to the door where I needed to be.

I spun around, squinting up at him, trying my best to intimidate him, which only seemed to make him laugh.

'You judged me,' I said, pointing into his chest. 'The second we met.'

'Did I?'

'Yes, you did.'

'I see, and then what?' Jay seemed invested in my recount of recent events, until I winced.

'Then I flashed you my boob.'

Jay burst out laughing, so loud it rivalled the muffled music from the roof terrace.

'It's not funny,' I said, hitting at him, but he was too quick, gripping my arms again and pinning me to the wall.

'Abby, go the ladies'. I'll wait for you here.' He said it in a no-nonsense tone, but he was still smiling, looking down at me like he didn't know what to do with me; should he keep me pinned to the wall or release a potentially wild animal?

'I don't need to go.'

'What?'

'It's just an excuse girls use to check our reflections and see if we still look pretty.' I blew a wayward strand out of my eyes, feeling anything but pretty. I felt hot and flustered, and dizzy, and I had a very sexy man pressed up against me, making me feel all sorts of strange things, especially with the way he was looking at me now. Gone was the humour of before, he simply looked into my eyes, the atmospheric lighting flickering across our faces in the dark, narrow hall.

I almost forgot to breathe, looking into the depths of his eyes. A shiver ran down my spine, only heightened by the smile that tugged at the corner of his sexy mouth.

'You still look pretty.' Spoken like a promise, his voice was low and deep, and he was standing so close that the heat from our bodies in this narrow space felt like a furnace.

'Pfft, that's just the alcohol talking.'

Jay smiled wide and bright, the way I loved, as he let my shoulders go and stepped back a little, rubbing at his jawline with interest. He moved towards the men's room, pausing before it. 'Yeah, but I'm not drinking, remember?'

Then, through my drunken socialising haze, I remembered. Jay was stone-cold sober, having opted for water or Coke all night. I blinked. So what had just happened between us – the way he had looked at me, how he had let me casually drape over him through the night – had nothing to do with Jay's choice of drink.

Oh God.

I felt my cheeks burn hot, my eyes flicking up to watch him push the door to the men's room.

'What are you doing?' I said, panicked all of a sudden. A rather stupid question, considering, but my mind was not my own, and my legs weren't either, as I had to use the wall for support.

Jay stilled, a cheeky grin forming as he looked back at me. 'Going to see if I still look pretty,' he said with a wink, before disappearing through door.

Smart ass.

Chapter Twenty-Two

'You're going to have to be quiet,' Jay warned, steering me into the courtyard by the arm.

'I am being quiet!' I insisted. 'Let go.'

'Abby,' Jay gritted.

'Geez, someone needs a drink.'

'And you definitely don't.'

'Pfft, okay, Grandpa. Ooooh, look at the pool!' The water sparkled, as if little white diamonds lay across its surface, enticing me like a magpie to tinfoil.

'Don't even think about it.' Jay steered me clear.

'Oh, come on! I've been near one all night,' I protested; I was starting to get really annoyed at my personal escort. I was fine, so fine, more than fine, and to prove just how fine, I ripped my arm free of his hold and bolted towards the pool, ready to show him just exactly how okay I was.

I prided myself on my grace and flexibility in many areas of my life: dance and gymnastics, ballet lessons, netball and swimming medals. Not going to lie, I was a massive overachiever in many ways, and all those achievements steered me towards the pool's edge. I would master the perfect dive into the pool, because I had done so a hundred times before. The ability to slice through the water with barely a splash was kind of my thing – my secret talent, if you will – but it was going to remain a secret no longer. Let Jay look on in wonder; maybe he'd even apologise for doubting my ability.

I was so confident, taking long strides to the pool, then moving into smaller, daintier ones, my arms out to the side, then sweeping up into position. It was like it was all happening in super-slow motion, my approach to the pool edge nearing, Jay calling out my name with no care or concern for who might hear, and what did I care? Let them see. Let them come out onto their balconies and see the master at work; it would be worth the 1 a.m. disturbance of peace to witness my prowess. And it would have been a thing of beauty had I not, on the very last few steps to the pool, tripped over a pool noodle.

I catapulted forward with a scream, before making the most inelegant entry possible. I hit the water so hard I barely had time to register that I was submerged, the air forced from my lungs as I sunk, face down. I found myself wishing for an out-of-body experience just to escape the burning pain that was coiling over my body.

I became overwhelmed with blind panic as I clawed at the water, my wet clothes and heels weighing me down.

So this was death? Aussie actress found floating in West Hollywood pool – how very *Sunset Boulevard*. Knowing my luck, someone would get video footage of my last moments tripping over a pool noodle and sell it to *TMZ*. I would be a little more famous after death; I only hoped *E! True Hollywood Story* wouldn't immortalise me as 'Noodle Girl'.

Just another broken dream in Hollywood – but not today. I felt a violent burst of water and a dark figure appeared next to me, then unceremoniously gripped me, yanking me up from the pool floor. As soon as I breached the surface and the cool night air hit my exposed skin, the pain was a hundred times worse, and with each cough and splutter I was convinced I had shattered every rib. I was merely a bag of skin with rubble inside; the result of such a brutal entry.

'You alright?'

All I could do was cough and wheeze as I tried to climb up Jay's torso.

'It's okay, I got you.'

Jay dragged me out of the pool and I collapsed, wincing, onto the concrete, still warm from the day's sun. I heard voices from above and I wasn't completely sure that I wasn't, in fact, dead, but then the very real feeling of Sorscha licking the salty droplets off my cheek snapped me back into reality.

'She's alright,' Jay shouted up to a balcony.

I opened my eyes, blinking through blurry, water-logged vision to see that I had quite the audience. A mixture of confused and angry faces: some seemed concerned but the majority seemed to wish I had drowned, and quietly.

'Sorry,' I croaked. Barely audible.

'It's okay, everyone, go back to bed,' Jay called out, and a man called back something that didn't sound all that friendly, but Jay's attention moved back to me, cupping my cheeks and checking my eyes for signs of trauma.

'Abby, can you hear me?'

I moaned because that's all I could do, and I wasn't too worried about being quiet about it.

'Where does it hurt?'

'E-everywhere.'

Jay's hands were gently skimming over me, examining with expert ease, until he disappointingly came to a conclusion.

All I could think about was how I had to see Ziggy tomorrow. A neck brace and a wheelchair was not going to be a good look. Seriously, why was life a cakewalk for some and a giant train wreck for me?

'I think you'll live.'

'What?' I squinted up at him.

'On the plus side, you're not orange anymore – you're more of a lobster red,' he said, lifting up my dress to show my red-raw thighs. I could only imagine what my stomach looked like after my epic, mortifying belly-whacker.

'Oh, great!' I said, lifting myself onto my elbows, wincing and surveying the damage.

'Don't worry, it will go, it'll probably have more of a purplish hue tomorrow.'

My chin began to tremble as the bruising of my ego came into full bloom. I lay in the courtyard in a wet, twisted mess, reflecting on my disastrous existence, and I began to sob in the worst possible way: the drunken girl sob. I covered my eyes with my arm, wishing that Jay would just leave me here.

'Hey, come on.' Jay pulled my arm away. 'You're alright, probably just in a bit of shock. Come on, let's get you home.' My protests fell on deaf ears as Jay, without apology, yanked me out of my puddle of saltwater and tears and, without giving me a moment to gain my land legs, lifted me up into his arms, forcing me to wrap mine around his neck to find purchase.

'It's okay, I got you.'

He said those same words again and I believed him. I felt safe in his arms, rock solid as he carried me across the courtyard and up the stairs as if I weighed nothing. I wasn't overly comfortable, but I felt comforted. I felt like I had been hit by a bus and, with the alcohol wearing off, I was well aware of how Jay's warm breath felt on my cheek, and the feel of his skin under my hands, and the way his heart beat so rapidly. I felt it all; it was a definite distraction from feeling like a drowned rat.

Jay unlocked his door with such ease it made me wonder if he made a habit of carrying girls to his condo. Wait a minute – Jay's door? Jay's condo?

I lifted my head, eyes widening at the sight of Jay's door slamming behind us, and being carried down a hallway that did not belong to me. I couldn't find the words of protest. I was totally void of thought and speech, especially when he carried me past the kitchen and plonked me on the leather couch.

'I'm all wet,' I managed, worried about creating a puddle in his sleek bachelor pad.

'So am I,' he said with a laugh. I looked down at his wet clothes, in particular the now-sheer white shirt that clung to every curve of his ripped body. I kind of felt bad that I was responsible for his sodden state but, staring up at him, appreciating just how good he looked wet, I can't say that I was suffering from a huge amount of regret.

He disappeared through a doorway, switching on the light to reveal his bedroom. A large black leather–framed bed, firmly made, without a thing out of place. It was a fleeting look at best but my interest was certainly piqued by this glimpse into his world. All too quickly he switched off the light and came back to me with a towel and T-shirt.

'Bathroom's there if you want to get out of your wet clothes.'

I blinked, confused, a wry smile forming. 'My clothes are literally through that wall.'

Jay cocked a knowing brow. 'Can you be trusted?'

I didn't know the answer to that – all I knew was that I felt something, sitting here in Jay's company, and I was enjoying being under his watchful eye.

'Do you think I might have concussion?' Was that another reason he was keeping watch?

'I think you might have more chance of alcohol poisoning.'

My eyes squinted. 'Oh, ha-bloody-ha.'

Jay smiled broadly. 'Bathroom,' he pointed.

~

I rinsed the saltwater from my hair over the tub, dabbing a bit of coconut-scented conditioner at the ends to help untangle the matted mess. Jay's black T-shirt swam on me, resting just above my knees. I took the black material belt from my skirt and loosely tied it around my waist; from a distance it looked like I had a dress on, but the fact that I was wearing no underwear made it feel very wrong. But it's not like I would be staying long – this was merely a neighbourly formality.

I opened the bathroom door, taking small, tentative steps and wincing at the bruising that was no doubt ready to make an appearance. I was momentarily distracted from my pain by the delicious smell of chilli as Jay appeared from the kitchen with bowl and spoon, a slice of bread sitting on top. Much to my disappointment, he had changed into a fresh T-shirt and a dry pair of jeans, ending the wet fantasy image that was burned into my memory.

'Enjoy,' he said, moving to the coffee table and placing it down, pulling the tea towel from his shoulder and placing it next to the bowl. He stood back, looking rather pleased with himself.

My nose creased, unable to hide my distaste for anything spicy. I edged forward and peered into the bowl. 'Are you having some?'

'Maybe later.'

'Later? What, for breakfast?' I laughed, then I made a mental note not to do that again – it hurt too much.

'I don't sleep much, so yeah, maybe.'

I winced as I took a seat, making sure to pull the tee down so as not to inadvertently flash Jay any more than I already had.

'You don't sleep?'

'Very rarely.'

'What, are you like an insomniac or something?'

'Maybe. I think it's more to do with late nights and the nature of my work.'

'Is that why you do laps of a night?' I said, tentatively loading a forkful of chilli into my mouth. I paused mid-chew, realising I had nearly confessed my new favourite ritual, the night perve. My cheeks went red; I hoped I could blame the chilli.

'So, what do you think?'

Jay sat on the single chair opposite me, nervous, looking like a *MasterChef* contestant serving a haemorrhaging apple strudel to the judges. It was quite endearing to see someone who was usually so cocksure seem a little doubtful. What was more surprising was that I actually enjoyed the chilli.

'It's really good.'

'Really?' Jay's brows rose in surprise.

'Really, like, really, really good. Not too hot, just tasty.'

'You're not just saying that because I saved your life?'

I sighed. 'Another thing I will never live down.'

Jay laughed. 'It's okay, I won't tell, but be warned: the gossip mill runs overtime in these condominiums. By morning, the story will be that you pulled me out of the water and gave me the kiss of life.'

'I am well used to the truth being twisted,' I said, dunking my bread into the spicy juices.

'All the more reason to align yourself with the right people if you're going to start afresh here.'

'Yeah, well, after tonight I am convinced that the #LAfamily are not my people.'

'So you make your own people.'

'And, pray tell, who are your people? Definitely not actors.'

Jay relaxed in his chair, linking his hands behind his head in deep thought.

'I wouldn't have imagined there was much to think about? Surely the answer to that is a resounding no,' I mused.

'What does it matter what I think of actors?'

It was an interesting question; it shouldn't matter and yet it did. I didn't want anyone thinking I was this giant cliché, moving here in the search of fame and fortune. It wasn't about that really. I mean, it would be nice, but just to be able to do what I love – that was the real dream. That was the reward. What did it matter if someone thought it was egotistical? For me it wasn't about being the centre of attention, it was the art form itself, the transforming, the world building – it was the ultimate adrenaline rush.

'It doesn't,' I said, finishing the last of the chilli and resisting the urge to lick the bowl. Best save some dignity tonight, if there was any left.

'You done?'

'Yes, thanks.' I was tempted to compliment the dish again, but I didn't want him to get too big a head.

'Hey, Jay, do you have a bag I could put my wet things in?' I called out, making my way back to the bathroom where my clothes were hanging over the bath. I gathered them up and wrung the excess drippage into the sink, before folding them and looking at my reflection in the mirror. I was definitely flushed: it broke through the still very unnatural glow on my skin and the lighting certainly didn't help. I ran the tap, bathing my face and rinsing my mouth out with a liberal helping of Jay's toothpaste to cool the subtle burn of the chilli.

Without thinking I opened the mirrored cabinet, not exactly sure what I was looking for – some remnants of an ex-girlfriend maybe. 'Ooh, cologne.' I took a sample of Hugo Boss from the shelf and sniffed. Yep, smelt just like Jay, clean and crisp. There was floss and mouthwash, too;

no wonder his teeth were so perfect – oral hygiene was obviously very important. Deodorant, aspirin, no bottles stating, 'Take one a day and if axe murdering persists see a doctor.' So that's always a plus. Much like his condo, everything was in its place, perfectly aligned and . . .

'Here.'

I jumped, slamming the cabinet shut and looking, stunned, at Jay's reflection, holding out a plastic bag.

'Oh, I was just . . .'

'Snooping.'

'Yes.'

'Find anything?'

'I was going to check your side tables next, that's probably where all the good stuff is kept.'

Jay broke out into a wide, immaculate smile. 'How did you know?'

I shrugged. 'Just a guess.'

I had a sudden image of what might be in his drawers, the drawers of a strapping, young, single man in West Hollywood, surrounded by beautiful people – a long line of condoms, no doubt. Unlike my bedside drawer, which was filled with empty chocolate wrappers and desperation.

I quickly took the bag from him, blinking out of my wayward thoughts.

'Thanks,' I said, turning and shoving my sodden clothes into the bag.

Feeling Jay's eyes on me, I lifted my gaze to his in the reflection of the mirror. His smile was gone, as if he, too, had realised how close we were in this small space, so close I could feel the heat of him through my T-shirt. My mind was wandering again, thinking about how easy it would be to break away from his eyes, to turn to him . . . So I did, slowly facing him, breathing deeper and feeling my body burn with a feeling that had absolutely nothing to do with the chilli.

Jay's mouth was so lush. I had noticed it before, but being as close as I was now, the air thick with a new kind of tension, I really, really noticed, and wondered what it might feel like. I swallowed hard, knowing I was staring at his mouth, making no attempt to hide the fact. What was he thinking about? My blotchy skin, half-dried hair and the attractive makeshift tee-dress I had fashioned? I doubt very much that he would be thinking about my bedside –

Jay kissed me.

Stepping forward, cupping my face, his mouth crushed against mine, and I finally got to experience exactly what his lips felt like and, oh my God, they were mind-splinteringly good, searing across mine, capturing, pressing, burning. Any doubt was completely obliterated in that moment as my fingers scrunched the back of his T-shirt, pulling him closer, as he pressed me against the vanity, the hard corner digging into my lower back.

Jay broke for a second, smiling and moving his head to the side to access my mouth better as his tongue reacted to my eagerness. He slipped his fingers into my belt, twisting and pulling me more urgently into his kiss.

My T-shirt shifted up my thighs, but I was so lost in the moment I cared little that there was no barrier between us. He lifted me onto the sink and moved into the space between my legs, deepening his kiss.

Oh God, this was bad, very bad. My bare skin felt so cool on the marble top, my legs wrapped around Jay's waist to keep my balance as the denim of his jeans rubbed a delicious kind of friction, making me gasp.

Jay stilled. 'Sorry, did I hurt you?'

He gently touched my side, thinking I may very well be broken, unaware of the real reason for my gasp, and I certainly wasn't going to tell him. He was going to find out soon enough, especially the way his hands were sliding back and forth over my thighs, causing my skin to prickle. I wanted him to go higher, but I also knew how deadly that would be.

I should really call it a night. Thank him for his companionship and hospitality and just get out while the going was good. But after just a little longer of kissing his mouth . . . After all, it was only a kiss – a kiss was harmless, a bit of fun, this I could do until, uhhhh . . .

Jay slid his hand under the hem of my tee only to discover exactly what wasn't there. He paused, a small smile tugging at the corner of his mouth, but he didn't say a word; instead, his hands simply squeezed my bare butt as his mouth found mine once again, this time more fevered. The pressure between my thighs was heavier and more distracting, feeling how hard he was in his denim, rubbing against me. Knowing what he knew now, I wondered if he would explore more, but he didn't. He simply cupped my hips to lock me in place, and as he kissed me I could feel his fingers indent my skin. I was going to have to worry about more than abdominal bruising in the morning – I was going to be branded by Jay – but I didn't mind. He was being so good, so controlled, simply kissing me in a way that had me begging for more, stirring up other feelings and robbing me of all my sanity.

As much as I wanted to keep telling myself this was just a kiss, it was not enough. Gone was any form of bashfulness as I pulled his firm grip from my hip, and guided it around to the front, pushing his hand between my thighs and allowing him in. To hell with first base. I blamed his lips, that tongue for seducing me into a wanton mess, breathing hard against his mouth as he slid his fingers inside me with ease. So hot and wet to his touch, pressing into him as he looked into my eyes, his own breath ragged, the friction building as he pumped and I rocked and our voices echoed in the bathroom. I had never been so happy to get a fake tan – it had led me to Mediterranean cocktails, to the pool, to right here, with no knickers and Jay between my legs. Nothing else might come of this but utter mortification and awkwardness between us come the light of day, but, by God, I was about to fall apart right now.

Grasping his shoulders and rocking into his hand, I was going to come, and I told Jay as much over and over again, my hand gripping the edge of the vanity and sending the toothbrush and aftershave flying as I fell back against the mirror.

Watching Jay, I pressed my head against the mirror, my scream echoing in the tiled room so loud that I figured I had woken the neighbours for the second time tonight. And as my screams petered out, Jay didn't let up, pushing me past the point of madness. I gripped his arm and pulled it away, unable to take it anymore. I distracted him with my mouth, sucking in his beautifully lush bottom lip, and giving it a nip, suspecting that might bring him back to me. And it did, with a blinding smile.

Jay moved back a little, but he never took his eyes from mine. I felt limp, drunk, but this was so much better than any cocktail. Gone was any thought of pain, only a rich, sated afterglow as Jay helped me slide off the vanity to stand on shaky legs. If he could do that with his hand and his mouth, what else could he do?

If I looked him in the eyes for long enough, would he guess all the things I wanted him to do to me? Maybe it was the post-orgasmic comedown, but if he could read my mind, I don't think we would be standing here right now. He would have spun me around, hitched up my shirt and taken me from behind. If that was what he wanted, I wouldn't fight it – I would bloody well welcome it.

Yep, utter madness. He needed to make the first move, because clearly my mind was in the gutter. He needed to be the sensible one, and thank God he was, moving away instead of having his way with me. He bent to pick up all the items scattered across the floor, including my bag of clothes. I tucked my hair behind my ears; the sight of the carnage on the bathroom floor made me blush. Did I do this, in my state of unadulterated bliss? Jesus.

Jay didn't seem fussed, though; if anything, he seemed rather pleased with himself. It made me wish that maybe he hadn't been so bloody clever, or me so willing. I cleared my throat, adjusting my belt and trying to appear cool and whatever.

'What time is it?'

'It must be nearly two.'

'Shit, I better go,' I said, grabbing the bag and tying a knot in it as a means to distract me from bigger things – like Jay's eyes on me, or the very present hard-on he was trying to disguise with his shirt. Now I was the one who was pleased with herself. Yep, I did that.

I hooked the bag over my wrist and stood there ever so awkwardly. How can you possibly wrap up a night like this? *Thanks for the lift, thanks for saving me from drowning, thanks for the mind-blowing orgasm.* It was clear that he wasn't going to break the ice; he was having way too much fun watching the cogs turn in my brain, seeing how I was going to make my move. So I did it in a very roundabout way.

'Thanks for the chilli. Might need a little more salt next time,' I said, measuring it with my fingers and spinning on my heel, strutting through the condo towards the front door.

Jay followed me. I tried not to smile when he moved past me and grabbed the handle of the front door. 'You know that chilli was perfect.'

I pushed my hair over my shoulder. 'It was . . . nice.'

'Nice?' Jay folded his arms across his broad chest; his tone incredulous.

'Yeah, nice,' I said, stretching past him and opening the door, forcing him to move aside.

'Ah, yeah, but the thing is . . .' he began.

I paused in the breezeway, turning to look at him expectantly.

Jay smiled, broad and wicked. 'Would you come back for seconds?'

My own smile faltered because I was pretty sure we weren't talking about chilli anymore. So instead of giving a clear-cut answer I breathed out and left him hanging. 'Maybe,' I said, turning to make the last steps towards my door, almost home free, until Billie turned the corner.

I skidded to a halt, my eyes snapping from her shocked state back to Jay, then to the T-shirt I was standing half-naked in, and back again to Billie.

Sprung!

Chapter Twenty-Three

My instinct was to blurt out, 'It's not what it looks like.'
But of course that would have been a lie, because
it was exactly what it looked like, and if I was hoping for any
form of backup from Jay, well, I'd be sorely disappointed.
He didn't seem the least bit embarrassed or panicked,
leaning in the doorway without a care in the world.

'How was work?'

Was he serious?

Billie seemed rather taken aback too, and clearly uncomfortable, moving to her door and averting eye contact.

'Good,' she said.

'Any dramas?'

'Nope.'

Oh God, this was painful. I was stuck in the breezeway,
not knowing what to do or say. I just wished that Billie
would hurry up and open the bloody door. While I was
keen to get inside, she did not seem happy at all.

'Goodnight, you two.' Jay said, but his eyes were on me until he closed the door. It was enough of a look to have my lady-bits clenching and want to follow him back into his condo but, seeing Billie rip open her door and throwing her things on the side table, I realised I would have to do some damage control.

I followed her inside, closing the door behind us. 'Are you mad at me?'

Billie opened the fridge and grabbed a water bottle and, instead of answering, she guzzled cold water until she had a brain freeze. 'Son of a bitch!' she said, clenching her temple, letting the door shut and plunge us into darkness.

I moved to the lounge room and switched on the light. 'Did you have a bad night?' I asked, trying for a supportive, 'let's focus on you' tone.

'No, actually, I was having a great night . . . until I got home.' She looked at me pointedly.

Aaaaand here we go.

'Look, Billie . . .'

'No, you look! I don't get you; one minute you can't stand the guy and the next minute you're hooking up with him? What happens when it all goes to shit, Abby? Seriously, of all the people, it had to be with my neighbour, my boss?'

'It's not like that, and besides, it's not going to affect you; I'd never let anything I do interfere with your life.'

'You've been in town for five minutes; I've lived here for three years and I haven't even moved beyond second base.'

I wasn't exactly sure what base I got to tonight but it definitely felt like a home run.

'That's because you don't put yourself out there: you work, you come home and you work.'

Billie scoffed. 'It's called the real world, Abby.'

I was a little taken aback, hurt even. 'Oh, right, because I live in fantasy land, is that what you're saying?'

Billie rolled her eyes. 'Don't twist my words.'

'But that's what you're implying.'

Billie simply stared back at me. Now I was starting to get angry.

'Not that it's any of your business, but I didn't sleep with Jay; we kissed. The reason I'm wearing his top is because my clothes got wet.'

I thought it best to leave out details like raging vanity orgasm and falling into the pool; after all, I didn't want to get her any more riled up.

'I met some really cool people tonight, made some new non–LA Family connections, thanks to Jay, one in particular that I think will excite you,' I said, rummaging through my plastic bag for my clutch, and retrieving the wet and slightly smudged business card. I handed it over to her. 'They're looking for an experienced make-up artist at the Star Network. I said you'd give them a call.'

Billie's eyes skimmed over the business card before looking back at me; it was like she thought I was pulling a prank.

'You're welcome. And look at it this way: at least Jay and I are getting along.' And with that, I walked away.

~

My fight with Billie haunted me, making me toss and turn until daybreak. I lay flat on my back, staring at the ceiling, my head pounding, my stomach churning, my eyes puffy from lack of sleep. On top of all that sat the weight of my dread at meeting Ziggy today. Usually this was something I looked forward to, but this time there was so much riding on her visit.

She was flying all the way to talk business and discuss my future prospects, and what did I have to show her? I was hungover, motley orange, with a barely functioning American accent in prep for one of the biggest auditions of my life. The one thing that frightened me more than anything was disappointing Ziggy. I had done it once before in my younger years; having slept in, I'd missed a really important magazine interview, and the aftermath had seen me bear the full brunt of Ziggy's disappointment. She'd threatened to drop me if I didn't pull my head in; it had been a huge step forward in my maturation.

Now, after being left to my own devices, I felt like I was right back where I started. Same shit, different location. There was no way of sugarcoating my bloodshot eyes, or the feeling of wanting to be sick from a hangover so epic I didn't know if I could claw my way out of bed, let alone meet for a luncheon with Ziggy.

I'd hoped to see Billie and clear the air before I left to make me feel better, but instead of finding her in her usual place, whirling around the kitchen and cooking up a storm, her bedroom door was firmly shut and there was no sign of life. There was that same empty feeling when I stepped out into the breezeway, where the hopeless romantic side of my brain wished that Jay's door might open, that he would offer me a cup of coffee and a friendly face. But there was nothing there to greet me, just memories from last night's awkwardness.

All of a sudden, despite my nausea and aversion to sunlight, I was actually glad to get away for a bit. Avoid Billie, avoid Jay and just concentrate on my career. I didn't know why I was so nervous about seeing Ziggy; I had done everything she had asked. Signed up for acting lessons, met with my voice coach, learnt my lines, prepped as much as I could. Hell, I had even met up with Sienna and networked, so yes, my groundwork was sound. I was doing good. *Lots of positivity*, I thought, no matter how clammy and bilious I felt about being trapped on a stuffy public bus, trying to listen to the calming sound of *The War on Drugs* filtering through my earplugs and concentrate less on where I was, and more on where I was going.

I had to hand it Ziggy: she never did anything by half-measures. When she came to town she really came to town, opting to stay and play at the LA icon that was the Hollywood Roosevelt Hotel. Named for President Theodore Roosevelt, the hotel had welcomed generations of VIPs, from the legends of Hollywood's Golden Age to today's hottest stars.

Arriving early, I wandered throughout the property, classic architecture meeting contemporary design in warm tones and rich textures. From the moment I stepped into its Spanish Colonial-style lobby, I was surrounded by Hollywood history. Ziggy had told me the first Academy Awards were presented at a private dinner in the hotel's Blossom Ballroom – the winners were announced three months before the ceremony, which took just fifteen minutes. Clark Gable and Carole Lombard carried on their infamous affair in the penthouse, which cost $5 a night. Marilyn Monroe lived at the hotel for two years as her modelling career began to take off – she was staying in one of the cabanas at the time of her first professional magazine shoot, which took place at the Hollywood Roosevelt pool.

Ziggy was staying in the Marilyn Monroe Suite; she was never ashamed to boast about her personal obsession with all things Marilyn. I had researched the accommodation myself and I had desperately wanted Ziggy to stay in the Gable-Lombard Penthouse, just so I could experience for myself a 3200-square-foot duplex with an outdoor deck tucked beneath the Roosevelt's iconic sign. The suite boasted spectacular views of the Hills and the Hollywood Sign, but of course Ziggy was adamant: it was the Marilyn suite or nothing.

We were to meet at the Public Kitchen & Bar, a luxurious vintage-style dining room with leather banquettes and gilt chandeliers, offset by a living wall of succulents and a historic mural that was uncovered during renovation – or so the waiter claimed when he noticed me admiring it.

'Have you been here before?'

'Ah, no,' I said, desperately trying to avert my attention from the bar, where a long line of glossy, well-lit alcohol bottles taunted me, instantly turning my stomach.

'Well, if you're looking for a recommendation you might like to start with an assortment of charcuterie, artisanal cheeses and house-made preserves, then tuck into some hearty meats and inventive seafood dishes.' The man smiled brightly, but I really wasn't in the mood for happy and helpful, I was in survival mode – and desperate for the fried stuff.

'Thanks, I'll just wait for my friend,' I said with a weak smile, thinking how hot it was. Was there a fireplace blazing somewhere? I rubbed my clammy hands on my legs, observing how everyone seated around me seemed relaxed and comfortable. I was definitely in The Horrors – of all days, what had I been thinking, to go out last night? I massaged my temples, contemplating whether to be sick now or after lunch. It was a very important decision, but one that was taken away from me the moment I heard Ziggy's voice from across the room. 'There she is!'

Oh God.

If there was a hint of silver lining in this cloud it was that she wouldn't be able to accuse me of being pale; my underlying post-hangover green would be tinted by the tan. Of course, I wasn't sure it was any more flattering. I was about to find out, watching as Ziggy strutted a long, determined line to the table. I stood to brace myself for the crushing hug I knew was coming, which wouldn't aid my bruising from last night's antics.

'Oh, Abby, it's so good to see you, darling. Let me look at you.'

Oh shit. Please, don't.

She stepped back, holding my hands, her smile alight as she examined me; it didn't take long for the smile to falter.

'Abby, are you unwell?'

Crap. I didn't know if honesty was always the best policy, but Ziggy had an excellent bullshit detector, which was not really great for me, considering that I earned my living by acting. Maybe that could be something I could learn in acting classes?

'It's been a big few weeks, just adjusting and getting my bearings. I caught up with Sienna last night!' *That's it, Abby, spin it into a positive – mention something she asked you to do.*

'Oh, so you're hungover, then,' she said, taking her seat opposite me. I sat down in kind, anxiety bubbling under the surface of my crawling skin.

'It was a big night,' I said, a memory of my head pressed against a vanity mirror surfacing. I slammed the memory down and leant forward, my elbows on the table. 'I'm not a saint, Ziggy. If I am going to go out and network, chances are there will be drinks and socialising.'

'Yes, and that's where you will learn how to pick and choose your battles. The LA Family might party hard, but they work hard too. They have jobs that fund their lifestyles – never forget that. Did you want something to drink now?' she asked, giving me a cheeky glance from the cocktail menu.

The very thought made me want to dry heave. I knew she was testing me, but I was going to be responsible. 'Just a water, thanks.'

Ziggy laughed. 'No hair of the dog?'

'Not until I'm earning to pay for it,' I said, showing her I heeded her words, however depressing they were.

'Now, just because you land a job doesn't mean you can hit it hard, either. It's all about remaining professional.'

I wanted to roll my eyes. I wasn't a complete idiot, I hadn't got this far by being a loose cannon; compared to some, I was a bloody angel. Taking a deep breath, I realised that Ziggy's tone was really rather motherly. She was lecturing me because she cared, because she was worried.

'Don't worry, Zig, I will not get led astray. I know why I'm here and I plan to balance my life.'

'Well, that's good, because I have a little something for you,' she said, lifting up a bag I hadn't even realised she'd carried in.

'Aww, Zig, you shouldn't ha . . .'

I peered inside, my words falling away. No, she really, really shouldn't have. I reached inside, pulling out the flimsy material.

'Oh, wow. Activewear,' I said, trying not to sound bitterly disappointed.

'Welcome to LA! There's also a drink bottle in there.'

'Oh, yay!'

Ziggy reached for my arm, bringing it to her face and turning my arm from side to side.

'What on earth?'

'Oh, yeah,' I said, pulling free from her and putting both hands in my lap. 'It's just a spray tan – it will come off.'

'It better come off. You look jaundiced.'

'Oh, wow, Ziggy, cheers. You really build me up, you know,' I snapped, instantly regretting my words, seeing her eyes lock onto me as if she had misheard me. She had an incredible ability to make me feel tiny, and I instantly wanted to apologise before she went Next Level Zig, as I had seen her do with producers on the phone. It was this 'other' Ziggy that had made grown men cry – I had witnessed it.

Something worse happened – she said nothing, unfolding her napkin and placing it in her lap. Her silence was far more brutal than a lecture, and I really didn't know where to go from here. All I wanted to do was to get back to normal with Ziggy. She'd always been my rock, my voice of reason, but ever since I moved to LA the conversations had been different; the stakes were higher and I felt like I was in her world now, not mine. This new world was harsher and unlike anything I had ever known. Even if she was using tough love to thicken my skin, I didn't have to like it.

'So, you met with Ray?' she asked coolly.

She was giving me a small reprieve, and I was going to take it with both hands.

'Yes! He has been so helpful, and I booked in with the small theatre group you recommended downtown. I start there on the fifteenth,' I said brightly, transmitting positive vibes, positive, positive, positive.

'So, hit me with some lines,' she said, clasping her hands together and looking at me expectantly.

'What?'

'For your audition on Monday – let's hear them.'

'N-now?'

'As good a time as any.'

I felt hot again, and I knew that it had nothing to do with my hangover and everything to do with the unbearable weight I felt resting on my shoulders.

My mouth gaped as my mind went blank – *oh shit oh shit oh shit*. But like a gift from the heavens I was interrupted by the floating, friendly waiter. 'Ready to order?'

'Yes!' I said, way too loudly, causing Ziggy to smirk knowingly.

'Well, okay then,' he said. 'I didn't realise you were hungry.'

'Starving,' I lied.

Ziggy shook her head, re-examining her menu. Yep, she saw through me.

Utter bullshit.

Chapter Twenty-Four

Despite the rocky start, Ziggy did eventually instil some confidence in me; she had hooked me up for some new headshot shoots, booked a meeting with an agency and a few interviews. The more we spoke about her plans for me, the more I realised just how badly I wanted this role. It was the same kind of yearning I'd had when I auditioned for *Ship to Sea*; I was born to play Annika just as I was born to play Cassie Carmichael.

Ziggy smiled, first at the waiter who cleared our plates, mine barely touched, then she turned her sparkly blue gaze to me, listening intently as she clasped her hands under her chin. I had poured my heart out over lunch, bucked up the courage to run some lines and let her know the research I had done, the motivation for the character I was portraying, and how I was willing to inhabit her, mind, body and soul. She belonged to me. I thought my speech might have earned me some kind of recognition, so when Ziggy smiled and said: 'Honey, you're going to need a day job.'

I could have fallen off my chair. 'What?'

'Look, great, fantastic, you are doing almost all the right things, and I am super impressed with how keen you are for this role, however . . .'

Oh, how I hated that word. *However.*

'This is not Australia and you don't have a foot in the door anywhere. I can line things up, connect you to the right people, appropriate jobs, and I have few in mind that I'm excited to tell you about, but . . .'

'But what?'

'You're going to have to prepare yourself for a lot of rejections.'

My back straightened. I know this was worst-case scenario stuff, but I wasn't like that. I had to keep positive – it was the only way I was going to make it through.

'That role is mine, Ziggy, and I will go down fighting for it.'

Her lips pressed together in a thin line. 'I just don't want you to be disappointed.'

What I was disappointed in was her lack of faith.

'Don't you think I can do it?'

'Just don't put all your eggs in one basket. Here,' Ziggy took an envelope from her bag and slid it across the table. 'Here are some other projects that will give you good auditioning practice and, with any luck – '

'A beer commercial?'

'A top beer commercial,' she pointed out.

'A non-speaking commercial.'

'It will be good exposure.'

'As what, flirty girl at the bar?'

Ziggy clasped her hands together on the tabletop; I could see her patience was wearing thin. 'Okay, so Monday, after your audition, what then?'

'I – '

'I'll tell you what you'll do: you go to another audition, then another, you audition for Burger King if you have to. You line up for as much as you can and submit those sparkly, beautiful new headshots to as many people as you can. You know why?'

'Because this isn't Australia, nobody knows me, I know.'

'Because it's not all sunglasses and autographs. If you want to make it in this town you have to work for it. Bloody hard.'

'Like Sienna,' I scoffed.

'Abby, jealousy doesn't become you.'

My eyes snapped up. 'I'm not jealous,' I squeaked, clearing my throat.

'Aren't you? You should be. There is nothing quite like the burning hatred of a nemesis to fuel the fire.'

I sighed. 'I just want to do good, give it my all.'

'Then, in that case,' Ziggy said, placing on her sunglasses and grabbing her bag. 'Keep fit, stay out of the sun, and spray booths, drink plenty of water, go to your classes and get a day job.'

'I never thought this would be part of the plan.' I sulked.

'Well, princess, if you want to survive then you're going to have to make it your plan. It's a dog-eat-dog world out there, where there are a million Abby Taylors; just let yourself be the smartest one.'

'I don't feel too smart right now.'

Ziggy moved, rubbing me on the shoulder. 'Don't be too hard on yourself. This is a tough gig. I want you to live as normally as you can in between all the insanity. Lap up anonymity, Abby, you never know how long it will last.'

'I never thought I would miss being the homewrecker.'

'Oh, wash your mouth out! Dinner tomorrow night?'

'Sounds good.'

'I promise we'll talk about more fun things next time.'

I knew it was all a part of the tough love she was providing, and maybe it was the hangover, the fight with Billie, and the stupidity of hooking up with Jay last night, but I felt miserable. I had wanted Ziggy to tell me everything I wanted to hear: 'you're glowing', 'this part is yours for the taking', 'Hollywood is lucky to have you' and 'of course Jay likes you'. Okay, now I was getting hysterical.

I left Ziggy to her afternoon of laptop by the pool – more Abby Taylors needing her sage advice, no doubt – to wander the city streets looking for some much-needed inspiration, the same warm feelings that had engulfed me when I'd first entered the Roosevelt, surrounded by the ghosts of Hollywood. I wondered how Marilyn felt living there. Her modelling career had been taking off; was she filled with optimism in the beginning? As I looked up at the dirty sky I wondered if it was really pollution or merely clouds of pent-up frustration from all the creative souls riddled with self-doubt. Maybe that's what the Hollywood sign symbolised: the ultimate, unattainable pinnacle of success, up above the smog, looking down on all the dreamers stuck here, choking.

Wow, I really needed to clear my black mood. And what better way than by passing through the busy intersection, wrapped up among the eager tourists, crossing over to the forecourt entrance of Grauman's Chinese Theatre, a key stop on the Hollywood Walk of Fame. Celebrations of the industry's best literally set in stone – well, concrete. Hordes of onlookers walked over imprints of the eyeglasses of Harold Lloyd, the cigar of Groucho Marx and the legs of Betty Grable. Western stars William S. Hart and Roy Rogers left imprints of their guns, while Rogers' horse left his hoof prints. Herbie, a Volkswagen Beetle, left the imprints of his tyres. John Wayne had surprisingly tiny feet, and there, of course, were Marilyn Monroe's dainty handprints.

I whispered a silent wish as I bent down, hoping against hope that our hands would be the same size, that if they matched it would somehow mean something, that I was destined for bigger things. But of course they didn't – my fingers were much longer than hers. It was clear I would not have made it as a Hollywood actress back in the day.

Taking a ride through the Hollywood Hills on a tour of celebrity mansions was tempting, but so was a nap. Clearly I had a lot to learn about living a rock 'n' roll lifestyle. Man, when had I become so lame? I was twenty-five years old; these were the best years of my life, and I should be really living them!

There was only one person I wanted to do that with, and, talking to me or not, she was going to start living too. Because I really didn't want either of us to end up like old Veronica on the lower floor, sharing dinners with a little dog and lusting after men forty years her junior.

Nope, nope, nope.

Time to jump on the bus and head back home. Ziggy had sparked something in me, something that had been a long time coming, and stepping into the footsteps (quite literally) of those who had made it set me on fire. I was going to give it everything I had, starting from now.

Chapter Twenty-Five

Ziggy had told me to prepare for the worst, and that was exactly the attitude I adopted going back to the condo. Prepped for the silent treatment, even the 'I don't think we should live together' speech, what I didn't expect were tears – colossal, sobbing tears.

I let my bag drop, quickstepping to the lounge, where Billie's head was buried in her hands.

'Billie, what's wrong?'

She was so upset. I had never seen her like this before; had someone died? There was no blood, no chopping accident in the kitchen – what could it be?

Billie lowered her hands; shaking her head, she looked at me and started to laugh, then cry again, and laugh some more. She looked like a mad woman.

'Billie, you're scaring me.'

She wiped her eyes, trying to contain herself before she gripped my hands tightly and looked me straight in the eyes.

'Abby, I got a job!'

'Um, okay?'

'No, more than okay – I got THE job, a make-up job, at the studio, from the person you met last night.'

'What?'

'I called him and he wanted to meet me straightaway. We spoke for over an hour, he gave me a tour, I did a test run on an actress, and then he said the job is mine if I want it!'

'Billie, oh my God!' I wrapped my arms around her; the universe might not have given me a sign, but this was even better. My best friend, who had been trying so hard for so long, had finally landed a proper gig. In the space of a moment I had gone from never having seen her so upset, to never having seen her so happy.

'Thank you, Abby, thank you so much. I'm so sorry about last night, the things I said were way out of line and so not true.'

'I'm sorry, too. I can't even imagine how weird it must have been seeing me and Jay together.'

An awkward silence settled between us, which told me exactly how awkward it had been. I cleared my throat as a means to break the long pause.

'Well, hey, you got a job! And not just any job, but THE job! When do you start?'

'Monday!' Billie squealed, and I squealed too, laughing like lunatics and squeezing each other.

'We have to celebrate!' I said, jumping to my feet and ducking to the fridge, retrieving two lame bottles of water. I handed one to Billie, who eyed it sceptically.

'Aah, I think we have two very different definitions of what celebrating is.'

'Think of it as a public service announcement; I wish someone had told me to drink plenty of fluids before I went out on the town last night.'

'You are a gem!' Billie took the bottle and took a deep swig, gasping before something seemingly horrifying occurred to her. 'Oh shit.'

'What?'

Her shoulders slumped. 'How am I going to tell Jay?'

The mere mention of his name tensed my muscles. 'What? Tell him you have your dream job, simple.'

Billie shook her head. 'There is nothing simple about it. I've always prided myself on being the reliable one, the one staff member he could count on. He is going to be so pissed.'

'He'll get over it,' I said, as if I really knew Jay, which of course I didn't; sure, I'd had his tongue inside my mouth, but that didn't mean I knew him. I had seen a few glimpses of niceness, but I had also seen plenty of the not-so-nice side of him.

I thought for a moment. 'Are you working tonight?'

'Nope.'

'Will Jay be at the Saloon?'

'I think so.'

'Well, how would you feel about celebrating at the Saloon?'

'Are you serious?'

'I know it's probably the last place you want to be, but trust me.'

'It's not the place – I love going there – I just . . . he is going to be so mad.'

'Most likely, but I think I have a plan.'

'Oh God, should I be scared?'

'No, but I probably should be.'

And as I took a deep swig of my own water, I reflected on my plan. No, I wasn't scared, I was damn well terrified.

～

So, my grand plan was more of a loose idea. I had no ample amount of energy, despite swallowing fluids and aspirin all afternoon. I did, however, have an obligation as Billie's friend to be her wing woman if she needed me to be. There was, I won't deny it, some butterfly action in my stomach at the thought of seeing Jay again. Before all this, I had tried to think of a solid excuse to cross his path, and now I had it. I would go to the Saloon Bar and support Billie in handing in her resignation; after all, it was kind of my fault – not that I was sorry, and I was sure Jay wouldn't be either. They had been friends for years, surely he would understand her need to follow her dreams. Oh, wait, that's right: Jay didn't believe in those things, even if he had helped me network the other night. Was there ever a more confusing man? I think not.

Getting ready, I pulled my hair from my ponytail; my headache wasn't quite ready for an 'up do' right now, and my stomach wasn't ready for a figure-hugging outfit. No, tonight I needed comfortable casual, so much so that I was tempted to borrow a kaftan from Veronica. Instead I chose a light shirt dress, and definitely underwear!

It was a mild summer evening so we decided to walk. After nearly a month in LA, I was beginning to see the other side of my neighbourhood. While there were celebrity spottings and nightclub openings, there was also a normal side to living here, the run-of-the-mill stuff that happened all over the world. People still did their food shopping, loads at the laundromat and prescription refills; they just happened to do it in the proximity of the epicentre of the movie industry. Walking past a street performer knocking out a tune on some empty soy sauce bottles, then a man reclining on a rubbish bin, who gave sass to anyone who wanted to throw away their garbage, I realised that this was a town of contradictions. You never knew exactly what you were going to get. I liked the absurdity of it all.

'So, Jay, huh?'

My attention snapped from the graffiti on the bent and broken fence we passed to Billie, who looked at me expectantly. I knew this was coming. I had coasted through the day without mention of last night, riding the excitement of

Billie's good news, but now, walking in the dusky evening towards the Strip, I finally had to face the music.

'It wasn't a big deal. Nothing much happened.' It felt like a huge lie but, unlike some women, I wasn't comfortable sharing stories of my sex-capades with the hot boy next door over cocktails. I had never been that kind of person and I wasn't going to start now, especially not with Billie, who knew both of us so well. It just felt weird.

'Well, he's a good guy.'

'Says the girl who is terrified of telling him she's quitting,' I mused.

'I'm not terrified, I'm just . . . I don't want to let him down. He's been so good to me. And I guess there's this part of me that is scared of change.'

'Change is good! And he'll understand. If he doesn't, then he really needs to get out of LA and stop being so sensitive.'

'I think everyone in LA is well versed in rejection; you don't have to be an actor to feel it. Apartment applications, job interviews, dating – it's all rather brutal. I mean, it's one the biggest cities in the world and there's so much competition.'

Billie's words felt like a knife twisting in my stomach. I was always about running my own race, convincing myself that 'I got this'. Despite Billie's and Ziggy's warnings, I was telling myself that the role of Annika was mine; I was born to play it. But, thinking realistically, how many other hopefuls were currently telling themselves the same thing? Girls who hadn't got a dodgy spray tan and then got drunk and hooked up with the boy next door. No, there were probably trained professionals with real American accents who were up for the role, taking it far more seriously than I was.

Walking to the Saloon Bar in the hope of seeing Jay, I had an overwhelming desire to turn back and go home but, glancing at Billie, I knew I wouldn't. She was next-level stressing, rubbing her hands on her jeans and taking slow, deep breaths as our feet landed on the Strip.

'Billie, seriously, you have nothing to worry about.' And I truly believed it. She had landed her dream role, her next adventure was just about to begin, and I hoped against hope that I wouldn't be far behind her.

But as we neared the corner, spotting the Saloon Bar in the distance, my plan in my mind, I couldn't help but feel that what I was about to do was a major step back.

Sure, change was good, but this time, for me, I wasn't so sure.

Chapter Twenty-Six

Maybe I liked the Saloon Bar because it reminded me so much of a Hollywood film set, like one of those old Westerns, minus the hookers dangling over the second-storey railings. It was also surprisingly gimmicky, not something I would have expected Jay to be a part of, given the sleek lines and clean edges that he liked so much. Still, he probably bought into it rather than built it.

From the small history lesson Billie had given me on the way, I knew that the Saloon Bar's reputation had grown from being commonly known as 'the Killing Floor' in the eighties, where there was blood on the dance floor most nights from wild bar-room brawls, to a deserted money pit in the nineties, only to be revamped, becoming one of the better places to be on any given night of the week. The Saloon Bar had Jay to thank for that, injecting good staff, good food and good music.

While Jay may have changed the Saloon Bar's clientele and reputation, he'd kept the theme. Standing on the second level and looking down at the sweeping bar that dominated the space, you could almost imagine cowboys playing cards at the tables as a piano played in the background and a handlebar-moustached barman cleaned a glass. There were some modern touches, like the gorgeous wait staff swanning around the place, the tattoo-clad bartender with a nose ring and lumberjack beard instead of a vest and moustache, and the waitress with Jessica Rabbit red hair and the lipstick to match. It made for a stark contrast visually, and I really liked it, just as Billie did.

'Well, he's expecting me,' she said, glimpsing at the door behind us; it wasn't until that moment that I realised we were standing in front of Jay's office. Shit just got real.

'You sure you don't want me to come in with you? I sort of wanted to talk to him too.'

'No, it's okay, I think I really need to give him the courtesy of a one-on-one, you know?'

'Okay.' I guess Jay was Billie's Ziggy, and I knew all about not wanting to let her down.

'Well, I'll be right here,' I said, squeezing her shoulder.

'Thanks,' she said, moving to the door and knocking.

'Come in.'

Hearing Jay's voice sent an electric shock through me, every nerve in my body alert to the fact that he was in the next room. I stood to the side, not wanting to be seen when Billie opened the door and went inside, giving me one last thin smile. I swore that if he made her cry, or just made her feel guilty, I would give him what for.

The waiting was interminable; my chin rested on my hand as I leant on the railing, lazily looking around at all the people moving below. I kind of wished it was the eighties – I wouldn't have minded seeing a bit of action, I was so bored. I had long since given up trying to listen to the inaudible murmurings from inside Jay's office. Instead, here I was, Billie's fantastic support service, feeling completely useless, waiting to see if she came out from the office crying or high-fiving.

After what felt like a millennium, the door opened behind me. I straightened and turned quickly to hear Billie laughing as she stepped out on the landing, Jay next to her. His smile slipped away as his gaze locked onto me. He was clearly surprised to find me standing here.

Was it a mistake to come here? I hadn't seen him since last night, and I could feel my cheeks flush, remembering how I had behaved. Maybe his intention was to give me a wide berth. I hope he didn't assume that I was here because I was obsessed with him. I knew what men were like – no-strings-attached hook-ups were all the rage – so I should have known better than to show up here so soon after our shenanigans.

'Oh, um, Jay, Abby wants to talk to you, if you've got a sec?'

It couldn't get much worse; Billie had obviously failed to mention me wanting to talk to him, and now the whole thing was playing out rather disastrously. I had grand visions of walking into Jay's office under the guise of supportive best friend, there to set him straight if he was going to be a jerk about it. And then – so went my plan – I would wrap up by offering him a deal, one that I hadn't even told Billie about.

'Ah, yeah, sure, I've got a few minutes,' he said.

Oh wow, a few minutes. How gracious of him. I was already feeling annoyed and I hadn't even ventured inside.

'This won't take long,' I said in my most business-like tone.

Jay nodded at me before turning to Billie and touching her arm. 'You good?'

Billie smiled, nodding her head. You could see the lightness in her, the relief as she spoke. 'Yeah, thanks, Jay.'

Well, I was glad everything was working out. It appeared I really didn't need to be here. I badly wanted to say 'I told you so' to Billie, but apparently the clock was ticking for his lordship and I would have to wait to talk to her.

When I went to move, Billie grabbed my hand; looking at me, her brows furrowed. 'What do you want to talk to him about?' she said in a low voice.

I glanced to the open door. 'I'll tell you later,' I said. Before Billie could respond, I stepped inside Jay's office and closed the door behind me.

I had felt fine before, but now a knot of tension was tying itself in the pit of my stomach at seeing Jay behind his massive wooden desk. I had expected that his office, at least, would reflect the décor of his home, but instead it had the same vibe as the rest of the Saloon; was that a picture of a cactus behind him?

'Have a seat.'

His voice snapped my attention away from the picture, and I moved to take the seat in front of his desk. It felt strange, formal, like I was in trouble; maybe I would be.

Jay sat there, unreadable, waiting for me to start talking. I'd been so focused on Billie's situation and my part of the plan that I hadn't put much thought into what my request for an audience would make him think.

'You wanted to see me?' The meaning of his question was clear, but the way he looked at me made me think he meant something else. Oh, how I wanted to wipe that smug expression off his face. *Yes, Jay, I can go a day without seeing you – my heart will go on.*

I shrugged. 'I need a day job, apparently, and now you have a vacancy.'

Jay's brows rose in surprise; he was not expecting those words to come out of my mouth.

'I believe I have you to thank for my best employee finding work elsewhere.'

'Her dream job? Yes, you do.'

'And now you have found yours . . . here?' he questioned, his words dripping with sarcasm.

I simply kept my cool and repeated, 'I need a day job.'

'It's not nine to five.'

'I know.'

'And I'm guessing you're going to need time off for auditions.'

My stomach dropped; I had thought that I was doing him a favour, filling Billie's spot, but now I wasn't so sure.

'Do you have a résumé?' he asked.

'No, but I can get one. I'll even provide a headshot, if you like,' I teased.

'That won't be necessary. Do you have any experience waitressing?'

'I am a fast learner and I can make nice really well.'

'Yeah, so I've seen. Is it possible that maybe you could just actually be nice?'

My brows narrowed; like genuinely be nice without faking it? It was a concerning revelation; my life had been filled with trying to please or impress people, socialising with people I didn't even like. Was it possible? Did I even know how to be nice?

'Abby.'

My eyes snapped up.

'These aren't difficult questions,' he said, clicking his pen and watching me seriously. Gone was the man from last night; all his sexy, smirky smiles and smoky hot stares. Jay in his office, at his work, was all business.

'I think sometimes in life you just need a change, or challenge, and I think that working here is exactly what I need.'

'Are you being real with me now?'

I straightened in my chair. 'What do you mean? You think I'm acting?'

'Well, sometimes it's hard to tell.'

'I assure you I am not.'

'Were you acting last night?' Something sparked in his eyes.

I could feel my cheeks warm at the memory.

'I don't think it's really appropriate to discuss that in the workplace.'

Jay leant back in his chair, stifling a laugh. 'Well, I was referring to you liking the chilli I made, but hey, if your mind is in the gutter, I can't help that.'

I shook my head. 'You *so* were not.'

'Wasn't I?'

'Well, how do I know when *you're* being real?'

He ignored the question and simply rolled his chair closer to his desk.

'If you're serious about wanting a job you're going to have to prove yourself. What I ask of all of my staff is that no matter what they have going on outside these doors, they show up and give a hundred percent.'

'I will – I mean, I would – I'll prove it.'

Jay seemed distracted. 'I don't think you'll like my usual initiation, but I do it with every staff member – and before your brain starts being inappropriate again, hear me out.'

It was a good thing he clarified, because my mind was beginning to wander. 'Initiation, you say?'

'I have a VIP event happening tomorrow night, and I'm going to need people who won't be starstruck.'

I smiled big; oh, I had this down to a tee. 'I accept the challenge.' If you could even call it that. I would be able to schmooze VIPs like a pro, thanks to my insider knowledge; it might even be a chance to secretly network on the side.

'Don't you want to hear the details before you accept?'

'Nope, just tell me where and when and I will be there.'

Jay looked at me like I was a mystery to him; I kind of liked that. He thought he knew my type so well, and I wanted to show him he was wrong. I could be real, and work hard just like anyone else – in fact, better than anyone else.

'Well, if you're sure.'

I held up my hand. 'I don't want to know – it doesn't matter who it is. I told you, I'm not someone who gets starstruck.'

I moved to stand, hooking my bag over my shoulder, feeling empowered.

'Okay, head out and find Deedee. She'll take care of the details and get you set up for tomorrow. It's a 9 p.m. start, but if you want to come in at seven, for a bit of orientation, that would probably be best. I know how you actor types like to prepare.'

I rolled my eyes, which probably wasn't a wise move, considering that Jay had just moved categories from 'neighbour' to 'boss'. Oh, and he had also spent a short amount of time in the 'lover' category, but I was trying not to think about that.

'Billie will show you who you need to speak to; no doubt she's lingering outside the door.'

I bit my lip, because I knew that was exactly what she would be doing, dying to know the outcome, just as I had with her. It was like waiting outside the principal's office.

Jay really was a busy man; he grabbed his keys and sunglasses and followed me out the door, where I was greeted by a very eager-looking Billie.

'Billie, do you want to give Abby a bit of a tour? You're looking at the Saloon Bar's newest recruit,' Jay said, shutting the door behind him.

Billie's reaction was priceless; her jaw dropped and her nostrils flared as she looked between the two of us. 'Are you serious?'

I smiled. 'I have mighty big shoes to fill, but someone's got to do it.'

Billie laughed, wrapping her arms around me. 'Oh, babe, you will love it here, and I am not just saying that because the boss is standing behind you.'

Jay sighed, putting on his shades. 'No doubt I will see you ladies later.'

'Actually, before you go, Jay – what are you doing Sunday night?' asked Billie.

Jay paused at the top the stairs. 'What's the occasion?'

'I was thinking of having a bit of a gathering, nothing too big, just a few celebratory drinks with friends; this job is kind of a big deal for me, and Abby has an exciting week ahead too.'

This was the first I had heard of planned 'celebratory drinks', and I certainly wouldn't have been endorsing it on the night before my audition. I seriously wanted to kick her.

'Sounds like a plan. See you then,' Jay said, and I swore he was speaking only to me. He turned and headed down the stairs. My heart clenched in a way that was reminiscent of my first schoolgirl crush.

I turned to Billie, who held up her hands in surrender.

'Before you start cursing me, first things first.'

'What?'

'You, me, a table, and cheesy, guac, sour-cream-smothered nachos.'

My shoulders slumped. Curse her. 'I told you, I'm on a health kick.'

'Yeah, and how's that working for you?'

My memory flashed to the cocktails I slammed down followed by the bowl of chilli and bread I scoffed last night.

'Utterly shithouse, actually.'

'Come on, then; diet starts Monday.' And with that Billie linked her arm through mine and dragged me down the stairs.

~

'Oh no-no-no.' I threw myself down in the seat opposite Billie.

'What's wrong?'

'I totally forgot I said I would have dinner with Ziggy tomorrow night.'

'And you can't?'

'I start work tomorrow night.'

Billie coughed mid-sip. 'What, as in here?' she gasped.

'Yeah, Jay wants me to work at some VIP party. I said I would totally do it, I was bringing my A-game. I really want to prove to him that I am not some brainless actress. Shit, I might have to see if Ziggy can do lunch. Shit, shit, shit. I hate being flaky with her.' I flicked out a napkin and rested it on my lap, then looked up to see Billie staring at me catatonically, her face colourless.

'Jesus, Billie, it's okay, I am pretty sure Ziggy will do lunch.'

'Ah, no . . . um, I was meant to work that VIP gig. Before I handed my notice in, that is.'

'Oh, okay.' Was she feeling funny about me working in her place? I thought it might have made things easier for her transition, but she looked really concerned, chewing her straw distractedly.

'Umm, Abby, did Jay tell you anything about the VIP party?'

I stopped mid-sip of my Coke, straightening slightly. 'I said I didn't want to know. Why?'

Billie looked like she was in pain, her face twisted. 'Abby, the VIP party – it's for Leon Denero and all the LA Family.'

Whaaaaaat?

I sat there, stunned, Billie's words ringing through my head like a death knell.

'Noooooooo. No!' I slammed my hands on the table, my rage and despair bubbling to the surface just as the waitress brought over our food.

'Is everything alright, Billie?'

Billie simply nodded, looking up at the waitress. 'I think we're going to need some more guacamole. A lot more.'

Chapter Twenty-Seven

Dreams do come true, and so do fucking nightmares.

'Just tell him you won't do it!' Billie had said the same thing a hundred times, and her words fell on deaf ears once more as I paced the balcony of her condo, biting my thumbnail.

'This is a test, a massive test,' I mumbled to myself.

'He probably has no idea what a nightmare this would be for you; just tell him.'

'Oh, he knows alright – we spent an evening with them, remember? He knows I don't like them and now I have to fucking serve them. Brilliant.'

'Well, if he knows, why didn't he tell you?'

I groaned, stepping back inside and face-planting in despair on the couch. 'He tried to tell me, but I was all like, no, no, I don't need to know, I can be professional, blah, blah, blerrggghhh. I could seriously poke myself in the eye with a sharp stick sometimes.'

'It would be preferable to hanging out with the LA Family, that's for sure.'

I closed my eyes, having visions of Leon ordering the most expensive bottle of wine and me having to pour it into Sienna's glass. I wanted to die.

'Abby, you do not have to do this.'

I rolled onto my back, staring up at the ceiling. 'Yes, I do,' I said, before rolling onto my side and resting my head on my hand. 'Hey, why didn't you tell me Leon and the LA Family were having a VIP party at the Saloon?'

Billie thought for a moment. 'I just assumed you'd be invited.'

That made sense, and then it had me thinking. I pulled myself up to sit on the side of the lounge, my bare feet resting on the rug. Delving into my pocket, I checked my phone – no messages from Sienna. The party was tomorrow night – why hadn't she invited me? Now that I thought about it, I hadn't heard from her since the gathering.

'Interesting,' I said, thinking how hypocritical it was that I didn't want to hang out with Sienna and her clique, and yet I couldn't help feeling a little offended that I wasn't invited to their get-together in my territory.

'Oh, fuck 'em – they are a bunch of bloody wannabes anyway.'

Billie was trying to help, bless her, but it still didn't quite pull me out of my despair. Maybe lunch with Ziggy might offer me some perspective, I thought, dialling her number. 'I can't believe I am rescheduling my dinner with Zig for this.'

'Please, don't.' Billie clasped her hands together in prayer but it was too late.

'Hey, Ziggy – guess who got a job?'

~

At least Ziggy was happy I had heeded her advice and got a day job, and even more impressed that it was somewhere that might have me interacting with the who's who – with the Leon Deneros of the world, ugh. Lunch was a fizzer so I invited her over to join the Sunday drinks session; it was going to be my only chance to do some prep before my audition on Monday, and potentially a counselling session should I survive my first Saturday shift slaving for the clique.

I was so disenchanted with the world that I didn't even check if Jay cut laps of the pool that night, my balcony door firmly shut in defiance. I didn't want to deal with him or anything else right now. Instead, I focused on my lines and tried to put myself into a more positive headspace, but something was niggling at me.

I picked up my phone, my thumb hovering over the keyboard. I thought long and hard before I started to text:

Hey Sienna, what are you doing tomorrow night? Want to catch up? Xoxo

Again, my thumb hovered over the send button until I thought, *What the hell, bloody send.*

This was a test: either she had forgotten to invite me to my supposed boyfriend's bar for VIP hangs, or she was deliberately excluding me, knowing I would find out. So much hung on her response. Soon I saw those three teasing dots dance across the screen.

Hey hey, sorry babe, busy tomorrow night – going out of town for the weekend, but let's catch up soon. Xx

'That lying little . . .'

Something hit my window.

At first I thought I imagined it, but then I heard the same clink again. Maybe someone was trying to get in, but I didn't think serial killers threw pebbles at your window. I peeled the blankets back and crept to the window, another rock hitting the glass. I unlocked the door and slid it open, tentatively stepping out.

Jay was standing below my balcony, poised to throw another pebble. He smiled as his eyes locked on mine.

'What are you doing?' I whispered loudly. My reputation for being a disturber of the peace was already confirmed; I really didn't need the residents to hate me even more.

'Come down,' he whispered back.

I rolled my eyes; this was not a John Hughes movie – what could he possibly want?

'Why?' I said, wrapping my arms around me. All I wanted was to stew in my own misery – didn't he know that?

He didn't answer; he simply motioned me to come down with a head tilt.

'For God's sake,' I gritted, turning around and reaching for my dressing gown. I really didn't need him seeing me in my Charlie Brown PJs.

By the time I reached the pool, the only figure I saw was the one freestyling through the water. I merely stood by the edge, crossing my hands over my chest and watching on in complete boredom until finally he stopped, blinking up at me, breathless.

'Is this what was so important for me to see?'

Because I had seen it many a time, but that was my dirty little secret.

Jay swam over to the ledge near me, lifting himself out effortlessly and sitting on the edge. It was one thing to see him half-naked and wet from a distance, but to be standing right next to him . . . well, I had to swallow very hard and try not to stare.

'So?' I prompted.

'I know you didn't want to know, but I think I should tell you about the VIPs tomorrow night.'

My head snapped to him.

'Why?'

'Because then you can decide whether you want to work that shift.'

'You mean, I get a choice?'

'Usually not, but I can shuffle a few things around. It's no big deal.'

The ghost of a smile traced my lips.

Jay was a good guy; I was so glad that I came down. He wasn't testing me – he was trying to protect me. He knew more than anyone how difficult it would be for me to serve the likes of Sienna and her crew.

I shook my head. 'Don't change a thing. I'll be there.'

Jay stood, droplets of water rolling down his smooth, chiselled skin; he was ever so distracting. It was proving difficult to remain calm, to pretend as if he wasn't towering over me with no top on, looking down at me with a sexy little smile. 'Are you sure? I really think you'll want to sit this one out.'

The more he tried to push me away, the more adamant I was about proving I could be professional. 'I am sure.'

'What if I told you that –'

I placed my hand on his mouth, stopping him from saying another word.

I laughed. 'Don't tell me.'

Jay's lips spread into a grin. I felt them move underneath my fingers; the feel of his soft lips against my skin made me shiver. As I slowly moved my hand, the tips of my fingers lingered to gently touch the curve of his lips. I stepped closer to him, my heart racing, caring little that we were standing in the courtyard, or that drops of water were pooling at his feet.

My hand ran along his strong jawline, touching the light dusting of stubble before my fingers danced down his neck and over his Adam's apple, which bobbed and strained under my touch. Maybe it was my skin on his, or the summer night air against his damp body, but his skin was prickled with goosebumps, making me smile as I traced his collarbone, looking up at him through heavy lids. Our eyes met, and there were no more sexy smiles, just questions: where to now? Whose move next?

Jay made it first, stilling my hand, which was moving down along his abs, exploring the dips and rises of his smooth skin. He squeezed my hand so tight that it bordered on pain. I looked up at him, confusion lining my face, increasing when he slowly shook his head. His meaning was crystal-clear.

No.

I felt my cheeks blanch as I pulled away, tucking my hair behind my ears. 'Wow, people warned me there would be rejection in this town, I just never realised how rough it would be,' I said with half a laugh, trying to look anywhere but at him, ready to run back to my condo. Pre-empting my flight, I felt Jay's warm grip on my arm as he motioned for me to look at him, placing his fingers under my chin and lifting my face up to look at him.

'It's not, believe me,' he breathed out heavily, like it physically pained him to do so. 'The things I want to do to you . . .'

I blinked, utterly confused. 'Then why?'

'As long as you are under my employment, last night, this,' he pointed between us, 'can't happen again.'

What?!

'Umm, okay. I guess I should have read the fine print. No sleeping with the boss, got it.'

'It just can't happen. It's something I feel really strongly about.'

I breathed out a laugh. 'I was so eager to sign on the dotted line, too.'

'If it makes you feel any better, I've never wanted to fire someone so much in my life.'

A small smile tugged at the corner of my mouth. 'Then why don't you?'

I could see Jay's jaw clench as he looked down at me, seriously considering it.

I shrugged. 'You can rehire me in the morning.'

Jay laughed, shaking his head. 'It doesn't work like that.'

I couldn't help but feel something inside me sink; apparently he really was a good guy, perhaps too good. But I wouldn't beg; after all, I did have some pride. Besides, I would use it as an even bigger driving force to land the role of my dreams on Monday and have great pleasure in handing in my resignation to the Saloon Bar.

'Well, boss, I'll see you tomorrow at seven.'

'Abby.'

I knew what was coming, the old 'come on, don't be like that' line, but instead I smiled, warm and genuine. Because I really wasn't being 'like that'. I wasn't mad. I wasn't upset. Horny? Yes! But I wanted to be clear that I could deal with this awkwardness, no worries.

'Night, Jay.' And as I turned away from him, heading across to the stairs, I knew I really was okay, because I had a plan. Instead of dreading the challenges of tomorrow or the next day, I was bloody well looking forward to them.

Chapter Twenty-Eight

I was surprisingly chipper, considering.

I'd started the morning with some yoga, then had my daily date with Ray, who had informed me that, as of today, I wasn't *that* terrible, which I eagerly accepted as it was by far the best compliment he had given me.

There was only one way to face the challenges of tonight and that was to go in as if I were going into an audition. Once you walk through those doors your prep is over – there is nothing else you can do to set yourself up for what you're about to face. A successful actor must be able not only to endure the pressure but to thrive on it, using it to perform at her very best. Our careers count on it.

Walking through the doors of the Saloon for the first time as an official employee, the bar crammed already, music thumping so loud the windows were vibrating, I'd never felt such pressure. I wasn't sure how I was actually going to learn anything – the crowd and the music were going to make it next to impossible to hear instructions. My voice would be hoarse before night's end, which worried me as my audition kind of relied on it. But I had to forget all that; I had to bury those nerves, switch off my fear and just do the job. Surely a crowd of loud, drunken patrons couldn't be any more offensive than some of the casting call agents I'd dealt with.

I reported to the main bar like Billie had told me to do; she'd prepped me well, though I had been adamant about her not coming tonight. I had to accept that there were some times in life when I had to stand up and do it on my own, without a wing woman or man, though I knew Jay wouldn't be far away, lingering somewhere and watching on. While I liked the idea of him being nearby to call on for help, part of me wished that he was far, far away; if I was going to royally cock up, then I really didn't want him to witness it.

There were two areas in the Saloon, the main circular 'front' bar where most of the action happened, and the private bars. Due to its size and the quick, darting movement of the staff behind it, the front bar reminded me of a giant fishbowl. It had the most staff and was manic yet well-ordered, the bartenders smashing out drinks and yelling 'behind' as they zig-zagged from station to station with military precision. Billie could have briefed me all week, but there'd still be no way I could keep up with them.

'Relax, you're with me,' said Deedee, the red-headed punk girl. 'VIPs are upstairs at the private bars.'

'Is it less crazy than this?' I shouted.

'Less crazy but more demanding,' she said, steering me towards the stairs. 'Dealing with some of the divas can test your patience.' She stopped and turned partway up, casting me a stern look. 'But however tempted you might be, you cannot spit in their drinks; that would be an instant dismissal.'

'Oh, right, well, I didn't plan on it; I mean, I definitely won't.'

Deedee nodded. If this was the main part of my orientation then I felt I would be okay. We walked past the closed door of Jay's office, further along to another room with opened doors.

'There are two main VIP parties tonight: this section Becky and Ana are managing, and the one at the end is for us; a couple of the guys from downstairs will come up later and help keep an eye on things, check out the vibe.'

I peered into the first room: it was large, with couches and a fully stocked bar, a full surround-sound system and a dance floor; it was a little world, far more sleek and neutral compared to the heavy Saloon theme downstairs, the perfect place to get some action without being annoyed for selfies and autographs. A dark-haired girl broke ice behind the bar, and the other, short-haired girl straightened the couches.

'Who's in this VIP tonight?' I asked.

'Ugh, the Real Housewife bitches of Hollywood,' the short-haired girl puffed while moving the last of the furniture.

'Becky,' Deedee warned.

'What? Well, they are. They were here last month and they were a bloody nightmare.'

'You all stocked up, Ana?'

The girl behind the bar rolled her eyes. 'Yep, we have all the pinot grigio on ice.'

'Hey, you sure you girls don't want to swap? I could think of worse ways to spend my night than with Leon Denero.' Becky sighed like a lovesick teenager.

'Oh, that guy is so hot!' added Ana.

Deedee never faltered. 'And that is precisely why you are in this VIP room,' she said, cutting them a dark parting look.

Deedee turned back to me. 'You can put your bag and personal items in the staffroom around the corner and grab a spare apron from the locker; do that and then meet me in the second VIP room,' she said, walking away.

It occurred to me that I had never once seen Deedee even crack a smile; this was going to make for a fun night. At least she wouldn't stand for any crap.

The staff room was really small but secure and I placed my bag into a locker, using my birth year as a code for the lock. Now free of my minimal baggage, I took a deep breath and headed back towards the VIP area, stopping when I thought I heard my name.

'Abby, was it? Is that her name?'

I lingered near the doorway of the VIP room Ana and Becky were in.

Were they talking about me?

I stepped a little closer but stayed out of sight.

'I don't know, dude, I so wasn't listening when Deedee told me this morning.'

'How does the newbie land a prime VIP gig anyway?'

'I don't know, but trust Jay to put the lesbian and some washed-up actress in Leon Denero's room,' Ana laughed.

'Washed-up actress?'

'Yeah, another Aussie thinking she's the next Margot Robbie trying to make it over here – it's so pathetic.'

I couldn't listen to any more; instead, I made sure I was heard as I cleared my throat passing their door, doubling back to see their horrified eyes flicking to each other.

'Hey, you ladies have a great night,' I said sweetly, before breaking away and heading towards the back room, my smile instantly morphing into a sneer.

Bitches.

~

After my run-in with my colleagues, I was just in the right frame of mind to face off with Sienna. I couldn't give a crap about the smug looks or snarky comments she or her posse might make tonight. This was a test, mainly for myself. If I could smile my way through this, then Monday would be nothing. It would be my new benchmark for any challenges that might come my way; at least, that's what I told myself. It was easy to be confident when you were stocking a fridge or wiping down a table; knowing the VIP crowds like I did, they wouldn't be rolling into the venue until much later. The LA Family would make sure they were fashionably late to make a grand entrance, pretending to hate the attention yet not-so-secretly loving it – no wonder Jay hated the scene.

Passing by Ana and Becky's VIP room on my way to get some more ice, a chorus of cackles sounded as the Housewives toasted one another. On my way back five minutes later, I saw two women shouting in each other's faces, false nails pointed at one another, a rather bizarre contrast to their long, elegant cocktail dresses and dangling diamond earrings. Becky and Ana worked on removing empty glasses to avoid breakage, or use as potential weapons.

I walked back into our quiet, darkened little VIP room, lowering the ice with a sigh. 'Well, things are kicking off in the other room.'

Deedee touched her earpiece; I'd have said she looked concerned but she always looked that way.

'Yeah, well, things are about to kick off here, too; Leon and his crew have just arrived.'

I dropped my bag of ice. 'Oh shit.'

'Oh shit, alright – they're early.'

'Oh shit.'

'Can you stop saying "oh shit" and start getting some glasses ready?' Deedee wrestled with the remote, changing what had been a lovely quiet room into a pounding nightmare, the surround-sound speakers flooding the space.

Yep, shit definitely just got real.

I din't know where Jay was during all this. I had hoped he might come up and give us some kind of inspiring speech about fortitude, and wish us the best. But as I watched Deedee take her place as 'door bitch' with a controlled fierceness, I realised that this was not her first rodeo; she did this every week, and these VIPs meant nothing to her. For her this was just another night on the job, but for me it was personal. I was about to serve and slave after my competition, people who had been my equals back home, yet were now my betters. They had made it, they were the elite, and I was at the bottom of the scrapheap.

'Here they come!' Deedee called from the door, and then I heard them. The catcalls, the woo-hoos and the 'yeah, brothers' were nearing, and all I could do was grip the handle of the soda gun with white-knuckled intensity. I squared my shoulders and shifted into my character for tonight. It was going to be my best performance by far.

There were so many aspects of this group that were predictable, and Leon leading the pack was one of them. He swaggered into the lounge with his arm hooked around the shoulders of 'his woman'. What I hadn't predicted was that the shoulders of his woman didn't belong to Sienna Bailey, but to a very tall, very blonde someone else.

What the hell?

Chapter Twenty-Nine

Maybe they were just friends? Okay, friends don't kiss each other quite like that; friends definitely use less tongue. Had they broken up? I quickly skimmed the group: Dion, Jake, Jess and Nicole were here – the virtual heart and soul of the LA Family – minus their Queen Sienna. What was going on? And why the hell was this girl sitting on Leon's knee?

I had no time to ponder what was unfolding in front of me. Jake and Dion were the first to slam into the bar, shouting over the music to each other, drumming on the counter with their hands. Their bloodshot, hazy eyes looking straight past me to the shelves behind, on a mission to hit it hard.

'Hey, babe, make it a triple shot of what you got. D-Man, you want one of the same?'

'One? I'll take five – line 'em up, sugar.'

I had no idea what any of that meant, so I opted for five shots of tequila, and they didn't seem to object. Providing the salt and lime for each made the scene feel more frat house than exclusive lounge.

'Hey, sweets, you gonna join us?' Dion winked, saluting me with his shot.

'Yeah, come on, batter up!' called Jake.

Babe, sugar, sweets . . . oh my God.

They had no idea who I was.

I had styled my hair into two long boxer-braids which hung down over my shoulders, but surely it wasn't the 'do that did it. I was dressed in the customary black skirt and Saloon Bar top that everyone wore a little too tight – that must have been it. They expected a bar wench so they saw a bar wench, end of story. I couldn't help but grin from ear to ear.

'Oh, boys, I totally wish I could, but my boss would kill me,' I said in the best American accent I could muster. Ray would have been so proud.

'Aww, don't worry about the bossman, we won't tell.'

'Yeah, it will be our little secret.'

Ugh, they think they're so smooth.

'Abby! Floor, now!' Deedee slammed a tray on the counter, shooting me a look that said, in no uncertain terms, to stop consorting with the customers. Geez, I couldn't be friendly *and* I couldn't spit in their drinks? I really couldn't win.

Deedee brought in some recruits from downstairs, which was a welcome reprieve. Trent and Jax actually knew what they were doing, and the boys didn't flirt with them.

Deedee sent me out for a drink run, tray in hand; it was the last place I wanted to be, circling around the lounge where Leon was being straddled by a flailing blonde octopus. I was swarmed immediately, the drinks taken at lightning speed, leaving my tray empty.

'Hey, I know you.' My heart stopped as I turned towards the voice. Nicole Towney looked at me with her head tilted, stirring her drink. 'Abby?'

The jig was up.

'Hey, Nicole.'

'What are you doing here?'

I lifted up the drinks tray and shrugged. 'Living the dream.'

I thought I might have received a head nod of pity, or a look of derision; instead, the reaction I got was somewhat surprising. 'Oh, cool. I have a gig at the Green Olive near my house – amazing breadsticks.' She chewed on her straw thoughtfully.

I shifted away from Leon's group. 'Hey, can I ask you something?'

'Yeah, sure.'

'Where is Sienna?'

Nicole's eyes shifted behind me and I knew exactly what she was looking at. 'Ah, she had to go out of town, for work.'

So, she hadn't lied to me.

'Okay . . . and have she and Leon broken up?'

Nicole chewed her straw more intently, her eyes darting over my shoulder again as she shook her head.

No.

I felt a deep-seated anger rise within me.

'Then who is that girl?'

Nicole grimaced. 'She's just someone he met before we came here. You can't say anything to Sienna – it will break her heart.'

I shook my head, looking at Nicole in complete disbelief. 'What happens in the VIP room stays in the VIP room, yeah?' I scoffed.

'Look, it's none of my business.'

'Sienna is your friend.'

'I know, but I'm trying to make my way in this town, and it's hard enough without making an enemy of someone like Leon.'

'Oh, fuck Leon!'

My voice echoed, bouncing off the walls of the lounge, loud and clear, because the universe, in its infinite wisdom, provided a dip in the music, so that my angered declaration could carry to each and every ear. All eyes were now on me. Dion's, Jake's, Deedee's and, as I slowly turned, Leon Denero's.

Noticing me for the first time, he was not happy.

Deedee was beside me in two seconds flat. 'Abby, take your break now!'

'But I've only just started . . .'

'It's not up for negotiation – downstairs.'

Deedee ripped the tray from my hand, and I had to endure the long walk of shame, skimming past Leon's entourage out to the hall. The last thing I heard was from the astute Jake, asking, 'What happened to her accent?'

I couldn't think, couldn't breathe. I walked a long, determined line past the other VIP room, where one woman was in tears outside the door, being comforted by two friends. 'Don't you listen to her, Dianne, she has no right to tell you and Ronnie how to live your lives . . .'

All of a sudden I was actually envious of the Housewives; at least Dianne had someone on her side. I paused near Jay's door, torn between wanting to confide in him and to keep the whole ugly mess to myself. I would take my break, clear my head and ready myself to be reassigned downstairs, but first I needed a quick pep talk.

I knocked on the door, hoping to hear Jay's familiar voice, but there was no sound. I twisted the handle, but it wouldn't give. The office was locked and there was no sign of him. It was clear I was on my own. No Jay, no Billie – no ally.

I continued down the stairs, moving past the crowd and weaving my way to the exit. I was almost home free when someone grabbed my arm, stopping me in place. I turned around to see the same angry eyes I had linked with only moments before.

Leon.

He started pulling me towards the exit. 'We need to talk.'

Chapter Thirty

didn't want to talk to Leon, but he had no intention of listening.

'What do you think you're doing?'

Was he seriously yelling at me?

'Excuse me?'

'Are you fucking spying on me? Did Sienna put you up to this?'

'Oh my God, I work here!'

Leon shook his head, pacing in front of me, running his hands over his head.

'Fuuuuuck!' he screamed.

People lining up outside stared on, the murmuring increasing as, one by one, the outside diners realised the identity of the man having a momentous meltdown in front of them.

'Look.' Leon got right up into my face, forcing me to step back. 'You can't say anything to Sienna.'

'Are you kidding me? If you don't tell her I sure as hell will.'

He looked at me for a long moment, his eyes boring into mine; his jaw was clenched so tightly I could see a vein bulge in his neck. 'That would be a serious mistake.'

In that moment, it all came flooding back. All the people I had trusted, so-called friends and colleagues, and all the secrets they had kept from me, covering for all of Scott's lies. They had protected him by blaming me, just as Sienna would no doubt be blamed, and Leon would come out unscathed. My blood boiled as I recalled the deception, the hurt, the embarrassment, the betrayal.

I looked Leon dead in the eyes so he could be sure I meant what I said. 'We Aussies have to stick together.'

He scoffed. 'I'll ruin you and your little buddies; you'll never work in this town, I'll make sure of that.'

'Chill out, Leon. You don't have to be a complete prick every day of your life.'

Much to my surprise, he broke into a wolfish grin; the rage had simmered as he stepped back up to me, running his finger along my arm. 'You know, it's a real shame . . . I think you and I would have made much more sense. Tell me, do you bite as well as you bark, babe?'

I laughed. Never in my wildest dreams would I have imagined that action superstar Leon Denero would want to hook up with me. I guess I should have felt pretty special, but I didn't.

Instead, smiling sweetly, I reached over to the table next to me, and surprised the diners by taking their pitcher of beer. 'Next one's on me.' I winked at the table, then turned to Leon and poured it over his head.

'ABBY, WHAT THE FUCK?!'

Light bulbs flashed as the paps emerged from God knows where, getting into our faces; the queue erupted into laughter and applause as I placed the jug down and dusted off my hands.

Leon furiously wiped beer out of his eyes, pulling at his sodden shirt.

'You stupid bitch! Don't you know who I am? I will fucking ruin you!'

I scoffed. 'Oh, Leon, that is so clichéd. Stop embarrassing yourself.'

I pushed past him, the hoots and applause deafening. The sound of it carried me through the restaurant and I took a deep breath of satisfaction – until I heard my name.

'Abby!'

I stopped, glancing up, my smile completely falling from my face as Jay stood before me, looking at me in utter disbelief.

Ah, crap.

If I had thought Leon looked angry, Jay was next level, his eyes darting between me and Leon, who pushed and swore at the cameramen surrounding him.

'Get out of my goddamn face, man!'

Jay's eyes dipped to the empty pitcher in my hand. There was nothing I could possibly do or say – he had obviously seen the whole thing. So I did the only thing I could do; I untied my black apron, placed it in the pitcher and handed it to him.

'You can use my wages towards table twelve – they've earned it,' I said, moving past him. I didn't go back inside, I didn't collect my things, I simply disappeared into the night.

~

'Oh my God!' Billie was as white as a ghost. 'Oh. My. God.'

'Yeah, you've said that.'

'Abby, what were you thinking?'

'Well, clearly it was more of a reflex than a thought process.'

'And Jay saw everything?'

'Yeah.'

'Oh my God.'

'Billie, you're supposed to be making me feel better.'

'I-I don't know how.'

'Yeah, I don't know how either. I think I've completely blown it.'

'Do you think Leon will make trouble for you?'

'Oh, screw Leon. I couldn't care less about him. Billie, you should have seen Jay's face.'

Billie winced.

'Seriously, I had one job to do. One. Job. Shut up and give people the VIP experience, but no, I couldn't even do that.'

'Well, in your defence, I like that you stuck up for Sienna. What a creep.'

'To be honest, if I had my time again I don't think I'd do it any differently. I am so sick of seeing the Dions, the Jakes, the Leons running around thinking they are these big VIPs, and for what? Pretending to be heroes and doctors and heartthrobs on a screen. None of it's real! We all just take ourselves so seriously. We think that we're something special, that our ridiculous stories of who's dating who is somehow worthy of a three-page spread.' I shook my head. 'I just don't know what's real anymore.'

'I think you know,' Billie said.

I looked up from my hands, the feeling of hopelessness washing over me. 'Jay's real, and I have completely ruined everything.'

'Talk to him.'

I shook my head. 'I don't think I could bear it,' I said, moving to stand.

'Where are you going?'

'Bed. Maybe I'll wake up and it will have all been a dream.'

'Or maybe you can just wake up and face the music.'

I cringed. 'Don't wake me up – I want to stay in bed as long as humanly possible.'

'Ignorance is bliss, huh?'

'Yeah, something like that.'

Chapter Thirty-One

'Abby, wake up!'

I rolled and kicked at the intruding voice. 'No, go away.'

'Abby, get up!'

I buried my face into my pillow, moaning. Maybe if I ignored the voice it would go away.

'Abby, get up – there is someone here to see you.'

I sat bolt upright in bed. 'Jay?' I croaked, squinting around the room.

'Get dressed,' Billie gritted, leaving my room.

I dived out of bed, tripping on the sheets that were twisted around my ankles. 'Shit, shit, shit.' What time was it? Daylight was streaming in my window and I couldn't find my phone. Where were my bloody pants?

With wild hair, wilder, sleep-encrusted eyes and still in my nightie, I burst through the door and skidded to a halt in the lounge room. Several sets of eyes watched me from the couch; for a split second I thought I was in the wrong apartment, until Billie appeared with a tray of biscuits and cheeses.

Oh crap, Sunday drinks!

'Did you just make that up to get me out of bed?'

Billie placed down the tray with a weary sigh. 'Front door.'

My heart pounded in my chest as I padded down the hall, smoothing down my bed hair. I wasn't all that worried about what I looked like; I just really needed to see Jay, to explain. I couldn't whip the door open fast enough, but Jay was nowhere in sight.

'Sienna?'

She had been crying, that much was clear. 'I'm sorry to disturb you, I know you have company.'

'I, no, gosh, that's all Billie. Hey, do you want to come inside?'

'Oh no, no, I'm not staying, I just wanted to stop by.'

'Oh, okay.'

I was wide awake now, bracing myself for yet another abusive tirade, or maybe a slap across the face. So when Sienna stepped forward and threw her arms around me I didn't know what to do. My arms slowly wrapped around her, and I could feel her shoulders shake as she tried but failed to keep it together.

'Thank you,' she said, pulling back, her watery eyes looking into mine. 'You did and said more for me than anyone of my supposed friends.'

'News travels fast, huh?'

She laughed. 'It does when you pour a jug of beer over Leon Denero's head on the Sunset Strip.'

'I wish I'd done more.'

'Well, if you're thinking about kneeing him in the nuts, don't worry, I've taken care of that.'

I smiled. 'Good for you.'

She nodded. 'So, yeah, I just wanted to say thank you.'

'Like I told Leon, we Aussies have got to stick together.'

'Yeah, well, I am certainly re-evaluating my circle,' she said, stepping away to walk towards the stairs.

'Hey, Sienna.'

She stopped, turning to look at me. She looked so sad, so broken, that my heart actually ached for her.

'Just run your own race. There is so much make-believe in our world, it's easy to get caught up in it. I think we really just need to surround ourselves with the right people and focus on the things that are real.'

Sienna smiled, but it was small. 'You are so lucky, Abby. All you have ever done is own what you do, and look at you: you have an amazing condo, a gorgeous boyfriend and a secret job opportunity I can only imagine is going to change your life. I have to say, I've always been so jealous of you. But I know that's crazy and I can work through it because our friendship means more than any silly rivalry. No, Abby, you are the real deal – thank you for making me see that.'

Sienna smiled again, and this time it was bright. The sadness had lifted. 'Brunch this week?'

'Sure, love to.' And this time I actually meant it.

Watching Sienna take the stairs and step out of view, a sickness began to stir inside me. My condo? My boyfriend? My secret job? Dear God, here I was telling Sienna to surround herself with what was real and I was living a complete fucking lie. Finally seeing my situation with clear eyes, I felt like the bottom had fallen out of my world. And the one person who had helped me realise just how ridiculous and shallow a life I had been pretending to live was gone now, too. I'd ruined the one true thing I'd had.

I went to walk back through the condo when Jay's door opened behind me. I turned around slowly, afraid to hope that he was there. The sight of him made me draw in a deep breath, one that I would hold onto because I was too afraid speak, to move, looking into his serious, dark eyes.

'I thought I heard your voice,' he said, his face cast in stone.

'Ah, yeah, Sienna just dropped by.' I crossed my arms, watching to see if that surprised him, but if it did he didn't show it. 'Jay, look, I . . .'

He walked back into his condo, my words fading away. I feared he didn't want to listen, but he was only gone a second before he reappeared, carrying something over to me.

'My bag?'

'You left it in the staff room last night.'

I opened it up: my keys, my phone, my life all inside. I pressed on my phone but it was flat, so I let it drop inside the bag again.

'Seems like I'm always returning your bag to you.' He smiled. It was such an unexpected thing, the way he was looking at me, but then something in his dark eyes dimmed.

'Y-you mean, you're not mad?'

'Mad?' Jay chuckled, and it was such a surprise that I thought he was losing it, but then he smiled again and shook his head, looking down at me with lightness in his eyes. 'Abby, I would have fired you if you *hadn't* poured that beer over Leon's head.'

'What?'

'You stood up for a friend, without giving a second thought to how it might have affected your career. In my world that makes you employee of the goddamn month.'

'Don't tease me, Jay.'

'I'm serious. You did alright, Abby Taylor, and had you not run off into the night I would have told you that.'

'You looked so mad, I thought that . . .'

'I was pissed – at Leon.'

'I still shouldn't have created a scene. It's probably all over the Internet.'

'I don't care.'

'Really?'

Jay shook his head, and I knew he really didn't care because that sexy smirk pulled at the corner of his mouth. He stepped forward, not quite touching me, just close enough for him to look at me, really look at me. We were okay, and I thought I might die from happiness.

'Sorry I'm late. Bloody Uber!' Ziggy's voice snapped me out of my euphoria, and Jay and I broke apart like a pair of naughty teenagers. Jay coughed, pretending to be casual, but Ziggy never missed a beat.

'Oh, hello,' she said, looking from me to Jay, then back to me. 'Sorry, am I interrupting something?'

'No, of course not. Um, Ziggy, this is Jay, my neighbour; Jay, this is Ziggy, my esteemed manager.'

Jay held out his hand. 'Nice to meet you.'

'Likewise,' Ziggy cooed. I could see the cogs turning inside her head, and I just knew there would be a thousand questions stockpiling in her brain. 'Are you coming for drinks, Jay?'

'Oh, no, I, ah, actually need to head into work for a bit, but tell Billie thanks, I'll catch up some other time.'

Jay seemed nervous under Ziggy's scrutiny. Her infamous 'peer over her red-framed glasses' was unsettling, that was for sure.

'What's your last name, Jay?'

It took a moment for him to answer, taken aback by the question. 'Ah, Davis.'

Ziggy stared at him for a moment before snapping out of her trance. 'Oh, sorry, I just thought I knew you from somewhere.'

I burst out laughing. 'Not you too.'

'Not me what?' Ziggy asked, confused.

'It's okay, I get that a lot,' Jay said. 'I must have a doppelganger out there or something. Listen, it was nice meeting you, but I better get going. Abby.' He nodded his head, and I loved the way his eyes connected with mine before breaking away, an invisible touch that stayed with me long after he disappeared.

Ziggy and I kinked our heads to watch him walk down the breezeway.

'Well, if he has a doppelganger out there I would sure like to find him.'

'Ziggy!'

'Beautiful people everywhere.' She sighed, before turning and taking in my bedtime attire.

'Bloody hell . . . well, almost everywhere. Darling, it's three o'clock in the afternoon. What gives?'

I bit the bottom of my lip. 'You know how you said to always be professional?'

'Yeeesss?'

'Well, you might want to come in and take a seat.'

I hooked my arm into hers and guided her through the doorway.

'Oh dear, I'm not going to like this, am I?'

'Don't worry,' I said, patting her hand. 'We have alcohol.'

~

If it didn't happen on YouTube it didn't happen.

We all crowded around Billie's phone watching the horrors of last night replay over, and it was oh so sweet, but I tried not to visibly enjoy it with Ziggy beside me.

'Look at the amount of views,' Ziggy gasped.

'How do they know my name?' That was the point I was most worried about.

'Well, you were afraid of obscurity – they certainly know your name now,' said Billie.

'I think I liked anonymity better. This is not quite how I'd planned to launch my Hollywood career.'

'I wouldn't stress too much,' said Billie. 'Check out the comments – they are totally giving it to Leon, particularly his "don't you know who I am?" line.'

'Well that's what you get when you act like a douche and cheat on your girlfriend.' I glared at the screen.

Ziggy took off her glasses, rubbing her eyes. 'I'll put out a statement. No doubt I will have a few messages waiting for me; I suspect more than a couple of people will want to speak to the agent representing the girl who put Leon Denero in his place.'

I winced. 'Do you think it will affect my chances at the audition tomorrow?'

Ziggy sat her glasses back into place. 'Now, Abby, if Annika was in your position last night, what do you think she would have done?'

Billie straightened. 'Yeah, you can just say you were method acting.'

'I think Annika would have glassed him, and thrown him over a table.'

'Oh, okay, maybe best not to channel her then.'

'Listen, it's getting late and I have stayed out way past my curfew.' Ziggy pushed up from the comfort of the couch. 'You should get some rest. Just concentrate on tomorrow and leave all the white noise to me.'

'Thanks, Ziggy.'

'I am in meetings all day tomorrow, but I will give you a call when I'm finished, and we can catch up on Tuesday before I fly out.'

'Sounds like a plan.' Before I was able to catch myself, I hugged her fiercely. She could be tough as nails sometimes, but when I needed her she was there, and I loved her for it.

'Break a leg tomorrow; remember everything we discussed and you will be fine.' Ziggy walked down the hall towards the front door. 'And no more YouTubing!' She called back.

Billie and I looked at each other with a little smirk, waiting for the front door to thud.

I bit my lip and moved to her side. 'Maybe just once more.'

Chapter Thirty-Two

This was it.

I was seated against a wall, in a long corridor with grey carpet and white walls. I remembered all that Ray had told me, and the advice Ziggy had given, but how could you prepare for a day such as this, for something that meant so much? I tried to block out the girl to my right, who was murmuring her lines under her breath, eyes closed, script in hand. The girl on my left had dozens of tiny little notes written in the margins of her script. Both were a stark contrast to my prep, which consisted of simply sitting calmly, focusing on breathing in and out. Ziggy had said not to overthink it, and that last-minute cramming would only over-stress my mind and scramble my lines, so I resisted the urge to run my dialogue one more time.

Some people sat on the floor, tapping their feet, some were pacing, and a couple of others were quiet like me. I left my script in my bag, the script that I'd had to reprint twice because the previous copies had been coffee-stained and crinkled beyond recognition. I didn't give myself permission to think about how much I hated the process, the nerves, the long waits, the demeanour of the casting director as he called people into the room. I looked away from the flushed faces that left the room after their auditions, not wanting to read into their expressions. I simply stared at the blank walls and thought about nothing. For the first time in a very long time I just let myself exist in the moment, enjoy it for what it was. *What will be, will be.*

'Abby Taylor?'

The ocean sounds playing inside my head stopped abruptly as I turned towards the voice that echoed down the hall.

'Good luck,' whispered the margin-writing girl.

'Thanks,' I said, grabbing and dropping my bag.

Get it together, Abby. Shut those nerves down.

I walked down the bleakest, longest corridor of my life, my shoes sounding painfully loud on the floor. I could feel several sets of eyes on me, assessing their competition, while others were no doubt trying to block me out and stay in their own headspace, just as I had. My script was in my hands now, beginning to droop a little in my moist fingers.

I walked through the door and saw my audience: three men, one woman and a camera operator.

'This is Abby Taylor reading for Annika,' announced the Casting Director's assistant.

With a polite and confident hello, I touched the back of the chair, using it as an anchor, then counted silently as I readied myself. *One*. I moved to the chair. *Two*. I sat down. *Three*. I took in one last steadying breath. *Four*. I lifted my eyes to the team assembled. *Five*.

Go.

~

Even though there was no real way of escaping the sound of choppers or the distant hum of street traffic in my little tucked-away corner of the leafy courtyard, the sounds of the city weren't enough to distract me from my thoughts. As long as I was on my own, away from conversation, I was happy to sit on the pool's edge, dangling my bare feet in, comforted by the cool water and the swirl from the filter jets that made the water dance along with the swishing of my feet. I placed my hands underneath my thighs; the concrete beneath was warm from the sunshine earlier in the day.

I had sat here for an hour, maybe more, and I was in no hurry to head back to the condo. I didn't want to experience any form of reality other than this. It was soothing, replenishing. I just needed a few more moments, but what you want and what you get are often two very different things.

I sensed his presence long before he was there, silently moving to sit beside me. He rolled his jeans up and lowered his legs into the water next to mine, mirroring my pose by sitting on his hands.

It was a long moment before Jay cleared his throat. 'Billie said Ziggy has been trying to get onto you.'

And there it was, that pesky reality.

'My phone is switched off.'

Jay nodded, silence falling again, which I should have welcomed, but now I was aware of the world creeping back in.

After a long moment, the tension so drawn out I thought Jay might leave, he rubbed his jawline. 'Abby, you're going to have to help me out here.'

I stared at my wriggling toes. How could I help him when I could barely help myself?

'Should I ask, or should we just sit here, staring and being weird?'

I shook my head, not really knowing what I was saying no to – all of it? Jay wasn't going anywhere soon, that was pretty clear. I really didn't want to look at him, to deal with anything outside of this comfortable little cocoon I had created, but then he turned to me.

'Abby, come on, look at me.'

Damn that gentle way he said my name.

Jay looked into my eyes as they brimmed with tears, and I felt the streaks of salt that had dried on my face from all the times I had cried before: leaving the building after the audition, texting Ziggy as I walked towards the bus stop, riding the bus where a little girl had touched my hand to comfort me. It was all too much, too much to hold in.

Jay's eyes were soft, his lips pressed in a thin line. 'No good?'

My chin trembled and I shook my head again. 'No good.'

And before the tears fell, Jay pulled me into the safety of his arms, enveloping me in his warmth and kissing the top of my head.

As good as it felt, I knew I was being stupid. I had gone to one audition, had one rejection, and now I was having a complete meltdown because I had messed up my lines. I'd been so confident, so focused, only to screw it up.

I didn't want to be that person who cried over a bruised ego, I wanted to have thicker skin, but I couldn't help it. It was more than wanting to show the LA Family, or the people back home, or Jay, that I wasn't just some struggling actress; I really, really wanted that role. And sure, Ziggy and Ray had warned me that you don't always get what you want, but part of me had thought that if I gave it everything I had I couldn't fail. Yet here I was, knee-deep in failure.

'Do you want to go for a swim?'

I lifted my head at Jay's words. 'Does that make you feel better?' I asked.

'Yeah, it makes me feel good. Why don't you head upstairs and get changed and – '

Before Jay had even finished speaking, in a desperate bid to feel better I pushed off the ledge and into the pool, submerging myself fully clothed. I let the shock waves of cold water wrap around me until my need for air brought me to the surface. Gasping, I pushed the hair from my eyes and blinked to see Jay staring at me, wondering what the hell I was doing.

'Or you can just jump right in.'

'You getting in?'

'No, I think I might sit this one out.'

I splashed him and he laughed. 'Alright, alright. You talked me into it.'

He stepped into the water, disappearing under the surface fully clothed, but he didn't come up straightaway; instead, a dark, blurry outline hovered close to me, then a hand touched my ankle out of nowhere and I squealed. Only then did Jay break the surface, breathing heavily and laughing.

'Stop it, you're freaking me out,' I laughed, my hands anchoring to his shoulders.

'Feel better?' he asked, spinning me around. I felt completely weightless.

'A little.' I linked my arms around his neck as he pulled me into the deep end.

'If anything, the cold water has knocked some sense into me. You must think I'm a right piece of work.'

Jay turned to me, but he wasn't smiling; his hands at my back, he looked me straight in the eyes. 'Don't ever stop caring about the things you love.'

Jay's hands were skimming along my skin now, riding up underneath my top and running along my spine. I shivered, tightening my hold on him.

'I don't want to care. I'm so, so tired of it all, and I have been here five minutes. Maybe LA just isn't for me.'

'Wow, you really are throwing a pity party.'

'I'm just being a realist.'

'No, you're being a quitter, and that's something I would never have guessed you'd be.'

I shrugged. 'Guess you don't know me that well.'

Jay's lips curved, and he locked his arms around me and spun me slowly once more. 'I know you. I know that you're impatient, and funny, and kind to your friends. I think you do like spicy food but you are too proud to admit it. I think you know what you want, but you just haven't quite cracked it yet. I also think that you are secretly obsessed with me but again, you'd never, ever admit it.'

I raised a brow. 'Wow, tickets on yourself much?'

'It's a sold-out show!' He grinned.

'Well, it's too bad that you're my boss; wait, hang on, are you still my boss? I wasn't fired, was I?'

'I told you, you're employee of the month; tourists have been taking selfies out the front of the Saloon, where Leon Denero got swilled by the crazy Aussie waitress. Customers are even ordering pitchers of beer and calling it a "Leon".'

'No way.'

'Sales have gone up and that's after one shift. I've even heard that old *Ship to Sea* clips have been trending on YouTube.'

'Oh God.'

'So, yes, I'm still your boss, if you still need that day job.'

'Yes, unfortunately so.'

'It'll be alright. You'll learn from this and take it into your next audition.'

'No, not that,' I laughed. 'I really don't want you to be my boss . . . *tonight*.'

It didn't take long for Jay to get the meaning, I felt it in the way his hands traced along my skin, saw it in his slow swallow.

'And I know you, too,' I said, cocking my head to the side and studying him intently. 'You take pride in all that you do, and take care of the people near and dear to you. You give a hundred percent and expect it in return. You're proud and punctual and you never break the rules.'

Jay laughed. 'You don't know me at all.'

'Really, why?'

Jay stopped moving me around in circles but the world kept spinning; the only thing keeping me grounded were my legs wrapped around his waist and my arms around his neck. His mouth was so painfully close to mine I could feel his breath brush against my skin as his eyes searched mine, and I didn't feel bad anymore. It was more than just the water that was wiping my cares away – it was so much more than that.

'Why, Jay?' I repeated, urging him to tell me where I had gone wrong.

'Because tonight I intend to break all the rules.'

And just like that, he broke the very first one: he lowered his head and kissed me gently, and I was never so happy to be wrong.

Chapter Thirty-Three

A trail of water snaked from the pool up the terracotta steps, along the breezeway and down to a door. Jay's door.

We were barely in the hall before the door slammed behind us, Jay lifting me against the wall, quickly peeling off my soaking top and letting it fall to the floor. Jay had been right about one thing: I was impatient. Impatient to get his shirt off, dragging it up so Jay could rip it over his head, throwing it to find good company next to mine.

His muscles were firm and defined under smooth skin. My legs encircled his waist just as they had in the water down below, but this time I felt the weight, felt the heat and pressure of him against me, the hardness between my thighs, gasping as he arched up into me, moaning against my mouth. He was still wearing his wet denim, but there was no mistaking the hard press of him through his pants, under my palm.

I wanted to set him free, to make quick work of his top button, but he didn't oblige; instead, he moved my hands and pinned them above my head, his tongue filling my mouth, inside me in a way that only made me hunger for more.

More, I need more.

'Patience really isn't your thing, is it?'

I could feel the vibration of his laughter under my lips, as I kissed along his neck, nipping.

'I know what I want,' I said, turning to his mouth; he let my hands fall then, and I wrapped them around him. Jay carried me down the hall through to his bedroom, crashing down onto the bed, caring little of the wet clothes we were still wearing. They wouldn't be staying long. Jay was already hooking his fingers into my waistband and dragging them down my thighs; only one leg was free before his hands pinned my thighs, his mouth on me.

Look who's impatient now.

My amusement morphed into something else the moment Jay's tongue pressed against me.

'J-Jay,' I gasped.

It was too much; my skin was damp, raw, overly sensitive with his hot mouth on me; I was going to come right now if he kept doing that. But I had no means to voice it, I was too busy rocking into him, silently urging him on despite the edge I knew I was crashing towards.

Reading my body, Jay pulled away just as my back arched and my moan sliced through the darkness of his bedroom. I collapsed, panting, protesting when he moved away, until I saw where he was going. Jay leant over to the bedside table, opening a drawer and retrieving a silver foil square.

'I knew you had the good stuff in there,' I giggled, and though it was dark, the sheer curtains drawn across his bedroom window allowed enough light in that I could see his smile, see him unbutton his jeans as he stood over me. He pulled them off one leg at a time, followed by his briefs, his long, hard length springing free before he sheathed it, then he bent to remove my pants completely.

Now I lay beneath him, still damp and salty from the water, my cheeks flushed, my nipples hard. I had never wanted a man like I did now, looking up at Jay, revelling in the feel of his hands on my thighs, sliding down to reach under my knees to pull me closer to him. I watched his darkened silhouette bend to capture my breast in his mouth, pulling and sucking gently at first, then move to the other, nipping and raking his teeth over the sensitive peak. He played my body like an instrument, attentive to the rise and fall of my breaths, the gentle moans that turned into begging pleas as his fingers and mouth found the right places.

His skin was salty to taste, and I would have welcomed him into my mouth, but for the hunger I felt when he rubbed his tip against me, testing, before pushing inside me. His movements were slow at first, being gentle with me, and maybe it was the guise of the dark that made me so brave, or just the feel of him inside me, but soon I was rocking up into him, wanting him hard and deep, my nails digging into his shoulder, my breath burning into his neck as he gripped my leg tight, pushing me wider to open for him, the tightness so intense he gritted his teeth.

'Abby, fuck, so good!'

Our bodies, once damp and cold, were now hot and slick, the friction between us so intense that I could feel him building, chasing my cries as he fucked me harder and harder like I begged. I yelled a mixture of God and his name, requests and demands, then pure, raw emotion that tore me apart as I came, harder than ever before, screaming into his skin. My cry vibrated against him and he thrust into me so hard the bed scraped against the hardwood floors. Jay's hoarse groan filled the air as he filled me with final brutal thrusts, before collapsing on me, his heart thundering through his chest.

I couldn't breathe underneath his weight, but I didn't want him to move, wanting him to lie there a little longer, inside me, filling me so completely. Nothing felt better than being in Jay's arms, but as comforting as that was, it also terrified me because, as I was coming to learn, anything too good to be true usually was. But as Jay pressed lazy, gentle kisses across my neck, I knew this was different.

~

'Don't answer it,' I breathed, begging Jay not to relent. His hands gripped my hips as he relentlessly rocked up into me, meeting me halfway while guiding me back and forth over him, urging me to ride him, and I did. The sunlight streamed in through the sheer curtain, heating Jay's room with the golden light of morning sun. I could see the sheen of perspiration across my bare breasts, and Jay could see it too, his hand sliding up to cup and squeeze them.

His face was a mixture of pleasure and pain as his phone rang for the third time on his bedside. Someone was really trying to get through and, as good as it felt riding Jay, my hands clamped on his chest, the ringing was starting to override the pleasure.

'Fuuuck,' Jay yelled. 'I better get it.' He reached over, taking a moment to still his breathing and smiling up at me.

'Hello?'

It took all of my willpower not to tease him, to rock in slow, torturing circles with him still inside me.

'Oh, hey, Billie . . . yeah, she's here.'

The mood was well and truly killed for the both of us; as I slid off Jay, he winced, and tried to keep the conversation normal.

'Sure, yeah – hang on, I'll put her on.'

I cringed, hoping I didn't sound like I'd been interrupted in the throes of passion, whatever that sounded like.

'Hey,' I said sheepishly.

'You didn't come home last night,' Billie said, stating the obvious.

'Ah, I know, I, ah . . .'

'No need to explain, I get it.' She didn't sound mad; if anything, she sounded downright amused. 'But listen, you're going to have to call Ziggy. She's been trying to ring you and has been driving me nuts. Aren't you two having brunch or something today?'

'Oh shit, yes – what time is it?'

'Eight forty-five – you better get a move on. Isn't she leaving today?'

'Yes, shit. Shit. Yeah, she flies out at lunch.'

'Right, well, you better make the long commute home.'

'Yes, on my way!' I said, ending the call, realising how ridiculous that sounded.

I looked back at Jay, stretching in the sunshine, smiling like the Cheshire Cat.

'What are you looking so smug about?'

His smile only broadened as he traced his finger down my spine, momentarily distracting me.

I sighed, leaning over him, giving him a chaste kiss on his lips. 'I gotta go. I have to meet with Ziggy before she flies out. I was so busy being a bloody diva yesterday that I didn't take her calls, not cool. And then there was that other, uh, distraction . . .'

With a sheet wrapped around me I picked up my damp, balled-up jeans, cringing at the thought of trying to get them back on. Last night there had been no thought of how my clothes would fare the next day; I hadn't been inclined to stop mid-way to fetch a clothes horse.

'Top drawer of the tallboy.' Jay pointed behind me, and I pulled on it to find a drawer of T-shirts.

'You'll have to start giving them back – I'll have nothing to wear.'

I pulled the tee over my head – again it swam on me – and turned expectantly to Jay.

'Plastic bag?'

I laughed. 'You know the drill.'

Chapter Thirty-Four

Ziggy's Marilyn Monroe suite was an open-plan loft-style apartment, with white furniture, sleek, hardwood floors, vintage Eames pieces and a wraparound balcony overlooking the Tropicana pool and café.

I could have thought of worse ways to say goodbye, watching as Ziggy poured me a hot black coffee.

'I feel like such an idiot,' I confessed. And I wasn't solely referring to my disastrous audition, more my reaction to it.

'The first of many hurdles, sweetie.'

'I know, but I'm sorry I didn't answer your calls. That's not cool and it won't happen again.'

'I'll forgive you this time, but do me a favour?'

'Sure.'

'Learn from this: bunker down, do your lessons, try out for the roles I send your way and stay humble.'

Now there was some good advice. The last thing I wanted was to turn into the LA Family, where the lines between truth and fiction were so blurred they didn't know the difference anymore. I didn't want to become one of those people who used others as stepping stones to get to the top. I had to believe that things happened for a reason, like my run-in with Leon and the audition that I'd thought belonged to me. Nope, I was going to do this the hard way – the right way.

'So this week you have that commercial, and another casting call through the Delaware agency I organised for you. Nothing heavy, just take a look, show up, do your thing, get some notches on your belt.'

All the things I would have turned my nose up at before but now grabbed with both hands.

'Okay.'

'Alright, then, well, I best go and make sure I have pilfered all the soaps and shampoos before the porters come. I want to maintain my Marilyn vibe for as long as I can back home.' Ziggy floated off into the bathroom, clanging and clattering about and scooping up anything that wasn't nailed down. Just because she was successful didn't mean she didn't like free stuff just as much as the next girl.

I nursed my coffee, staring into its depths, thinking of Jay's eyes and smiling, eager to see him again. I was ready to front up to the Saloon Bar, this time hoping to get through an entire shift without making a scene; facing Deedee would be far more terrifying than any audition I was likely to do.

Ziggy's voice rang out from inside, but I couldn't quite hear what she was saying.

'What's that?' I called over my shoulder, refocusing on the poolside cabanas below, seeing if I could celebrity-spot among them.

'I said,' her voice called out clearly as she stood in the doorway, 'why didn't you tell me?'

'Tell you what?'

'About Jay; it bloody bugged me all night until I figured out.'

I tore my gaze from the view and turned, confused. 'Figured what out?'

'Oh, I don't know, the fact that Jay Davis is the son of Alexander Davis, the lead villain of – '

'*Hollywood Heartbreak*!' I cut her off.

I knew the show, hell, everyone did – *Hollywood Heartbreak* was one of the longest-running scripted television programs in the world, airing every weekday. The show was a mix of drama and romance, the main, ongoing storyline following two feuding families in the entertainment industry. My mother and nan had been addicted to it for years, and Alexander Davis – or, as we all knew him, Victor Nankervis – was the most notable patriarch and villain on television. He was a handsome man with salt-and-pepper hair, a very impressive goatee, and dark, brooding eyes – Jay's eyes.

'Oh my God!'

'I know! Why didn't you tell me he was born into Hollywood royalty? That means his mum is – '

'Amber Foster Davis.'

'The multi-millionaire make-up, diet and fitness guru who assaults our television sets with her "only four instalments of $59.99" products; we even had a few in our house.'

'OH MY GOD!'

After my second exclamation it dawned on Ziggy. 'You didn't know?'

'What, that salt-of-the-earth Jay grew up in a Hollywood mansion surrounded by industry pros? No, I didn't fucking know!'

I scooped up my bag so fast I nearly took the chair with me.

'Oh dear,' grimaced Ziggy. 'Well, I'm sure he had his reasons.'

I paused at the door. 'Yeah, I am sure he had his reasons, while judging me as being nothing more than a pathetic actress trying to make her way in this town. How bloody dare he?'

'Right, well, umm, do you want to maybe calm down before you walk into traffic on the way out? You're starting to worry me.'

'Sorry, Ziggy, I gotta go, I just . . .' I hugged her then walked out of the suite, dodging the porter in the hall and storming into the elevator. I was so angry I couldn't even bring myself to hold the doors for a young couple who were running to catch a ride. My hands were balled into fists at my side; my pulse thudded in fury.

'Victor fucking Nankervis.'

~

I waited out the front of Madame Tussauds on Hollywood Boulevard, declining a snapshot with Thor and Iron Man. I looked up and down the street, not sure from which direction my saviour might come. A car horn sounded, and I turned to see the flailing arms of Sienna as she pulled up outside of LA LA Land souvenirs in her little white convertible.

'Hey, sorry I took so long, traffic is – ' She peeled her glasses down, examining me as I slid into the passenger seat. 'Hey, are you okay?'

I didn't speak, I simply pressed a map against the dashboard, poring over it.

'Abby?

I pointed to the map. 'Here. I need to be here.'

'So we're celebrity stalking?'

'Sienna, please, I just need you to take me there.'

Sienna must have read something in my eyes, as she simply nodded and pulled back out onto Hollywood Boulevard.

Never argue with a crazy person.

As a new citizen to LA I had fully intended to, on a spare day, nose about some celebrity streets, gasping and pointing at the views of the stunning mansions en route to the Hollywood sign; I mean, I was only human. But I had not envisioned it quite like this – zooming around in Sienna's open-top convertible down Sunset Boulevard, past Rodeo Drive, the sun beaming down as we sped past palm tree after palm tree, the wind whipping my scowling face. I felt Sienna giving me the side-eye, much like any nervous driver who had picked up a crazy, unpredictable hitchhiker.

After squinting at the Hollywood sign from afar, we continued along Mulholland Drive, passing the mansions of Katy Perry, Bruce Willis and Quentin Tarantino, and even the house where the freakin' *Fresh Prince of Bel-Air* was filmed! But there was only one house – mansion, really – that I was interested in, and, without questioning me, Sienna pulled up outside the place I had flagged on the map.

'Are you sure this is it?' I asked.

'This is it.'

I couldn't bring myself to move – I was too busy staring. My eyes followed the gated circular driveway, the immaculately-kept grounds, the soaring fountain and, finally, the sprawling white two-storey home. The mansion featured large arched windows and a grand double-door entrance that was bigger than Sienna's car. I envisioned Jay as a small child splashing around in the front-yard fountain, but he probably didn't need to do that; no doubt there were several pools out back, along with tennis courts, maybe even a bowling alley.

I felt sick. This couldn't be true. The Jay I knew was a self-made, hardworking, condo-living bachelor in West Hollywood who recoiled from the entertainment industry. This was not him, not possible; Ziggy must have got it wrong.

'Holy shit! Jay's parents' house?'

My head snapped to Sienna, who was looking at her phone. I took it from her while she recovered from her shock. I saw an old photo on the screen, probably from the nineties, of Alexander, Amber and Jay at some red-carpet event. Jay looked like a sullen fifteen-year-old, flanked by his dad in a double-breasted suit and his mum in shoulder pads and *Dynasty* hairdo.

'Holy crap, Abby, that's the dude off – '

'I know,' I said miserably.

'I told you I knew Jay's face.'

I scoffed. 'You and everyone else, it seems.'

'Mind. Blown.'

We both looked from the map back to the mansion.

I shook my head in utter disbelief. 'Wait until Billie finds out about this.'

Chapter Thirty-Five

I had wanted to cry, scream, vent and rage over Jay's secret life to Billie, but after I had poured my heart out, then showed her the map, read out all relevant Wikipedia listings and gone deeper into Google than I ever had before, I was ready to be consoled in the way that only a best friend could. So when, at the end of my tirade, Billie sat there expressionless, saying nothing, my stomach dropped.

'You knew.'

'I have known Jay a few years, so naturally I know some things.'

'And you didn't tell me?'

'Well, does he know about your parents?'

'My dad laid cable for Telstra and my mum worked in a video shop – it's hardly the same.'

'Why should it matter where he comes from? I don't see what the big deal is.'

I couldn't believe her! She was taking Jay's side, like always.

'Look, I don't care, but I do care about the fact that he was so high and mighty about what I do and the industry as a whole. He's a bloody hypocrite.'

'I think you're reading way too much into it.'

'No, no, I'm really not,' I said. I moved to my bedroom, snatched Jay's cleaned T-shirts and headed for the front door.

'Abby, where are you going?'

'To put in my resignation,' I called back, slamming the door.

~

'You sure have some nerve coming back here.'

If Deedee scowled any longer, she'd strip paint from the bar.

I sighed. 'Is Jay upstairs?'

'Coming to beg for your job?' she sneered.

'Obviously you're not as important as you think you are, as you haven't been kept in the loop. I'm still an employee, Deedee.' I smiled sweetly; little did she know that I wouldn't be for long.

I didn't knock, I simply twisted the handle and stepped inside, my brow creasing at seeing Jay at his desk wearing reading glasses, peering at paperwork – a regular Clark Kent. Guess I really didn't know him at all.

He peeled off his glasses, his smile making my traitorous heart clench until he saw my face, thunderous and betrayed. His eyes dipped to the three T-shirts I held – two of his, plus my Saloon Bar uniform.

'Laundry day?'

'I'm giving these back,' I said coolly, placing them on his desk and stepping back.

'I was only joking about you taking my clothes.'

'No, it's okay. I don't want anything from you, including this job.'

Jay pressed back in his chair. 'Right. You have another offer?'

'Nope, absolutely nothing.'

'Well, we can keep talking cryptically or you can sit down and tell me what's on your mind.'

I scoffed. *What's on my mind – is he for real?*

'I actually had a bit of an epiphany today.'

'And?'

'And I reckon I am being way too narrow-minded. I came to LA thinking I was going to nail some big movie deal or epic Netflix original series, but you know where it's really at?'

Jay watched me quietly, sensing the trap.

'Daytime television!' I saw something flash in Jay's eyes and I knew the penny had dropped. 'But, you know, it's just like anything in this industry, it's all about who you know, and I thought that you might have some connections – '

'Abby.'

'Or maybe some tips, you know, some tales from the trenches?'

'Abby, stop.'

'No, you stop! Stop lying to me,' I shouted.

Jay stood. 'I have never lied to you.'

'Oh, right. Well, stop pretending, then.'

'Pretending?'

'Jay, ever since we met, you have mocked my profession, sneered at the entertainment industry as nothing but a bunch of pretenders out to boost our egos. When you – YOU – have been the biggest pretender of all.'

'Abby, this is me, this is who I am.'

'Yeah, a poor rich kid from the Hills wanting nothing more than to fit in with the common man.'

'And why do you think I'm here? Why do you think that I rebel with every fibre of my being against the entertainment industry? Because I have had it shoved down my throat from the day I was born. I didn't grow up with normal parents, I grew up with my father being a TV villain. Their life choices are not mine, all I have ever wanted was something real, and despite what you may think, I found that the day I met you.'

I laughed. 'You made it perfectly clear that I was the biggest fake of all.'

'I was an idiot – I still am. I should have told you, but I didn't want things to change.'

'To change?'

'Everything always changes when people know.'

It all made sense now, his reluctance to be around the paparazzi, his coyness at the possibility of recognition.

Jay had become what celebrities feared most – normal. While most of us were running towards a future, he was running from his past.

'I'm not living on my daddy's trust fund. Everything I have is my own: my car, my business, my condo. I've fought to be independent, to be humble. I like to think I still am.'

Humble.

The word rung in my mind – the one piece of advice that now made the most sense.

Stay humble.

'I've been lied to before, and I promised myself that I would never let that happen to me again.'

'Abby.'

'Look, it's probably just as well this has happened. I'm in a really confusing place right now. I really should just be focusing on my career and adjusting to LA, and to do that I think I need to keep it simple.'

'Abby, don't do this.'

'Jay, you're never going to fully accept what I do, and I get that. And it's not your fault – it makes sense now – but face it, you're never going to be standing at my side on the red carpet, are you?'

Jay's jaw clenched, his eyes burning into mine; his silence was my answer.

I nodded. 'It's strange, I thought we were from two different worlds, but we're far more alike than I realised.'

Jay breathed out. 'It's complicated.'

'Too complicated.'

Chapter Thirty-Six

Moving to Hollywood to pursue acting was a giant cliché; okay, I got that. But I never really expected it to be this hard – I know, another cliché. The competition was fierce and the market was oversaturated. Today's line-up was for the beer commercial that Ziggy had promised and – as Jay had predicted – that didn't require a script, simply 'a certain look'. I had felt dirty 'auditioning', which meant merely standing before a panel of men and being looked up and down, judged solely on my appearance.

Ziggy had lined it up because it was a good brand and a way to build my stateside exposure. If, by chance, the commercial landed at the Super Bowl, then maybe it would be worth the ego hit the audition promised. Though, staring up at the flickering fluorescent light of the seventies' veneer-panelled office building, I seriously doubted this commercial would be making it anywhere near the Super Bowl.

As I walked to the bus stop, I wondered what Ziggy was thinking. Was she just out to find me a paying job, no matter the moral turpitude? Was this what I had to look forward to, a starving actor lining up for whatever came my way? Worse still, what if I couldn't even land a non-speaking role? What would that say about me? I had thrown myself into my acting lessons, and my American accent, according to Ray, was almost convincing, but maybe it was all for nothing.

Billie and I were like ships in the night most days. She was thriving at her job, which saw her on location for much of the week, and it was wonderful to see her so happy. We never touched on our conversation again; we were clearly never going to see eye-to-eye, and that was fine. I had always been adamant that my relationship with Jay would not affect our friendship, but it kind of did. Maybe if I hadn't been so self-centred from the get-go there wouldn't be the underlying strain we had between us now. It was one of the many things I wished I could go back and change.

Sienna was a surprise package: she'd eschewed the superficial bullshit of the #LAfamily and come down to earth – I mean don't get me wrong, she still had her bitchy moments, but she was learning not to be so judgey. On the days we both had free, we were bona fide tourists together, exploring everything from Malibu beachfront wine tastings to improv shows downtown. After her disastrous, and much-publicised, break-up with Leon, and my whatever-it-was with Jay, we made sure to keep each other busy.

A couple of weeks had passed, but my failings still felt very raw.

'Abby, you can't give up – you are going to be a superstar!'

I laughed, my feet resting on the wrought-iron railing of my balcony. 'I don't feel like much of a superstar; anyway, that's not what it's about.'

'Then why the crazy talk of quitting?'

'Not quitting, I just don't think LA is for me. I'm not being emo about it, but life is so short, so why not explore other options and find something that feels right?'

'You had something that felt right,' Sienna murmured to herself before she took a drink.

'Do. Not. Say the "J" word.'

'Have you seen him?'

I had been good, locking my balcony door and pulling the curtains across to avoid the spectacle of Jay's late-night laps. On the third night, however, I broke, peeking through the curtain and opening the door, only to find he wasn't there. He'd not been there any night since, either.

I always knew when his car was out front and, when it was, a part of me hoped that I might bump into him on the stairs or in the breezeway, but it was pretty clear that he was avoiding me as much as I was avoiding him.

'Nope, he must be pretty taken up with work,' I shrugged, ready to move on from the forbidden subject. I certainly wouldn't be discussing the fact that I had been secretly YouTubing episodes of *Hollywood Heartbreak*. No one needed to know that.

'How about you stick it out another month? That means you would have given yourself at least three months here. A lot can happen in a month.'

I had thought about staying for six months, but I liked the sound of three; better to rip off the Band Aid quickly.

'Have you mentioned this to Ziggy yet?'

'No way – I don't need any more pressure.'

'Fair enough. Now, are you over being all doom and gloom?'

I laughed. 'Yes, for now.'

'Well, you better be, because if you are going to be a total Debbie Downer then I will not be taking Cinderella to the ball.'

'What?'

Sienna grinned from ear to ear, jumping up from her seat and skipping to her handbag.

'Ta-da! Two tickets to the Hollywood premiere of *Forget Me Not*. Starring Oliver Drake and Mary Masterson.' She dangled them in front of me.

'Are you freakin' kidding me?'

'Nope! Doug, who is head of publicity, wants some of us to walk the red carpet at Grauman's Chinese Theatre, and who was I to argue?'

'This is awesome! I am dying to see this movie.'

'Well, you won't just be seeing it, you will be rubbing shoulders with the stars.'

'I'll more likely get ushered out of the way so they can take pictures of you, but that's okay.'

'Are you kidding? They get a whiff of you being "Pitcher Girl" and they'll swarm you.'

I cringed; I really didn't want that to be my claim to fame.

'Don't worry, I'm just teasing; it will be a really good way to network, and you get to wear a pretty dress.'

My eyes widened. 'Oh shit, what will I wear?'

Sienna smiled mischievously. 'You leave that to me.'

~

There was something to be said for drinking water and not having guacamole with every meal; the red dress that Sienna loaned me actually fitted, now that I was being a little kinder to my body.

Though I didn't feel like I belonged in Hollywood, standing in Sienna's dress, moving from side to side, I felt as if I at least looked the part.

'Wow!'

I turned to see Billie in the doorway, her smile of approval evident.

'Isn't it beautiful?'

'Sienna done good.'

'You're not booking into that same godawful salon that did your tan, are you?'

'Oh, hell no – I think I will just keep it simple.'

'Simple, yet stunning,' Billie said, standing to my side and admiring my dress in the reflection. 'If you want, I can do your make-up?'

'Really?'

'Sure, it's kind of my thing.'

I laughed. 'That would be amazing.'

'Good, because Freddy's coming over at four-thirty,' Billie announced, leaving my room abruptly.

I did a double-take, gently gathering my skirt and following her out. 'Ah, who's Freddy?'

'He'll be doing your hair; I work with him. He's amazing. Used to do J-Lo's highlights.'

'You've had this planned?'

Billie shrugged. 'Only for the past week. Didn't think you'd object.'

The awkwardness of the last few weeks fell away and I could feel my heart soar; without the ability to put the feeling into words, I shimmied over and wrapped my arms around her instead.

'You're welcome,' she said, wiping the corner of her eye. 'Now, let's channel some classic Hollywood. This is going to be your first red carpet, so let's make it one no one will forget.'

Chapter Thirty-Seven

'What do you mean, you can't make it?'

Keeping my voice even was impossible, and I sounded as horrified as I felt.

'Abby, I am so sorry, I have been sick all day. I wanted to leave it for as long as I could, hoping I would feel better, but I just can't keep anything down.'

Sienna sounded awful, her voice weak and weary. I really wanted to be a good friend but I was standing out the front of the condo, in an evening gown, waiting for a limousine to take me to a premiere. It wasn't like she was bailing on a night of ice-cream and bad TV.

'Look, don't panic. Carl Moran knows you're coming – he will tell you where you need to be. Just think of this as a really luxurious trip to the cinema.'

'With celebrities, paparazzi and film crews?'

'Thought you didn't get starstruck.'

'I don't!' I said, way too defensively.

'I'm sorry, Abby.'

'It's okay, it's not your fault. Just get better, okay?'

'I want a serious debrief tomorrow morning, if I haven't perished through the night.'

'Okay, deal.'

I ended the phone call just as a black limousine rounded the corner of the street, heading in my direction to pick me up – at least my ride hadn't bailed. I shook off my nerves and stepped into the car. I was all dressed up with somewhere to go, and I was going to embrace it fully. I would rub shoulders with the stars, practise my poses, schmooze with the elite, totally judge others' fashion choices and report back to Sienna tomorrow – because that's what friends do.

~

The limo crept forward along Hollywood Boulevard, the muffled squeals and flashes getting louder and brighter as we edged closer. I sipped on a steadying champagne, only to panic and check my lipstick – thankfully, there was none on my teeth. The door opened on the car in front to a cacophony of screams and yet more flashing bulbs. I tried to peer through the heavily-tinted glass, wondering what all the fuss was about, until Dom, my driver, enlightened me.

'Oliver Drake, ma'am.'

'Ah, yes, well, that makes sense.'

I couldn't help but laugh, thinking how disappointed they were going to be to see me alighting from the next limo; it was the equivalent of the unpopular kid being picked last for the sports team. But there was no time to care – it was my turn to make a grand entrance, and I was too busy worrying about how I'd get out of the limo without tearing Sienna's dress or landing flat on my face. I was way out of practice; the Logies was the last similar event I'd been to, and that was a backyard barbeque when compared to Grauman's Chinese Theatre.

The car stopped, and just as I had at my auditions, I took five seconds of grounding time, reminding myself to breathe. Casting my eyes down, I positioned my dress, then heard the door click and pull open.

Go.

There was no way of preparing for this: the blinding flashes, the calling of my name – wait, how did they know my name? The people behind the cameras had obviously done their homework, their calls attempting to drown out those of the fans packed behind barriers, hoping to grab a selfie with a celebrity. Stepping onto the walkway, I knew I was a nobody, but I still stood there, hand on hip, my smile bright, pivoting and posing at various angles. The cries from the barriers signalled that they obviously thought I was a somebody. Not wanting to miss an opportunity, they yelled out, 'We love you,' and 'Can you please sign this for me?'

It was confronting, and beyond anything I might have imagined. During my time in Hollywood, my expectations had so often been obliterated, yet this was something else entirely. It was like the world was moving around me in slow motion, the flashes, the yelling from ushers, the microphones shoved at me while large square lights shone hotly on me; it was utterly overwhelming. I knew I should have been enjoying it, putting particular care into my pose or smile, but I hadn't even hit the red carpet and I already felt completely at sea. I watched on as Oliver charmed and worked his adoring fans like a professional, like he was born to do it.

I simply stood frozen, blinking and staring. My pose was lost, my smile small and weird. I didn't know what to do or where to stand.

A man with a headset screamed at my side, 'Move on or get off.'

I stepped forward, feeling like cattle being herded to the slaughter. *Just walk, walk through, walk on, lift your head and look forward.* The moment I was finally able to lift my eyes, I stopped, blocking the red carpet once again and sending the man with the headset into a fit of rage. But I cared little about him, or about the flashes or the incoherent, maddened screams; all I could do was stare at the vision in front of me.

Standing there, at the top of the red carpet, was Jay, dressed in a gorgeous tailored black suit and black tie.

The world fell away. As the shock rolled through me, everything faded to white noise and shadow, and all I could do was smile. I watched him walk the wrong way down the carpet towards me, breaking all the rules as only he could. It was easy to think I imagined it, but when he grabbed my hand and looked down at me for a long moment, I knew he was real. He lifted his darkened gaze to the tiny man with a big mouth behind me.

'She's with me.'

'Oh, sorry – I didn't – nobody told me.'

I laughed, following Jay, walking along, stopping and smiling for paparazzi, leaning into him and posing for photos, taking in every bit of this crazy, surreal scene. We were ready to move through the last section, nearly home free, when I stopped. Jay looked back at me, his eyes questioning.

'You're on a red carpet.'

Jay's brows rose as he inspected his feet. 'So it would seem.'

'You said you would never do that.'

'No, you said that.'

Jay stepped closer, cupping my face, caring little for the cameras or the crowds, for who people might think he was, or I was, because in that moment it was just us.

'I'd walk over fire for you, Abby Taylor.'

I would say it was in that moment that I knew, but that would be a lie, because not so deep down I had always known. Jay was not Scott. My fear of betrayal was not born from his reluctance to be in the spotlight, from his need to be anonymous – if anything, I had known better than anyone the need to be a nobody, even if just for a little while. No, he was different. Jay Davis was the real deal.

'Good, because I'm going to need a leading man.'

Jay smiled, pressing a kiss to my forehead, squeezing my hand tightly as we walked on.

'I can't wait to tell Sienna about this.'

Jay laughed. 'Why don't you tell her now?'

I followed his gaze to see Sienna and Billie standing up ahead, screaming out our names.

'Jay, Jay, this way!'

'Abby, please, can I grab a selfie? Please, please, please?'

'Abby, who are you wearing?'

'You've got to be kidding me,' I said, moving towards them and whacking them with my clutch. Jay was their saviour, coming up behind me and pinning my arms to my side.

A very healthy-looking Sienna snatched my clutch from me. 'Surprise!'

'What am I going to do with friends like you?' I shook my head, turning towards Jay, who seemed just as pleased as the girls were.

He scooped his arms around my waist, lifting me onto my tippy toes.

'How about live happily ever after?' said Billie.

I wrapped my arms around Jay's neck, smiling brightly at the idea.

'Now that's what I call a Hollywood ending,' I mused.

Jay shook his head, lowering his lips to mine, ignoring the whistles and catcalls from our idiotic friends. 'No, it's only the beginning.'

Chapter Thirty-Eight

Two weeks later . . .

'Again, why are we doing this?' I groaned, dragging my feet and leaning against Jay, hoping he might carry me the rest of the way.

'Peer pressure.'

As I climbed the dusty hills of Mount Lee, experiencing slight heat exhaustion, I couldn't help but question my sanity. Jay was right. This was most definitely not my idea, and I let them know as much, my eyes boring into the back of Sienna's and Billie's perky, swinging ponytails as they hiked on with ease.

'Man, I am so unfit. Remind me to start cutting laps with you,' I puffed.

Even though Los Angeles boasted pumping clubs, Michelin-starred restaurants and the glamourous abodes of some of Hollywood's biggest names, here I was hiking three miles up a dusty, rattlesnake-prone path.

Awesome.

Despite the extreme conditions (and sunburn), I had to admit that there was something rather poetic about seeing the iconic Hollywood sign up-close, and having a sweeping perspective over the city.

'Come on, keep moving.' Jay steered me from the shoulders, pushing me up the slight incline, putting up with my whimpers and protests like only a good boyfriend would. I heard the enthusiastic calls of Sienna and Billie up ahead, pointing to the sign.

It sure was something to see, and it lit a spark inside me. I increased my pace.

'That's it, move that ass,' Jay yelled, smacking my butt and jogging ahead, but I had to stop to wrestle with my backpack. 'Hang on, I'm vibrating. Shit, wait.'

'Seriously, now?'

'Two seconds,' I said, searching for my phone; the interruption of technology in the serene surrounds seemed unforgivable, but I answered it anyway.

After a short conversation, I ended the phone call. I couldn't move, not an inch, and something about my posture drew Jay back to my side.

'Everything okay?'

I slowly looked up at him, completely catatonic.

'Abby?

'What's going on?' Billie's voice called down.

I blinked, then my eyes fixed to the Hollywood sign and I broke into a slow, probably scary smile.

'A sign.'

Jay followed my eyes, confused. 'Right?'

I started to laugh, grabbing at Jay's shirt and jumping up and down. 'It's a sign, a sign!'

Billie and Sienna came back down to us, watching as I started to cry.

'What's going on?' asked Sienna.

Jay shook his head. 'I think she's had too much sun.'

'Who was on the phone, Abby?'

'Jerry fucking Bassman! He wants me to do a call-back for the role of Annika! They reviewed my tape and they want to meet with me.'

'Holy shit.' Jay rested his hands on his head, barely believing my words as Billie and Sienna leapt on me in a big, sweaty group hug.

'I knew you'd do it, you bloody superstar!'

Cupping my cheeks in complete disbelief, I tried to draw in breaths through my sobs. 'I thought I had completely ruined it. I can't believe it.'

Jay laughed, drawing me into his arms. 'So humble.'

'No, seriously, I thought I sucked.'

'Come on, you two, we have to commemorate this amazing moment in time!' called Sienna, starting up the hill.

We ran the rest of the way up to the lookout, a group of Japanese tourists flinching at our approach. We caught our breath, only for it to be taken away again by the glorious view, the sun beginning to set. We asked the tourists, through a series of strange gestures, to take our photo, then shuffled into position, ensuring the Hollywood sign was the ultimate photobomber in the background.

Putting our arms over each other's shoulders, our smiles brighter than the California sunshine, our impromptu photographer counted down:

'Three, two, one – say "Hollywood"!'

'HOLLYWOOD!' *Click*

Acknowledgements

To my loving husband Michael, for braving the turbulent waters of an often-tortured artist – fourteen books on and you still check on me at ridiculous hours of the day asking if I need a drink or some chocolate; you are lovely!

To my wonderful publisher, Hachette: Fiona, Kate, Sophie, Haylee – thank you for all your passion, support and encouragement.

To my beautiful bookish friends Anita, Keary, Jess and Lilliana – this gig would be impossible without you.

To my amazing family for putting up with my lockdowns and never-ending deadlines, for constantly reminding me of things I tend to forget; you remind me to live and be balanced, your love is the best anchor I could wish for.

To all the readers, bloggers, reviewers of my stories, for taking something away from my words and for loving and embracing the characters, for wanting to read Australian voices, no matter what city they may stand in.

C.J. Duggan is the internationally bestselling author of the Summer, Paradise and Heart of the City series. She lives with her husband in a rural border town of New South Wales. When she isn't writing books about swoon-worthy men, you'll find her renovating her hundred-year-old Victorian homestead or annoying her local travel agent for a quote to escape the chaos.

CJDugganbooks.com
twitter.com/CJ_Duggan
facebook.com/CJDugganAuthor

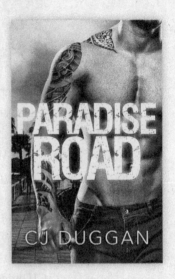

If you enjoyed *Hollywood Heartbreak*, you'll lose yourself completely in the rest of the Heart of the City series.

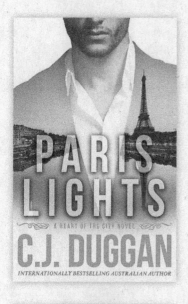

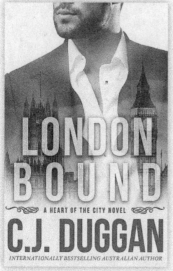

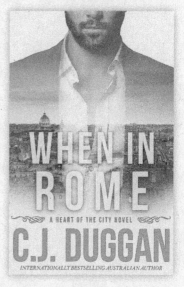

Read on for a sneak peek of *When in Rome . . .*

Chapter One

It struck me as a wondrous talent that Jan was able to type anything on her keyboard with her manicured hot-pink talons. Her entire focus was on her computer screen; her short coiffed hairstyle partially blocking the palm tree–lined beach backdrop. Dressed in a stiff navy jacket and cravat and wearing heavy eye make-up, Jan prided herself on looking the part, though I desperately wanted to reach out and blend her foundation line into her neck. John and Jan Buzzo's travel agency looked like the place where airline staff who couldn't quite pass the test came to live out their days, fulfilling their own crushed dreams by living vicariously through other people's travels. At the back of the room, just before the curtained alcove that didn't quite hide the view of the kettle and cup-a-soups, John Buzzo banged on the top of the printer and swore under his breath at the paper jam.

'Stupid piece of—'

'Here you go!'

A stapler punching paper drew my attention back to Jan, who, with much care, folded the stapled sheets and slid them into a complimentary faux leather binder embossed with the company's motto.

No regrets.

'You're all set!' Jan beamed, handing over the blue pouch with a silent fist pump for her commission earned.

I stared at her outreached hand for a long time, blinking as if I was having an out-of-body experience. I took it from her gingerly, barely believing what I had done. In an attempt to escape another one of my mother's lectures about what I was doing with my life, accompanied by the drone of the vacuum cleaner as she sucked up wayward chip crumbs from under my feet, I had gone out for some much-needed fresh air and sunshine. Now it seemed I would be basking in Italian sunshine, thanks to the budget 'Bellissimo' tour that I had just booked.

Like, seriously, I had only been making an enquiry, right? Walking past the travel agency, I entered on a whim, thinking only to ask a couple of quick questions, and maybe grab a brochure to take away. But as I opened up the travel pouch as if I was standing on a grand stage readying myself to announce 'and the winner is', there it was in bold print:

Shorten/Samantha Miss

Economy

Boarding Pass

Melbourne–Rome

Oh, God.

I felt all the blood drain from my face, the horror registering as I mentally began to calculate how many days I had until I would actually be scanning this very ticket.

What have I done?

Jan leant on her elbows and looked at me across her desk. 'Sammi, you are going to have the best time.'

I blinked, double-checking the date on the ticket against the calendar on Jan's desk, then looked up to her kohl-rimmed sparkling blue eyes.

'Remember,' she said, reaching out and tapping one long fingernail on the binder. 'No regrets.' Tap-tap.

Then why did I want to vomit into her wastepaper basket?

~

'Rome?!' My mother's predictable tirade echoed in the kitchen. 'That money was meant to be for a car, or a deposit on a house! Bill, talk some sense into her.'

Dad sighed, rubbing his hand over his beard, weary from the conversation already. 'Give her a break, love. You told her you wanted her to go out, so she went out.'

'I didn't expect her to book a ticket on some binge-drinking, orgy party-bus to Rome.'

'That's not what the brochure says, is it?' I quickly flicked through the booklet. 'Oh, yes, that's right, binge drinking day one. But to be fair, according to the itinerary, the orgy doesn't commence until day three.'

I slid the booklet over to Dad, who played along, nodding his head with interest. 'Well, you have to get settled in first,' he added.

Mum snatched the brochure away from us. 'I am so glad you two think this is funny. Have you given any thought to how you're going to prepare for this? Monday, Sammi. You fly out next Monday. You have no Euros, no travel adapters; what season is it over there? Are there travel bans in place? I bet you know nothing of all of this.'

Truth be known, I hadn't given a single thought to any of those things—I was busy trying not to freak out about what I had just done. But as I watched Mum look over the travel documents in horror, it occurred to me that this was as much about proving to my family that I could indeed make adult decisions as it was an attractive escape route. It all seemed so impossibly grown up, to book a trip away on the other side of the world. I didn't do these kinds of things; I was the baby, the homebody, strictly anti-change. Unlike my sister, Claire, the globe-trotter, I was happy staying at home. I sat on the stool next to Dad at the kitchen island, my attention drifting between my parents. Was it really such a shock that I could do something like this? That I, Sammi Shorten, could be so spontaneous and whimsical as to book a European adventure? They clearly didn't think I'd go through with it; I could see it in their eyes.

Mum squinted at the documents at arm's length, struggling to see without her reading glasses. 'You must be able to get your money back somehow . . . surely there's something in the fine print.'

Something inside me shifted, a feeling that drew my weight down onto my elbows as I leant on the kitchen countertop. 'Mum.'

'There must be some kind of cooling-off period . . .'

I sighed. 'Mum.'

'Surely a special circumstance where they can refund your money or . . .'

'MUM!'

Mum snapped up from the documents, blinking, then looked at me closely as if seeing me for the very first time. 'What?'

I smiled, small and sad, seeing everything that lay behind her eyes. In her gaze I saw her pleading for me to stay; that I could binge-watch all the TV I wanted, eat out of the fridge, make a mess, leave the hall lights on all night if I wanted—*just please don't go.*

I slid off my stool, rounded the kitchen counter and wrapped my arms around my mum; she seemed so small and fragile against my towering frame. I wasn't sure where my height came from, but it certainly wasn't from Mum.

I kissed the top of her head as she slowly, and some-what reluctantly, put her arms around me; in 'Mum-logic', hugging me back meant admitting defeat.

'I won't even be gone that long—it'll be a whirlwind trip. I'll be home and leaving crumbs on the carpet before you know it.'

Mum pulled away. 'Yes, well, that's what your sister said.'

My smile dimmed, thinking of Claire, who had ended up in Paris, madly in love and shacked up with a gorgeous Frenchman.

I laughed. 'Ah, I don't think you have to worry about me following in her footsteps.'

'Really?' Mum looked dubious.

I grabbed my mother's shoulders and looked her square in the eyes. 'I may not know anything about anything, but the one thing I do know is that I will not be falling for some gorgeous Italian man on my trip.'

Dad folded his arms across his chest, looking ever so stern.

'Seriously, this trip is about me, not about finding love.'

Mum looked at Dad, defeated but still resolute in her worry as she mumbled, 'Famous last words.'

Chapter Two

Jan had failed to point out in her sales pitch that my trip of a lifetime would begin with me standing in the sweltering reception of a flea-bitten hotel, sweaty and jet-lagged, waiting for the tour guide for a meet-and-greet. My parents needn't have worried; there was no chance of me finding love in a place like this.

At first I thought that there had been some mistake. I had stared at the catalogue long enough to memorise the glossy snapshots of smiling, tanned, carefree twenty-somethings with sunglasses and perfect white teeth having the time of their lives. Alongside these images was a picture of a quaint cobblestone street nestled in the heart of the city, indicating where our accommodation was: it said nothing about it being a hole in the wall with dodgy signage. I know I wasn't exactly well travelled, but when a murderous scream echoes from the top floor, followed by what sounds like a brawl, causing the house clerk to scream up at the guests, one isn't exactly

filled with warm, fuzzy feelings. I half expected to find
police tape and chalk outlines of bodies upstairs. For the
past week I had dreamt of a concierge flanked by marble
pillars floating behind the front desk welcoming me to
Rome; there would be 1000-threadcount Egyptian cotton
sheets, and a fluffy white robe and minibar. But there was
no floating welcome; in fact, as yet I was unable to book
in as a man and woman argued over the computer screen.
I had no idea what they were saying, but I hoped they
couldn't find me on the system because there had been
some mistake, and I was about to be accommodated at a
more upmarket establishment.

No such luck.

I was instead given a welcome drink, an unexpected
inclusion which was sickly sweet. Not wanting to look
ungrateful, I took a second sip, and then reminded myself
that accepting drinks from a winking stranger probably
wasn't a great idea, despite the official-looking, faded gold
name badge.

'Please, sit. It won't be long.' He gestured toward the
lounge area, where a cracked brown leather wingback chair
had my name on it. I smiled gratefully at Gabriello (at least,
that's what I thought I read on the man's name badge).

Arriving in the dark of night, the city had seemed beautiful and electric. My initial excitement was subdued as
soon as I entered the taxi, the fear of certain death soaking
my already dampened clothes as the driver darted, weaved
and honked through city streets. It had been a complete

miracle that we had arrived in one piece, and I wanted to kiss the filthy stone floor of the foyer.

The hotel was a narrow, faded building that looked more like a boarding house for ex-cons than the opulence I had been promised. My desperate thoughts were interrupted by the clicking of heels as a group of English girls strode in off the street and headed for the stairs, the elevator cordoned off with crime scene tape. I watched them linking arms, laughing, seemingly uncaring that they were about to spend the night on stained, grubby mattresses. Maybe that's why they were drunk? Loaded up to forget their regret of having booked into such a place. But then I had a thought: maybe they were part of another tour group, on an empowering girls' night out, bonding while enjoying the city sights. Maybe there was hope yet? The tour guide would soon make him or herself known, and with a friendly smile and an enchanting accent, he/she would lead me onto an exotic balcony where all the other travellers waited, making lifelong friends whilst supping on delicious antipasti and toasting the beginning of a grand adventure.

Or maybe not.

I pulled my suitcase closer to me in the lounge, waiting for someone else who looked just as dishevelled and lost as I did. Instead I saw the back of a man's shoulders, square and broad in a well-cut navy jacket. He wasn't a bewildered foreigner like me—there was certainly nothing dishevelled about him. Even without seeing his face I could tell he was at ease. As I took in the tall, lean man, all the way down to his expensive Italian leather shoes, I realised he stood out for all the wrong reasons. He didn't belong here at all. What was a man like him doing in a place like this? Again, I let fantasy get the better of me; maybe this was my travel guide? The tall, dark, gorgeous Fabrizio would soon walk over to me to confess that I was the only person who had booked the tour so I would have my own personal guide. I smiled to myself, my imagination giving respite from my squalid circumstances. Or maybe he was a spy? Bond. Gino Bond. Checking into the neighbouring room with a sniper rifle, waiting to catch out a sleazy con. Rather disturbing that the latter scenario seemed more plausible.

I groaned, rubbing my eyes, never knowing such tiredness. I was hot, gritty, exhausted, hungry: was this what jet lag felt like? I had never travelled further than interstate before, so I'd never experienced it. I was way out of my comfort zone for so many reasons and I could feel the panic rise up in me.

What have I done? What was I thinking?

I had checked the itinerary a thousand times. Right date, right hotel, right time: where was everybody? Why was I stuck here in this hotel jail all alone? I dragged my hands through the darkened, messy curls of my wayward hair, fighting back tears of fatigue and hopelessness. It was then that I realised I wasn't exactly alone. Lifting my face up from my hands, I took in a deep, steadying breath as I glanced upwards and stilled. For a long moment that was more than just deliriousness or fantasy I locked eyes with the tour guide/spy. He was no longer turned away from me, but looking—no, make that staring—at me. I turned around, thinking maybe there was some mistake, that there was a beautiful, leggy blonde woman in a mink coat and diamonds standing right behind me, but after a quick glance over my shoulder, I realised this was not the case and once more my eyes locked with the man's.

In my fantasies, the spy guide would summon a waiter from nowhere and, before our eye contact broke, an exotic cocktail would arrive 'with compliments from the man at the front desk', as he acknowledged me with a cheeky little wink. I, of course, would clutch my pearls (that I didn't own) and send back a coy message of thanks and a request to join me.

But this was reality, and there was no drink, no invitation, there was just a long, lingering stare from both of us that bordered on the ridiculous, as if neither one of us wished to break the contact out of fear of defeat. The strangeness of the situation was apparent to us both; the man's mouth tugged a little, and my brows furrowed with a 'What are you looking at?' scowl. I decided to be the bigger person, lifting my chin and turning away as I nestled back into my wingback chair, feeling vaguely superior as I imagined him looking on with an amused and impressed expression. The exchange with the sexy stranger had been the highlight of my day so far. I breathed out a laugh, crossing my feet at my ankles and feeling so utterly smug—until I looked up.

'Oh, Christ.'

There before me, a full-length reflection near the fireplace mirrored my gaping face. My eyes stared wide at my mussed halo of hair, a knotted-up curl protruding from the top of my head like the crest of a cockatoo.

Oh, my God—how long had I been walking around like this? From the plane? In the taxi? Sitting here for how many hours? I clawed at the mess, fighting against the frizz in an effort to tame the horror, thinking back to how the beautiful stranger had stared at me. He wasn't going to send me a drink: he was going to send me some hair product. I wanted to die. I pushed myself way back into my chair, my hands on my head with my eyes closed, hoping against hope that he wasn't watching me now. *Oh, dear Lord, please make him be gone, let my humiliation die.* I slowly peeled my eyes open thinking I could spy his reflection in the mirror, but the angle was all wrong and I couldn't see the reception desk.

No big deal—he was there or he wasn't; what did it matter what some stranger thought, some sexy-sexy, tall, dark stranger. I would never see him again. We were just two people in a shitty hotel, never to be known to each other. There was an upside to being in Rome: no one knew me, or my story; I was a complete enigma. I could be whoever I wanted to be and no one would be any the wiser. I could simply float under the radar and lose myself in this city. At this point in time, losing myself sounded like a bloody lovely idea.

I inhaled a deep breath, calming myself. Yes, that's what I would do: I would simply lose myself. I felt better already, calmed by my own logic. *Wow, I am so grown up*, I thought to myself with a nod. *This trip has matured me already.*

'Samantha Shorten?'

I stiffened in my seat, as if someone had poured ice water down the back of my shirt.

'Is there a Samantha Shorten here?'

I slowly peered around the corner of my chair towards the voice, dread heavy in my stomach.

I was no longer anonymous.

Chapter Three

'Ciao, Samantha, *come stai?*'

There was no time to react, no time to run through my mental archive of Year Eleven Italian lessons to gather a response to the woman who approached me, a smiling vision in canary yellow as she took my hand and shook it vigorously. Instead, I blurted out the usual reaction to hearing my full name.

'Please, call me Sammi,' I said, taking in the petite, attractive brunette with the high-wattage smile and twinkle in her eyes. I felt like a bag lady next to her.

'Welcome to Rome, Sammi. *Mi chiamo* Maria. Is this your first time?'

Looking at my scruffy, creased clothes and weary, clammy disposition, it wouldn't be hard to gather that I wasn't a high-class traveller. Still, it was a polite icebreaker.

'I've never been anywhere,' I confessed, glancing up, relieved to see the man was no longer at reception. I was safe to be as tragic as I wanted. Not that I cared what he thought, I lied to myself.

'Ah, well, you are in good hands then; Bellissimo Tours is the best way to start your Italian journey, embracing the local attractions, culture, food and people.'

The fact that Maria had left out the word 'budget' was not lost on me. I could imagine her repeating this speech a fair few times, but she had it down pat, even if I did see her eyes glaze over a bit as she rattled off the details for probably the hundredth time that night.

'Sounds great. So where is everybody else?' I asked, hoping against hope that I had, in fact, arrived at the wrong hotel, and that everyone was waiting for me across the road, in a vine-covered four-and-a-half star oasis, getting drunk on wine and eating pizza while dangling their legs into a fountain. But I should have known better than to let my imagination run away with me.

'Oh, they are all out in the courtyard; there are two entrances into the hotel.'

'And I just happened to take this one,' I said, glowering at the reception.

'Never mind—you are here and that is all that matters.' Maria clapped her hands together as if something truly amazing was about to begin. Maybe I had entered into the bad side of the hotel. Everything has a good and a bad side—even I had a bad side. It just so happened that of all the entrances in the world that I could have walked into with my matted, curly Mohawk, I had to choose the same entrance as the smiling, Italian sex god from across the way. Still, he was a distant memory now, and my night was about to kick off finally. With newfound energy, I grabbed for my suitcase, only to be waved away from my handle by Maria.

'No, no, Sammi—let the porters take care of that for you.'

My brows rose. From my experiences thus far, I couldn't help the reaction: I guessed the man lingering out the front, laughing and smoking with the doorman, was the porter. Nothing had inspired any confidence until Maria had emerged like a sun from behind a cloud, quite literally; her bright yellow sundress was almost as blinding as her smile. That smile was now absent as she made short, determined steps in her heels towards the front desk. Gone was her warm, carefree, welcoming air and reborn was Maria, Roman warrior, breathing fire in loud and quick Italian at the staff. Italian was such a romantic, beautiful language, even in such a tirade.

I was tempted to slink off into the night, cringing at the thought that I might have got them into trouble. I mean, I probably could have been a bit more inquisitive, looked around, asked more questions from more people, tried my luck with my fragments of remembered Italian. But all I had the energy to do was slump into the well-worn, yet very comfy chair in the lounge area and hope against hope that the answer would come my way—and it had, in the form of Hurricane Maria. An impressive little pocket rocket, she didn't appear much older than me, and yet she seemed infinitely more streetwise.

Now action began all around me: the smoking porter quickly extinguished his cigarette and hopped into action, and the flustered man behind the desk, who until now had been struggling between flailing through paperwork and skimming over wall keys, was aided by the young receptionist, who handed him the correct key. His face plum red, he handed the key to Maria with what seemed to be a thousand apologies, apologies that Maria turned her back on. Facing me, she smiled brightly, and there again was the flawless professional tour guide; it was as if I had imagined her fiery outburst, though the ringing of my ears told me otherwise.

'Sammi, why don't you freshen up and come meet everyone in the courtyard?'

I didn't know if it was the warmth of her accent or the notion of freshening up, but I immediately felt better. A nice hot shower to wash away the plane grime, and lathering of conditioner to sort out the curly mess on my head. That Claire had inherited Mum's non-offensive waves and I had been stuck with Dad's mop of dark curls was another way Mother Nature had conspired against me. I should have thought to ask Jan how a Roman summer would affect my hair. You know, along with all the other important things like tourist visas, airport transfers and luggage allowances.

My attention snapped to the smoke fumes emanating from the porter as he skimmed past me with my suitcase, motioning me to follow. I glanced at a reassuring Maria, whose smile seemed to magically appear anytime my confidence was flagging; she was programmed so well. 'When you are ready, just head down past the bar and out the back to the courtyard. You cannot miss it, there is a sign with "Bellissimo Tours"—it's a private function.'

I felt like such an idiot; a mere wander and I could have found them myself instead of sitting in reception like a bag lady getting laughed at. Still, at least I hadn't wandered into the courtyard looking like a rooster to a group of strangers. I guess I had to be thankful for that, but, following the skinny porter up the narrow, rusty, winding staircase, I couldn't help thinking back to those eyes, sparkling and amused, and it made me wonder. Perhaps I would have preferred the eyes of a thousand strangers, instead of that very vivid pair I couldn't quite shake.

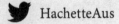
hachette
AUSTRALIA

If you would like to find out more about Hachette Australia,
our authors, upcoming events and new releases, you can visit
our website or our social media channels:

hachette.com.au

HachetteAustralia

HachetteAus

HachetteAus

HachetteAus